OSCAR LOOKED DOWN INTO THE DARK HOLE.

"I don't even know where we're going!"

"I'm taking you home, Oscar. My home."

"But you can't live inside Fenway Park," Oscar said.

"But I do," his father said.

"It's not possible. No one lives in Fenway Park!"

"I live in Fenway Park. Trust me. It is the most dangerous place I know."

OTHER BOOKS BY JULIANNA BAGGOTT

(written under the pseudonym N. E. Bode)

The Anybodies

The Nobodies

The Slippery Map

The Somebodies

Julianna Baggott

HARPER
An Imprint of HarperCollins*Publishers*

The Prince of Fenway Park

www.harpercollinschildrens.com

Library of Congress Cataloging-in-Publication Data

Baggott, Julianna.

The Prince of Fenway Park / Julianna Baggott. — 1st ed.

p. cm.

Summary: In the fall of 2004, twelve-year-old Oscar Egg is sent to live with his father in a strange netherworld under Boston's Fenway Park, where he joins the fairies, pooka, banshee, and other beings that are trapped there, waiting for someone to break the eighty-six-year-old curse that has prevented the Boston Red Sox from winning a World Series.

ISBN 978-0-06-087244-1

[1. Boston Red Sox (Baseball team)—Fiction. 2. Baseball—Fiction. 3. Orphans—Fiction. 4. Fathers and sons—Fiction. 5. Time travel—Fiction. 6. Supernatural—Fiction. 7. Fenway Park (Boston, Mass.)—Fiction.] I. Title.

PZ7.B14026Pr 2009 2008019666

[Fic]—dc22 CIP

AC

Typography by Ray Shappell

16 17 18 19 20 CG/OPM 10 9 8 7

❖

First paperback edition, 2011

This book is dedicated to Red Sox Nation—
its New Englanders and nomads—
especially the fans dearest to my heart:
Phoebe, Finn, Theo, Otis, Dave, Steven L.,
and Alyson P., the Baggotts and Trossets
of Massachusetts, the Gallatis of Delaware,
the Sobels of NYC, the ever-insightful
Carolyn Hector, Greg "The Closer"
Ferguson, and Stearnsy-boy, who now has
no choice but to be a true fan.

And to the heroic 2004 Red Sox team
and the heroic players in this book.

(And, yes, for *that* Theo, too, of course.)

Faithfully yours,

J.B.

There was a curse.
It was reversed.
And this is the boy
who did it.

CONTENTS

CHAPTER ONE

The Future Condo Prince of Baltimore

THE BOY WHO WOULD BREAK the Curse didn't know that he was the boy who would break the Curse. He was just himself, Oscar, who, at this particular moment on this particular day, was watching his mother, who was standing beside her El Camino, caught in the dark exhaust fog at the end of the line of buses. The school day was over. It had been an awful day, the kind that is so awful that it blots out everything else. There was a bruise from a knuckle punch on Oscar's back that still throbbed, and that hadn't even been the worst of it.

Oscar knew about the Curse, of course. It seemed as if everyone was well aware of the Curse that fall, especially in Boston. But what everyone didn't know was that the Curse itself was so real and tangible that it could be held in someone's hand. It existed in a dusty golden box. What everyone didn't know was that the Curse was waiting for the boy who would break it.

Meanwhile, here was Oscar, his mother waving to him from her spot by the El Camino. It was a wild, flapping wave that embarrassed him, and then she slipped into the driver's seat and honked the horn. He was going to turn twelve the very next day, and so this meant he would go visit his father, who would be giving him one of his sad presents—something secondhand but made to look new: an old watch with a new, handmade wristband, a freshly washed Windbreaker with someone else's initials penned onto the tag. His father's presents always made Oscar feel terrible. He knew his father didn't ever have much money, but still Oscar hated having to pretend how happy he was about old watches and Windbreakers. It made him feel like a fake.

When Oscar opened the car door, he saw his suitcase wedged in between the front seat and the dash. It was an ancient suitcase—wheel-less and plaid, with a zipper and plastic handle. His mother had bought it at the Salvation Army the week before. He'd thought it was strange when she came home with it. He didn't need a suitcase. He never went anywhere. He and his mother lived in a steamy apartment in Hingham Centre above Dependable Cleaners, where his mother worked. He ate at Atlantic Bagel & Deli & Coffee Co., got his hair trimmed at Hingham Square Barber Shop, traveled daily to Hingham Middle School. The farthest he'd ever gone was the forty-five-minute trip to visit with his father in Boston each Thursday at Pizzeria Uno near Fenway Park.

"What's with the suitcase?" Oscar asked, trying to position his legs around it.

"You're going to stay with your father, just for a month or two. It'll all work out." She put on the car's blinker nonchalantly—as if this were a normal thing to say—and turned onto Main Street.

But it wasn't normal at all. Oscar had never spent the night at his father's place—had never even seen it. His parents had been divorced for as long as he could remember. Oscar stared at the suitcase as if it were the real problem. The suitcase seemed all wrong. He wanted to tell her he didn't like the idea of being shipped off and not told till the last minute—had his father actually agreed to this?—and that he was a little scared of the whole thing; but all that came out was a small complaint. "It's an old man's suitcase," he said.

His mother said, "Look. Nothing's perfect. But let me explain something about love."

Oscar didn't want to talk about love. He knew what she was going to go on about: Marty Glib, the Baltimore King of Condos. His mother had met him in an online chat room; and whenever she talked about him, she fiddled with the beads on her necklace. He'd come up on business a few times; and his mother had gone on dates with him, meeting in restaurants in Boston, so Oscar had never seen him. More importantly, Marty had never seen Oscar—did his mother arrange it that way on purpose?

Oscar caught his reflection in the side mirror. His own face sometimes surprised him—the fullness of his lips, his dark eyes, his small nose, his freckles on his dark skin, his tight, black hair. Oscar wondered if his mother had told Marty everything about Oscar, if his mother—a pale woman with straight, reddish hair—had mentioned that she had a mixed-race child. Oscar's parents had adopted him when he was a baby—a bald, creamy-colored baby. Oscar had always wondered if they'd really known that they'd adopted a mixed-race child or if it had sunk in slowly as Oscar grew up. He didn't doubt that they loved him—his mother in a jittery way, his father with a distracted sincerity. He just wasn't sure if they felt somehow tricked, and if they blamed him a little, as if he'd been the one to do the tricking. Now Oscar wondered if his mother was tricking Marty Glib, too.

His mother had been different ever since meeting Marty Glib. Oscar's mother was in love, and this was her excuse for lateness. Love made her dawdle in department stores. Love made her flighty. She'd promised to sign up Oscar for the Hingham Little League; but love made her miss the deadline, and so he'd missed the season. He went to the games, watching from the sidelines. He could feel the running sensation in his legs, the stinging reverberation of the bat in his arms. But he could only watch. Oscar still fumed about it each time they passed Hersey Field on Thaxter Street, which was usually a couple times a day. In fact, on this awful day he was wearing his jersey from the summer before—ROCKETS was written on the front, TARZIA AND GILBERT TRASH, their sponsors, was written on the back. Oscar was a good baseball player, and without him the Rockets stumbled. The uniform shirt was a little tight now. He'd outgrown it and was picking at the frayed hem on the drive into Boston as his mother explained that love had made it necessary for her to spend a few months in Baltimore with Marty Glib, the Baltimore King of Condos.

"I'm bringing that big framed picture of you and me on the water slide," she said, "so he'll get used to the idea of you being around."

Oscar wasn't sure what this meant exactly. How could someone get used to him being around because there was a framed picture of him? Was this her way of telling Oscar that Marty would know he existed, know he was of color?

Oscar's parents never mentioned that he was half black. People stared a lot, trying to figure out how Oscar and his parents fit together. The bold ones would try to get an answer by saying things such as, "My, isn't he handsome!" "What beautiful skin." "What pretty brown eyes!" His mother always called this "fishing." She'd say, "Why do they have to fish like that?"

His mother always said the same thing to the fishers, right away. "Thank you. He's adopted." Oscar was tired of this answer, especially the way it seemed like a relief to his mother—she said it in an airy sigh. And Oscar always wondered if she was embarrassed that people would think that she was his birth mother, that she'd been with someone who looked more like Oscar, and here was the proof.

Oscar's father would just say, "Thank you," or "He is a beaut, isn't he?" And that was the end of that, which Oscar preferred.

What didn't help was that just this year it seemed as if the white kids he'd been friends with in elementary school didn't have as much to say to him anymore, and there weren't many black kids in Hingham Middle. Occasionally a Hispanic kid would ask him something in Spanish, assuming he spoke it. He'd just shrug. There were a few nice kids he wouldn't have minded chumming around with, like Steven Lannum and Alyson Perry. But he wasn't sure how to make friends. He felt kind of stuck in his life—trapped.

The problem now was Drew Sizemore, a mean kid in Oscar's class. He liked to pick fights, and just that afternoon he'd leaned forward in the line for gym and whispered in a quiet but menacing chant right behind Oscar's head, "Who's your daddy? Who's your daddy?" The chant came from the Yankees fans. Toward the end of September, Pedro Martinez had said in a press conference after a 6–4 loss to the Yankees, "I just have to tip my hat to the Yankees and call them my daddy." That wasn't so bad in itself. Oscar understood what he'd meant; there was a certain humility about Pedro that he liked. But now the playoff series was on; and just that Monday the Yankees fans had started chanting "Who's your daddy?" while Martinez was pitching. Drew Sizemore had hooked onto it and turned it on Oscar.

Oscar hadn't said anything. His father was Malachi Egg, who lived near Fenway Park. His father was someone who sat across from him in a pizza parlor, a man he didn't really know very well. But Oscar knew that he wasn't who Sizemore was asking about. Sizemore had seen Oscar's mother. He knew she was white and that Oscar wasn't, or at least not completely. He was asking about Oscar's *real* daddy, who Oscar didn't know. Oscar ignored him. Sizemore didn't like to be ignored. He punched Oscar in the back with a knuckle punch.

When Oscar had turned around, Drew shoved him. Oscar fell backward, knocking down Alyson Perry, who was a really nice girl with braces who wore her Girl Scout uniform to school sometimes. She knocked down Steven Lannum, a die-hard Sox fan, who was wearing a sweet new Pedro Martinez jersey. And Steve knocked down the next person, who knocked down the next—a domino effect—until all of the kids were sprawled on the floor.

Coach O'Donnell had shouted at Oscar, called him forward, and said, "You've bought yourself a one-way ticket to the principal's office."

Oscar had never been sent to the principal's office before. Coach O'Donnell had filled out a form with Oscar's name on it. He called the office through the intercom that was screwed to the gym wall and told them that Oscar was on his way.

Once Oscar had rounded the first turn in the corridor, he unfolded the form. His name had been printed in messy letters at the top. Under COMMENTS Coach O'Donnell had written: *Oscar Egg is a violent presence this afternoon, and he needed to be removed for the safety of the class.* This stung. It wasn't true. He hadn't gotten violent. It had been Drew Sizemore's fault, and he could feel the hot bruise on his back from Drew's knuckle.

The principal was away at a conference, the secretary told him. She pulled out his chart and thumbed through it on the counter. The phone rang; and when she went to answer it, Oscar glanced at his chart, all official and typed up: his homeroom number, his parents' names, his address, his birth date. It was all the regular information. He almost looked away, but something at the bottom of the form caught his eye. There was a code for race, and the tidy letters were all lined up: Black. He'd never seen it written before. There was a spot for it on the MCAS, the standardized tests they had to take every year, and Oscar usually left it blank. The previous year he'd lightly marked both white and black and then smudged them on purpose, which seemed the most honest answer he could give. But here it was, decided for him. Black. He was black.

Oscar hadn't been sure what to do with that information. The secretary came back and told him to have a seat. He sat in the office the rest of the afternoon. When he got a hall pass to go to the bathroom, he looked at himself in the mirror. Oscar hadn't only read about the Red Sox. He loved Jackie Robinson, too, and had read a bunch of books about him. Oscar wondered what Jackie—the first black ballplayer in the major leagues—would have done today on the way to gym class with Drew Sizemore chanting in his ear, knuckle punching him in the back. Oscar pulled his full lips into a tight line. He patted his hair. Why did his mother always keep it so short? Was she trying to hide something?

Even though his parents never mentioned his background, he was always waiting for them to. And so all of his conversations with each of them—always separately—were strained and heavy with the weight of something that was always just about to be said but then never was.

His mother took the stop-and-go route through Hingham and Cohasset and all the south shore towns along Route 3A. Fiddling with the air-conditioning vents at a red light alongside the ocean in Wollaston, she finally got to her point: "Your father doesn't really know you're staying with him. But you'll ask. He can't say no to you." Oscar guessed that this meant she'd already asked and he'd said no to her. And because his mother already had Oscar's suitcase packed and her time with Marty Glib planned out, it didn't matter what Oscar's father had said. He'd have to take Oscar home with him. Wouldn't he?

"What about school?" Oscar asked, trying to come up with a logical obstacle.

"Your father will set you up in a new school, temporarily. This is all very temporary," she said, waving her hand in the air as if brushing away the problem.

"A new school?" Oscar said.

"Well, not right away. You can get used to living with your father first. Maybe have a little vacation from school altogether."

Oscar liked this idea, but still he felt as if it was all too rushed. It wasn't thought out. It didn't seem like a real plan.

"Did you quit your job?" he asked. The reason they lived in the apartment over Dependable Cleaners was because his mother worked there.

"They said they can't guarantee the job'll be there when I get back. But maybe I won't need it," she said.

"What about our stuff?" Oscar asked. "I don't have my books with me."

"The only one you ever have your nose in is that Red Sox book. Well, I'm sure you have it memorized by now," she said, looking out the window, fiddling with her necklace.

She was right. Oscar pretty much did have all of the stats and stories memorized. Not having his favorite book was the least of his problems. He was going to have to ask his father if he could live with him. His father made him feel uncomfortable. He was pale and had bony shoulders. He slouched. He always seemed to have a terrible cold and a hacking cough. He was downtrodden. The waitress never got his order right—and he never asked her to take it back. But he never ate the food, just pushed it around on his plate nervously. He always looked overheated, sweaty, as if he had a fever. He was blinky, and he flinched a lot. He looked lost a lot of the time, as if he was surprised to find himself where he was. And when he looked at Oscar, even if he was smiling, he looked so terribly sad that Oscar sometimes wanted to cry for him.

When the subject of his father's place came up, his father would tell him he was lucky that he'd never been there. "Dangerous. Filled with tough customers," he'd say. "Cursed. If I could get out, I would."

It was this comment that made Oscar wonder if his father was a gangster. It was a strange thought. Even Oscar knew it was strange when he first thought it. But Oscar's father would never talk about his job. In fact, Oscar had no idea what his father did for a living. Once when Oscar mentioned Career Day at school, his father simply said, "I work the ground. I keep it the way it's always been. Who would want to hear about that?" Oscar figured "work the ground" meant that his father had a specific turf, and "keep it the way it's always been" meant protecting it.

The truth was, deep down, Oscar liked the idea that his father didn't ever take him to his home because he was a gangster. This was better than the other thought that sometimes crossed his mind. It went like this: His father didn't take him to his home because he was ashamed of his son. His father never mentioned that Oscar was different, but he was. It was like what his mother, in the dry cleaning business, had learned to call a returning stain. You could think you got it out, but it would always come back.

And so Oscar invested a lot of time in the idea that his father was a gangster. There was the way his father was always so nervous (was someone after him?), the way he only had certain days free, even the duffel bag he always carried. What was in it? A semiautomatic?

Although he liked the idea of his gangster father, Oscar really didn't want to live on dangerous turf filled with tough customers.

As usual on Route 93, there was a clog in the artery and they were stuck in traffic, not far from the blue gray buildings of Boston pointing up at the bulging clouds. He looked out his window at the huge oil tanks and Boston Harbor beyond that, and the undersides of airplanes as they descended toward Logan Airport. It suddenly seemed like a massive, wild city. He turned to his mother in the car. He said, "I don't think I can live with Dad."

His mother glanced at him. "Why not?"

"It wouldn't be safe," he said.

"Are you kidding?"

"No," Oscar said.

"Your father's always taken the safe route! You know that!"

"No," Oscar said. "I don't know anything about him." He meant it as an accusation, meaning ***Why haven't you ever told me anything about him?*** But his mother didn't take it that way. She didn't like blame. She'd read books on it, and they told her things like: *The past is the past. You can't live in it, so move on!*

She said, "Well, then, this is the perfect opportunity!"

They rode on in silence for a while. Route 93 stumbled into the chaos of the Big Dig. Someone had painted over the V in a Reverse Curve sign, making it read REVERSE CURSE.

The Red Sox were getting close again this year—Game 3 of the American League Championship Series against the New York Yankees was going to be a home game the next night. The Red Sox had lost the first two games, and so things weren't looking good. The Boston Red Sox hadn't won a World Series in eighty-six years—ever since trading Babe Ruth to the Yankees. The Red Sox had come close a number of times, but in the end they always lost. And this particular fall, the Red Sox had gotten close again, but they were now losing to the Yankees in the playoffs, two games to zero.

Everyone's mood was bleak. The die-hard Red Sox fans were morose. They shuffled around in their bulky coats and ball caps already glum and despairing. If they held on to some hope—a leftover bit from their childhood—they kept it hidden away. It was fragile, delicate—a glass-blown version of hope. Oscar hid his hope, too; but when he thought of the Red Sox—how close they were—the hope swelled in his chest. It made his throat ache and his eyes tear up, just a little bit.

Oscar didn't want to believe in the Curse, but he liked something about the idea of it. The Curse went something like this: Babe Ruth had been a standout young pitcher with the Boston Red Sox. During Babe's time in Boston, the Red Sox won the World Series twice—in 1916 and 1918. But then owner Harry Frazee sold Babe to the New York Yankees to fund his Broadway show *No, No, Nanette*. The Yankees went on to win twenty-six World Series, while the Red Sox found various torturous ways to lose.

Oscar thought about all of the big names: Ortiz, Damon, Martinez—how they must have felt in last year's playoffs when Aaron Boone hit a home run off Tim Wakefield in Game 7 of the ALCS. When it happened, when Boone's bat hit the ball, Oscar had been alone, watching the game on TV above the dry cleaners and its noisy hum of machinery. To feel cursed was the worst feeling in the world. He sometimes felt that way himself.

There was one thing he knew about the Red Sox: They would disappoint him. They would always seem as if they might win, but in the end they would let him down. Oscar thought that this wasn't such a big deal to other kids. He heard the way they talked about the Red Sox, the way they'd spout off about wins and losses; but he knew that they weren't really feeling it deeply in their souls. It wasn't an old scar. They didn't really understand. And it had dawned on Oscar recently that maybe this was true because these other kids who talked about being Red Sox fans had families who didn't disappoint them. But Oscar did, and so it seemed like being doubly hurt. Yet he couldn't stop hoping. That was the hardest part of all—he couldn't stop hoping that his mother and his father and the Red Sox would all come through for him someday.

His mother pulled up to the sidewalk at the Hotel Buckminster. Pizzeria Uno was on the ground floor, but Oscar finally had a view of the tall lights, the scoreboard, the green walls of Fenway Park off to the left. He'd never been inside Fenway Park, and in that way the visits with his father at Pizzeria Uno were torture—to be so close.

His mother put the El Camino into park. They were idling outside of Pizzeria Uno. Oscar could see his father's profile through the plate glass window.

"Don't ruin this for me, Oscar," his mother said, twirling the beads on her necklace. "I'm actually going to go somewhere. I'm actually going to be happy. And if everything goes just right, you'll be the Baltimore Prince of Condos one day. And we won't have to rent some awful apartment that stinks and work in a place that'll kill me with its hot fumes. And you'll sell condos when you grow up too. I'm doing this for us. I can't risk messing it up!"

Oscar was staring at his father through the window and then at the old-man suitcase between his knees. His father was holding the menu up but not really reading it. Maybe it wouldn't be bad to be the Condo Prince of Baltimore. He didn't like being stuck in the life that he had. Maybe it would work out. Maybe it would be better. He didn't want to mess things up for his mother.

"Please, Oscar," his mother said. "Just ask. If he says no, well, it'll be fine. We'll work it out. Just go and ask."

Oscar nodded and got out of the car. He looked at his mother and she waved out the open window. It was an even bigger, grander wave than at school, bigger and grander than the moment called for—even for his mother, who was becoming more and more dramatic these days. It was the kind of wave you give to people onshore when you're on a ship that is setting out to sea. His suitcase was still in the front seat, though, so he knew she wasn't leaving him. It just felt that way.

CHAPTER TWO

The Dusty, Golden Box

OSCAR PUSHED OPEN THE GLASS door of Pizzeria Uno. Bells wired to the door handle gave a weak jingle. He didn't want to look at his father, because he knew his father was smiling in his sad way, and so Oscar kept his eyes down and walked fast. He was used to walking this way at school. It was one way he tried to be invisible. He slid into the booth, picked up the menu, and hid behind it.

"Hey there, how are things?" His father had this way of speaking that sounded as if something was broken inside of him—even when saying the simplest, most commonplace things.

"Fine," Oscar said.

"Slow in here today," Oscar's father said.

“The Sox have the night off.”

“Yep, I guess so. No game.”

His father coughed, a little rattle in his chest. His father didn’t like to talk about baseball. But Oscar knew he was a serious fan, deeply pained by each loss, because sometimes he’d slip and give some very specific fact. Once he told Oscar that the field grass was 85 percent rye and 15 percent Kentucky bluegrass. Still, Oscar was sorry he’d brought up the Red Sox, especially now as they were down in the series against the Yankees and news was out that their prize pitcher, Schilling, had a bad ankle. Oscar wanted to be the perfect kid so that when he asked if he could stay with him, his father would say: *Yes, of course. I wouldn’t have it any other way!*

Oscar didn’t know how to be perfect, though. His mother didn’t want him to mess this up, but he felt pretty sure that he was going to. And he wasn’t sure how to ask his dad if he could stay with him. Should he mention Marty Glib? No, he decided quickly. Oscar’s father didn’t want to hear about Marty Glib. Sometimes Oscar thought his father was still in love with his mother (even though he’d been the one to leave), and that was even more painful than baseball talk.

His father placed a present—a big box wrapped

in comic book pages—on the table. "How about we wait until the end of the meal. Something to look forward to," his father said.

"Okay," Oscar said. He wasn't looking forward to it. He dreaded what might be wrapped up in the box. It wasn't so much that he was looking forward to it as he was putting it off. Oscar decided that he should put off asking his dad about staying with him too. That way his answer—surely a no—wouldn't hang over the whole meal.

Oscar ordered a couple of slices of pepperoni pizza. His father ordered the chicken parm sandwich (and the waitress delivered a meatball sub). This time Oscar didn't eat much either. His father asked about school, and Oscar went into a lot of unnecessary detail about how much he loved gym class even though the mats smelled like terrariums. He stretched the truth a little, too, saying that he'd accidentally knocked over Alyson Perry in her Girl Scout uniform during a game of tag but they were still good friends, and that he and Steven Lannum talked all the time about Martinez's pitching stats.

His father nodded along.

"Coach O'Donnell sometimes gets mad about things that he shouldn't. He gets things all wrong,"

Oscar said. "I don't think he should get like that. I mean, I'm always trying to do the best I can."

His father said, "I know. I know. Why do people get so angry when things don't go the way they want?" He looked down at his duffel bag and patted it twice.

Oscar didn't understand what that could mean, but this part of the conversation seemed like an opportunity. He said, "I think people should just deal with the situation they're given and do the best they can, don't you?"

"I do," his father said, now fiddling with the zipper on the bag.

"Like," Oscar said, as quickly as he could, "like how Mom's going away for a few months and she wants me to stay with you. Like how she wants me to go home with you today. That's not what I want," Oscar said, beating his dad to the punch. But then the next part came out as a question: "And it isn't what you want either, right?"

His father's head snapped up. "What did you say?"

"I said, like how Mom's going away and wants me to stay with you. She's got an old-man suitcase all packed for me. She wants me to go home with you today."

Oscar's father slid out of the booth. He stood there with his hands on his hips, his face pale. It glistened with sudden sweat. He turned away and then back again. "It's too dangerous. I can't risk . . . I told her this already. Today? Home with me today?" He turned away again and then came back. He stared at Oscar as if he just remembered something—something very important. "Are you the one who will save us?" he asked. "Could it be you?"

Oscar wasn't sure what to say. "Save who?" he asked. "From what?"

His father shook his head. "It can't be. Not possible. We just have to face facts. This is forever." He paused and then said, "Excuse me." And he walked across the restaurant and disappeared into the men's bathroom.

Oscar had no idea what had just happened. How dangerous would it be? What couldn't his father risk? Oscar looked out the window for his mother's El Camino. He'd have to tell her that it hadn't gone well, that they'd have to come up with another plan.

Her car wasn't there, though. Oscar wondered if she'd run off on a last-minute errand.

Oscar kneeled on the seat to look up and down the street in both directions. And that's when he saw that his father had left behind the duffel bag. He'd never done that before.

Oscar wanted to look inside of it, of course. He knew he shouldn't. It was private property. And yet he had to know what was in there. He had a right to know if his father was a gangster carrying guns with him all the time, didn't he?

Oscar got off of the seat quickly and went around to the other side of the booth. He glanced at the men's bathroom door. His father wasn't coming and so he quickly unzipped the bag. He looked inside, just peeking at first, scared of what he might find. But it wasn't what he expected at all. It was just a box. Dusty, made of metal—in fact, gold in color. Could it be made of gold? Oscar went to open it, but it had an old, dented lock. He rummaged around in the bag for a key, but the bag was empty. Oscar zipped up the bag and scooted back to his own spot, and just in time. His father was at the cash register, paying. Oscar stared at him, and—he couldn't help it—Drew's Sizemore's voice was in his ear. "Who's your daddy?" the voice chanted like a crowd in a stadium. "Who's your daddy?"

When his father was done paying, he walked back to the booth slowly. He'd wet his hair and combed it. He didn't sit down. He just stood there.

He raised one hand, ready to explain. His hand was shaking. He said in a quavering voice, "This won't work, Oscar. I'm sorry. You know how much I'd love for you to be with me, but, well, it's just . . ."

"Too dangerous," Oscar said.

"Yes, I mean . . ." His father started mumbling to himself. "How would you ever get back to your life? You'd end up stuck, like me. It would be . . ." He stopped himself.

Oscar wasn't sure what all the mumbling was about. His father picked up the duffel bag, swung it over his shoulder, and grabbed the present. Oscar was wondering if he'd get out of opening the gift in front of his dad. He could just duck into the car with his mother, take the gift, and they'd drive off; and Oscar wouldn't have to feel like a faker. "C'mon. Let's go meet up with your mother. I'll explain it to her one more time." He coughed nervously. "I can't believe she'd spring a thing like this. She should know by now that I can only do what I can do. Plus, what about school? Did she think of that?"

"She said I'd take a little vacation, and then you'd set me up somewhere near you." Oscar felt hot and nauseous. "This would all be very temporary," he said, waving his hand just like his mother had in the car. "She said we can make other plans if you said no."

His father smoothed out some crumpled bills and left them on the table. They walked out of the restaurant together, the bells jingling again. Rain sizzled on the pavement. When they got outside, they both stopped. Sitting on the sidewalk under the awning was an old-man suitcase—wheel-less and plaid, with a plastic handle.

There was a note attached to its handle with a rubber band. Oscar ran to the suitcase. He pulled out the piece of paper. The note was simple. It said:

Oscar,

I love you! This is all for the best; you'll see!

Love,

Mom

Oscar looked up and down the street, but his mother was nowhere in sight.

Oscar and his father waited under the awning of Pizzeria Uno for two hours.

"She's got to come back," his father kept muttering. "This isn't funny, you know."

Oscar knew that his mother wasn't trying to be funny. She wasn't the type. And he knew that she wasn't coming back. But he still wasn't sure that his father was going to take him home. While pretending to keep an eye out for the El Camino, he watched his father out of the corner of his eye. *Malachi Egg,* he thought. *Who is Malachi Egg?*

His father paced, staring at his watch and then flicking it with his finger as if the thing were broken. His cough seemed to be getting worse. He went on a long, hacking jag. His cheeks flushing deep red, he doubled over, wheezing and hacking. When he finally stopped, he was breathless. He straightened but seemed woozy.

And then the wind kicked up, pushing the rain sideways. Plastic bags in the gutters swirled and sailed down the street. The rain beat on the awning overhead, on the street and the roofs of cars. It was so loud that it sounded like a roar all around them.

Oscar shouted over the rain, "She isn't coming back!"

His father nodded as if he'd known it for a long time. And Oscar wasn't sure what to say next. It occurred to him again that maybe it wasn't so much that his father was afraid to take him to his place as it was that he was ashamed of his son. Wherever his father lived, did he have a picture of Oscar like his mother had promised to show to Marty Glib? Did people in his father's other life—gangsters or tough customers or whoever—know that Oscar was his child, his black child. Did they even know he existed? The idea made Oscar's stomach turn. He sat down on his suitcase. He was suddenly worried that he was going to start to cry. He could feel his face tightening up. He didn't want to cry in front of his father. He pulled his lips in tight. He wanted to be matter-of-fact, grown-up. He said to himself, "I don't care what happens." But he didn't mean it. His father didn't want to take him home. His mother had left him. His chest felt constricted, his throat cinched.

He said, "I've had a really bad day. I got punched in my back and sent to the principal, and my mother picked me up and told me she was going to leave me with you. And you don't want me. And it's not like this is the first time someone didn't want me. I'm cursed," Oscar said. The tears were streaming down his face now. He backhanded his wet nose and sat down on his suitcase. "I'm the kind of kid that nobody wants around. Look at me!" Oscar said, staring down at his ski vest and his too-tight baseball uniform shirt. "I'm stuck like this. Like me. Cursed forever."

When he looked up at his father, he was surprised at what he saw. He wasn't sure what he'd been expecting, but it hadn't been this: his father's face streaked with tears too, but his face shining, hopeful, a smile lifting his cheeks, his eyebrows. Oscar wasn't sure what to do with this odd, affectionate look. He stood up abruptly. And then feeling awkward, he stuffed his hands in his pockets.

"Maybe we have no choice for a reason. Maybe this is all adding up to something. Do you believe in fate?" he asked Oscar, his eyes glistening.

"I don't know," Oscar said, but there was something about this moment that seemed completely different from any moment that had come before it.

His father held the duffel bag with the dusty box inside of it close to his chest. "Let's go, Oscar," he said; and, head down, he stepped out into the rain.

Oscar wiped his tears from his face, picked up his suitcase, and hustled after him.

The rain soaked them fast—their shirts, pants, hair. The comic strips on the newspaper-wrapped gift smeared and began peeling away, leaving only a white box and ribbon.

Oscar wiped the rain from his face so that he could see. They were walking toward the bridge over the Mass Pike, toward Fenway. The suitcase was heavy; and when one arm got tired, Oscar would put the suitcase down and switch hands.

Then he would have to jog a little to catch up to his father's long strides. They crossed the bridge onto Brookline Avenue and turned left onto Lansdowne. Fenway Park ran the length of the street, looming like a silent, green cathedral.

Oscar paused for a moment under the seats that jutted out over Landsdowne. These were the new Monster seats. They'd been put in just the year before so that people could watch the game from right on top of the Green Monster: the famous towering wall in left field, the highest wall of all Major League Baseball fields. He knew that the wall was exactly thirty-seven feet and two inches high. He'd seen it a million times on television. The scoreboard was built into it—a manual scoreboard; and Oscar had imagined the people who worked it put up the scores through the slits in the wall. He'd imagined the small, dark, mysterious room that existed inside of the massive wall. Occasionally, he could see the slits cut into the lower part of the Green Monster, where the people working inside had a view of the game—a view like no other. And, of course, he'd seen the powerful home runs that were hit over the wall.

Oscar knew that the enormous wall was called the Green Monster because of its intimidating size, but he also felt as if it were a monster of some kind, as if it were truly alive in some way—a living, breathing presence.

"Hurry up," his father said.

Oscar jogged to catch up to him. At the end of Lansdowne Street they turned right onto Ipswich, past an empty Red Sox parking lot just down from a bus stop—all blurry from the driving rain—and they stopped in the middle of the empty street. Oscar's father was standing near a long line of official Red Sox garbage cans all locked together. He was looking down at a manhole in the center of Ipswich Street. They were both drenched, their shirts and pants sticking to them. His father noticed the ruined wrapping job on the present. He unzipped the duffel bag, which had remained slightly dry, and stuffed the gift inside.

"Guess we can wait for your actual birthday now," he said. He hugged the duffel bag to his chest again and hunched over it. "Okay," he said. "Stand here a minute. Keep an eye out."

"An eye out for what?" Oscar asked. But his father didn't answer.

He pulled an orange safety vest from his pocket and put it on. It made him look official. Then he reached down, stuck his fingers into holes in the manhole cover, and lifted it with a groan, pulling it to the side and then letting go so that it made a heavy clunk. Oscar looked down into the dark hole.

His father said, “You first.”

“Me? Why me?”

“Because I know how to cover the manhole back up after I’ve headed down. That’s why.”

“I don’t even know where we’re going!”

“I’m taking you home, Oscar. My home.”

“Down there?”

He nodded.

“You live down there?”

“No, this just happens to be the way I get in.”

“Where?” Oscar asked.

His father sighed. It seemed as if he didn’t really want to answer the question. As if he’d been avoiding it for years. But he couldn’t anymore. His father lifted his finger and jabbed it straight behind him, pointing quite clearly to Fenway Park.

“But you can’t live inside Fenway Park,” Oscar said.

“But I do,” his father said.

“It’s not possible. No one lives in Fenway Park!”

"Many live in Fenway Park."

"But it's not a rough neighborhood, you know; it's not dangerous turf."

"Dangerous turf?"

"You said you lived in a dangerous neighborhood!"

His father was confused. "I never said that."

Oscar thought for a moment. He was right. He'd never said this, not exactly. Oscar wiped his face, but it didn't do any good. The rain was coming down so hard that his face was soaked again. "You said you lived with tough customers. That you lived someplace dangerous! Too dangerous for me!"

"I live in Fenway Park. Trust me. It is the most dangerous place I know."

CHAPTER THREE

The Underlife of Fenway Park

OSCAR CLIMBED DOWN THE LADDER connected to the edge of the manhole. His knees felt loose in their joints. His arms felt rubbery. Maybe it was the feeling of being drenched, but it seemed as if he hadn't climbed down a manhole as much as into the blowhole of a whale. He worried that a flume of water was going to force him up and out. He looked around at the cement walls, the dripping tunnel ahead, then back up at the hole where his father was waiting.

His father lived in Fenway Park?

It didn't make sense.

Oscar was more than a little terrified; but it felt good, as if he wasn't just trying to avoid being tormented by the likes of Drew Sizemore. No. He was heading into an adventure. It felt like waking up from a long sleep—when he hadn't known that he'd been sleeping.

"Stand aside!" his father said. "Down she comes!"

The dim shaft of light and rain coming down through the manhole was blocked for a moment as Oscar's father jammed the suitcase into the hole. Finally the bottom bent in enough so the handle could pop through, and it landed on the hard, cement floor at the bottom of the ladder.

There was light and rain again, and then his father shifted halfway into the hole and dragged the cover across the manhole. Once he'd dipped down and the cover had clunked into place, everything went dark. Oscar heard his father walk down the rest of the rungs, then a click, then another, then his father cursing a little under his breath; and then there was a spark, and finally Oscar could see his father's face, the duffel bag, and his father's meaty hand holding a small cigarette lighter.

"I don't need the light. I know this route by heart, but I thought you might like some."

"Are we in a sewer?" Oscar asked.

"Nope. This is an access to electrical services, phone lines, utility cables, that sort of thing."

As he held up the lighter like a torch, his father looked tall all of a sudden, as if he'd grown a couple of inches. At first Oscar wondered if it were just an illusion—set off by his father being in such a tight space. But then he noticed that his father wasn't slouching. He was standing up straight. It was strange. He'd never seen his father stand up straight. He walked ahead, taking long strides. Oscar picked up his suitcase and followed.

The walls were strung with wires and cords and cables of different colors. The tunnel twisted and turned. They went on and on. There were offshoots and jagged turns; and as they went, the wires turned into vines. Then they became barbed and grew thorns. The edges of the tunnel were lined with nettle bushes. The vines blocked some of the light from the bare bulbs, and the tunnels grew dim and overgrown like a jungle. One of the burrs snagged Oscar's pants, tearing them.

"Watch out for that," his father said.

"It's a little late for the warning."

"Well, if you like your warnings ahead of time, then I'd say watch out for weasels and the Banshee—the Lost Soul of the Lost and Found—and a lot of other Cursed Creatures. Hmm, and, let's see . . . the mice come in waves. And if you hear hooves coming behind you, crouch down. It's the Pooka, and it won't be a good ride if he grabs you."

Oscar stopped in his tracks. "What are you talking about?" He felt his heart thudding in his chest.

"I told you it was dangerous," his father said.

"What's a banshee and a pooka? I don't even know what words you're using."

His father sighed. "Nothing to do about it except follow along." His father started walking ahead. "C'mon. Keep moving. That's best."

Oscar ran to catch up. He was trying to remember the way—left, left, right, right, right. But it became too complicated. He was disoriented. He couldn't tell if they were heading closer to the middle of the park or if they were skirting the edges.

Then there was some organ music. It seemed to be piped in from unseen speakers. Oscar recognized the tunes—rally songs, the same ones he'd hear in the background as an announcer was calling a game. But these were warped versions. The notes went flat. The tempo would speed up and then grind down; but it sounded purposeful, artistic.

"Where's that music coming from?"

"The horned organist. He plays when the official organist isn't around. You can hear it underground, though."

"It doesn't sound right," Oscar said.

"He plays the only way he can; his heart is twisted, you know."

"Did you say horned organist?"

"I did. Sad but true. Smoker."

Oscar let this sink in. Did he really mean "horned"? Did he mean that the organist had horns on his head? And smoked?

His father stopped abruptly, and Oscar nearly ran into him.

"Do you hear that?" his father asked.

"Hear what?"

Then Oscar heard a distant whining, a little chorus of sad yips that seemed to go with the awful, warped organ music.

"That," his father said.

"Is it an animal?"

"Not just one."

"What is it?"

"Weasel-man," his father said. "Hurry up. Let's go this way. Maybe we can avoid him."

But when they headed down the next chute in the tunnel, the whines grew louder.

"This way," his father said, turning in the other direction.

But again the cries only got louder.

"He's onto us," his father said.

"Who's Weasel-man?" Oscar asked.

"He's not evil," his father explained, now turning again, picking up the pace, getting a little breathless. "He's just . . . like . . . all of them. Good and . . . bad."

"All of who?" Oscar asked. His suitcase was heavy. It was weighing him down.

"We're the flip side of Fenway Park, the underbelly," his father said, pausing at a T, then darting left. "Everything they have up above we have down below. They have an organist. We do, too. They have folks who work in Lost and Found. We have one, too. They have concession workers. We have one, too. Weasel-man is our concession worker—a thief, some would say. It's how we survive."

"Do they know that you all exist?"

"They could, if they were smart. But, no. They don't. We take over when they're not here. We roam mostly in the dark hours. Each of us has another place besides the one they share, a place we've dug out for ourselves. When the outsiders are here, we head underground to those spots."

"Do you get to see the games?"

"Who would want to see the games? It's hard enough to listen to Radio tell us the news. Heartbreaking."

“I’d love to see them play,” Oscar said.

His father looked at him quizzically. “It’s heartbreaking,” he said, as if Oscar hadn’t heard him correctly.

The whining was growing louder, as if they were heading right toward it, and so his father turned again and walked around a corner, Oscar at his heels. They both collided with something massive.

Oscar bounced backward and fell down, his suitcase skidding across the floor, under a nettle bush. When he looked up, his father was brushing himself off, as was an enormous man. The man was bent almost in two, trying to fit in the small tunnel. He wore an old metal change maker on his belt and a grimy Red Sox baseball cap on his head, which was small compared to his body. He was holding a cooler and walking a pack of rodents on leashes. Weasels, Oscar guessed, as he supposed this was Weasel-man. The weasels poured over one another like fish. They pawed at Weasel-man lovingly and made soft, trilling noises now, as if whistles were caught in their throats. The leashes were tangled.

“Hey, watch where you’re going!” Weasel-man said.

“Watch where *we’re* going? You were the one who was after us.”

"I wasn't after you! I'm just walking the weasels and bringing Fedelma a cooler. I stole it from Concessions last night. She said she wanted a cooler."

"I'm headed home now, so I'll bring it to her," his father said. Oscar stepped out from behind him.

"Who's that?" Weasel-man asked gruffly.

"That's my son. Oscar. He's staying with me for a bit."

"He is, huh? He doesn't look like you."

"No," Oscar's father said. "He doesn't."

"What I mean is, he don't look like he's yours . . ."

"Nope, he doesn't."

"What I mean is, he can't be . . ."

Oscar's father raised his voice. "I know what you mean, Weasel-man. I know what you mean!" He sighed and grabbed hold of the cooler, and Weasel-man let him take it. The cooler looked heavy, but Oscar's father was strong. Oscar had always thought of his father as bony and weak, but his arms were actually quite muscular. "I'll take it to Auntie Fedelma."

"No need to get huffy. Be sure to tell her that Weasel-man got it for her. The weasels miss her." He bent down and petted a few of them. They all jumped for his affection.

"I will. Don't worry," Oscar's father said.

Weasel-man leaned in to look at Oscar more closely. "Nope," he said. "Not a chance."

Oscar wanted to say, *A chance for what?* But he was scared of the giant; plus, Weasel-man smelled so badly of weasels and fried food that Oscar's voice caught in his throat.

"Knock it off," Oscar's father said to Weasel-man.

Weasel-man leaned in to Oscar's father's face. "Why don't you like me?" he said. "You ought to. We're all in this together, you know. We should make the best of it!"

Then both men froze. They whipped their heads around. Oscar's father put his hand to the wall.

"A wave," his father said. "Where's it coming from?"

Weasel-man smiled. "Good-bye to you both," he said. He tipped his hat, and Oscar saw two yellow nubs, slightly pointed, that poked up from the top of his head. Horns? Oscar sucked in his breath. Weasel-man smiled, and then he walked off quickly with his pack of whining weasels, his change maker jangling.

Oscar wanted to ask about the horns, but they couldn't have been horns. No one has horns. But no one walks weasels on leashes either. Oscar cleared his throat to ask, but he stopped himself. He didn't want to sound silly in front of his father. And it seemed as if there was something more urgent going on. The tunnel was shaking ever so slightly now.

"What is it?" Oscar asked.

"A wave!" his father shouted urgently. "Get your suitcase."

Oscar had seen these on television: baseball crowds raising their hands so that a wave traveled around the stadium. But there was no game, so how could there be a wave? He would have been excited, but his father's face looked terrified. Oscar reached under the nettle bush where his suitcase had come to its stop, and he pulled it out.

"Best thing to do," his father shouted over the noise, "is to lie down in the dirt and let them pass over us."

The tunnel was trembling even more violently, and the organ was surging overhead with a grand finale of notes. "What?" Oscar said.

His father's mouth kept moving, but Oscar couldn't make out the words. His father had dropped the cooler and was down on the ground now, reaching for Oscar's hand, still holding tight to the duffel bag. That's when Oscar saw the wave.

It filled the tunnel. It seemed at first like a large animal made of small, whirring body parts. Oscar's father turned around and looked back. His face was red, his mouth moving urgently, the cords of his neck standing out. Oscar knew that his father was shouting. He knew that his father meant for him to grab his hand and that his father would probably pull him down to the ground, but Oscar was frozen. He could see now that there wasn't one large gray animal but many small gray animals—mice, thousands of them—coming at him with the force of a river.

At the last moment his father leaped up from the ground and grabbed Oscar and his suitcase with one strong arm, holding the duffel bag with the other. It seemed as if his father was lifting him up higher and higher, but it wasn't his father doing the lifting. It was the force of the wave of mice. Oscar and his father were buoyed up on the wave, bobbing violently, soaring down the tunnel. The cooler had been lifted up too. Faster and faster they rode. Oscar felt the mice, their small, furry bodies flowing all around him, the nips of their tiny nails, the snaps of their tiny, whiplike tails. The chorus of squeaks was almost deafening. His father's arm held him firmly around his waist.

"Hold on!" his father shouted. Up ahead the tunnel came to a T. "We're going to hit hard!"

Oscar threw his hands up to block his face. His father turned so that his body was between Oscar and the approaching wall. They did hit hard—the cooler making a loud crack—and fell to the ground. The mice split off in either direction, forming two smaller waves that roared on without them.

Oscar and his father stood up, brushing the loose fur and dirt from their clothes.

"Well," his father said. "That one wasn't so bad, was it?"

Oscar looked up at his father. He heard Drew Sizemore's chant in his ear again—*Who's your daddy? Who's your daddy?*—but it didn't mean the same thing to him now. "Who *are* you?" Oscar asked.

"You know who I am," Oscar's father said, a little confused by the question but smiling. "I'm your father." And then he stood up. "Well, well," he said, looking around. "We're here."

The tunnel looked the same as all the other tunnels they'd been in—the nettles, the vines. "We're where?" Oscar asked.

"Home, of course!"

CHAPTER FOUR

Home, of Course!

OSCAR'S FATHER VERY CAREFULLY FIT his hand through some barbed vines. He found a cord and gave it a tug. Oscar heard a distant, warbled chime, like the recorded song from a dying ice-cream truck—the opening notes of "Take Me Out to the Ball Game"? But it was so muffled and warped that he couldn't be sure.

A voice piped up. It was a woman's voice, gravelly and raspy. It sounded out of what looked like an old tin funnel—an old-fashioned fluted speaker—mounted above the pull cord. "Who are you?" the voice said. "Do you realize what time it is? Who wants to be woken up at this early hour!"

This was strange to Oscar. He didn't know the

exact time, but it had to be close to dinner.

Oscar's father gave a sigh. "Let me in," he said.

"Let who in?" the voice said.

"It's Old Boy," his father said. "I said I'd be back, and here I am."

"You're late!"

"I'm sorry. I ran into trouble." Was that what Oscar was to him? Trouble? This stung.

His father seemed to know he'd said the wrong thing. He looked down at Oscar, put a hand on his shoulder—just for a second, as if to say he was sorry for that. He looked at him, and the sadness was back, just briefly. He seemed to want to say something to Oscar.

Another voice shouted out from the speaker, a more lilting, dithering voice. "Are you sick? Are you unwell? You've been gone so long! I've been up for hours, worrying!"

"I'm fine. I'm hungry," his father said, and then Oscar noticed again that his father hadn't coughed at all since they'd entered the manhole. He didn't look sickly the way he always did in Pizzeria Uno. He looked tall; and with his shoulders pushed back, he looked broad, too.

"What did he say?" the lilting voice asked. "I

couldn't hear him!"

"He said he's fine. Whoever he is!" the gravelly voice shouted. "How do we know it's you?"

"Because you do."

"If you aren't who you say you are, then, then"—the gravelly voice grew deeper and venomous—"may your own horse kick you in the head in your very own fallow potato fields and may your wife beat you with a pan and may your . . ."

Oscar's father leaned against the tunnel wall. "Auntie Fedelma, we don't have potato fields anymore. We don't own a horse. I'm divorced. You haven't had the power to curse in ages. You know that."

"Wicked, you are, Old Boy! Can't you let me enjoy my worthless curses in my old age."

"Can I let him in?" the lilting voice asked.

Someone must have said yes, because just then a crack in the shape of a door formed in the wall; and Oscar's father fit his fingers into the crack, lifted some wires over the top of the door, and pulled.

Warm light spilled into the tunnel—heavy with the scent of hot pretzels, cocoa, buttery popcorn, and hot dogs—and something else, something medicinal and sharp. His father stepped in and set down his duffel bag. Oscar walked in behind him, holding on to his antique suitcase. Compared to the dark tunnel, the room was so blindingly bright that Oscar could only make out three old wizened faces staring at him—ancient old ladies.

They were wearing old uniform jerseys; and their long skirts, like quilts, were made of bits of cloth with numbers and Red Sox insignia stitched together. They wore cleats that were too big for them and curled up at the toes. They were seated in what looked to be a short row of bleacher seats, and they'd been eating from large, rectangular plates. It took Oscar a moment to see that the plates were made of scoreboard placards with the edges turned slightly upward.

One old lady was thin and pruned, with a crooked jaw and a sour expression. She adjusted her thick eyeglasses and squinted at Oscar. "Wait a minute. I see two figures! What have you brought, Old Boy?" Oscar recognized her as the gravelly voice that had uttered curses at them in the tunnel. "Have you brought a small beast? What is that fuzzy form? I can't make it out!"

His father whispered to Oscar, "That's Auntie Fedelma."

Oscar didn't think he liked her much. He didn't like being called a small beast.

"What did you say?" asked the one with the lilting voice. "What is that boy doing here?" She was hefty. Her puffy chins ringed her neck like mini flotation devices, holding up a sweet, rosy face. She lifted a tin funnel to her ear and waited for someone to answer her question.

"And that's Auntie Oonagh," Oscar's father whispered.

"Boy?" said the gravelly voiced old woman, rubbing her eyes. "Is that what it is?"

Now that he'd gotten used to the light, Oscar could see that the room was small and cluttered, near crumbling. He took it all in as quickly as he could. Next to the row of bleacher seats were three hammocks. Their wooden frames had been fashioned from baseball bats and the hammocks themselves from old netting that looked like it had been used around a batting cage. Quilts were draped over the hammocks. The walls were covered with yellowed newspaper clippings, and radios from all different eras were scattered here and there. The cracks in the walls had been filled with baseballs and wadded-up newspapers. Oscar could see through a tilted door frame into the kitchen, where a popcorn machine popped, pretzels hung under a warming bulb, and hot dogs turned on wire rungs.

There was only one old lady whom he hadn't yet met. She cleared her throat but didn't say a word. She was very small and was perched in the middle of the short row of bleacher seats. She looked unhealthy. Her breathing was wheezy and strained. His father again whispered, "And that's Auntie Gormley." Then he smiled, his chin up, looking as proud as Oscar had ever seen him. "This is my son. Oscar."

Auntie Fedelma gave a huff, crossed her arms, and glared at Oscar. "That is the Other? That is your Outside World Obligation? Why is he here? What are we going to do with him? I hope he doesn't eat a lot."

Auntie Oonagh clapped her hands, tappity, tappity.

And Auntie Gormley, who looked the most ancient of all, stared at Oscar, her eyes wide, and then lifted her small, wrinkled hands to her mouth—and smiled so broadly that her cheeks pinched small tears from her eyes. Oscar didn't understand it exactly, but he felt as if he'd known Auntie Gormley for a long time, forever maybe; and in this moment he felt warm in his chest.

At the same time everything was so foreign, he felt disoriented. "Where are we?" Oscar asked his father quietly.

"Fenway. I told you," his father said, and then he pointed to a potbellied stove in the corner. "Warm up, dry out. That used to be in the locker room; but when they put in central heating, we took it for ourselves. Still works!" he said, banging on the wrought iron with his knuckles.

Oscar stood in front of it and held out his hands. The old ladies were watching him. He kept his eyes on his father, who walked into the kitchen. Coolers leaked small puddles on the floor, which was tiled in five-cornered rubber mats—home plates. His father set down the extra cooler next to the others.

"Present from Weasel-man," Oscar's father said.

"For who?" Auntie Fedelma asked.

"For you, of course," Oscar's father said.

"Weasel-man's crazy," she said. "I don't need another cooler!"

"He said you wanted one," Oscar's father said.

"Did I?"

Oscar felt dazed. His body echoed the feeling of riding the wave of mice. How had he wound up here in this small, underground hovel filled with Fenway Park castoffs? He asked again. "I know we're in Fenway, but where?"

“We’re under the mound,” his father said.

“We’re under the pitcher’s mound?” Oscar asked.

“Yep,” his father said.

“And you all don’t go up and watch the games?”

They stared at him with a mix of shock and sympathy, as if he were a foreigner from some distant land who just didn’t quite understand. Aside from the looks they gave him, the question was ignored.

“Fairies live under fairy mounds!” Auntie Fedelma said, staring hard at Oscar through her thick glasses. “It’s a fairy mound first and foremost!”

“Fairies?” Oscar asked.

Auntie Oonagh sang, “Fairies! Fairies! Fairies!”

“I don’t like the term ‘fairies,’ ” his father said. “You know I don’t.” He’d gotten two pretzels out from under the bulb and now handed one to Oscar. It was warm but a little tough.

“We are what we are!” Auntie Fedelma said. “And proud of it!”

Auntie Gormley caught Oscar’s eye and blinked at him. Oscar wasn’t sure what that meant exactly. He took another bite of his pretzel.

“We’re only half-and-half of what we are,” Oscar’s father corrected.

"Half fairy and half human," Auntie Oonagh said.

"It's how we got kicked out in the first place," his father said. "We didn't fit in, and so now we're here."

This struck Oscar. He felt half-and-half, too. He knew why he didn't seem to fit in, but he didn't know why his father felt that way. What did it mean to be half fairy, half human? And what land did they get kicked out of? He reached up and pressed down his hair, and he immediately wished he hadn't. It would only draw attention, but he couldn't have stopped himself anyway. It was a nervous reaction.

"Fairies! Fairies!" Auntie Oonagh sang.

"Living under a fairy mound as fairies do and have always done!" Auntie Fedelma said, still eyeing Oscar suspiciously.

"You look like regular people to me." Oscar felt strange saying it. He decided that they were all pretty crazy—maybe his father, too. He was twelve. He didn't believe in fairies, really. Weren't they children the size of mice with wings, who fluttered around in gardens? What twelve-year-old would believe in fairies?

"Yes, we look like humans," Oscar's father said. "We got the human height and bulk, mostly." He glanced at Auntie Gormley, who was quite small.

"But . . ." Auntie Fedelma stood up. "I was born in 1846, I think. I don't know when. I stayed a girl for thirty years or so. Your father here was born . . . when was that? 1913? He should be an ancient old man, or dead already. But he isn't. He only looks to be about forty."

"Fairies live forever," Auntie Oonagh explained. "And half fairies just feel like they do."

"We age slowly—the human part of us kicking in. And we can die," Oscar's father said. "We all do eventually die."

And here Auntie Gormley lifted a finger in protest.

Oscar's father corrected himself. "Well, we're not sure that we're able to die right now. Because of the Curse, we're stuck here . . . in many ways."

"And we have plenty of fairy in us too. Don't forget these," Auntie Fedelma stood up from her chair and turned ever so slowly. On her back, Oscar saw what seemed to be a pair of crumpled, decrepit, pale-colored umbrellas—spiny legs with thin material stretched between. They sprouted from two small holes in her shirt. She spread them open a bit, but they only looked more pathetic. "Wings!" she said.

"Wings?" Oscar repeated.

"Mine have nearly shriveled up from disuse," Auntie Oonagh said, showing her wide back, where two wizened wings the size of handheld fans sat limply.

Oscar turned to his father. He couldn't remember ever seeing his father without a shirt. In fact, his father usually wore a jacket, too. Had he been hiding wings all of these years? "Do you have wings?" he asked.

"I keep them to myself," his father said, obviously embarrassed by his aunties' displays.

Oscar looked at Auntie Gormley. "Me, too," she mouthed.

Oscar was so surprised, he wasn't sure what to say or do or even where to cast his eyes. And although some part of him felt a little betrayed by his father's secret—why hadn't his father confided in him?—he was also relieved. His father understood what it was like to be two in one. His father had wings. His father had a part of himself that he wasn't sure what to do with.

The wings seemed so personal. Oscar didn't want to be caught gawking like those fishers who were always trying to find some trace of him in his parents. He decided to change the subject. "Where's the pitcher's mound or, um, the fairy mound?" He wasn't sure which one was the proper term now.

"It's up there," Auntie Oonagh said reverently, raising her eyes to the ceiling. "Old Boy was given the gift of the land; he knows the secrets of the ground above us."

Auntie Fedelma cut in. "What good is the gift of the land to us here? He was supposed to be a farmer one day. We used to have *real* land," she said. "He's nothing more than a groundskeeper!"

Oscar's father explained. "There's a tradition among our branch of you-know-whats that when a child turns twelve, his aunties give him a gift, a blessing. Mine was to know the secrets of the earth, the gifts of the land—a typical gift to give a boy from landowning fairies." He sighed heavily, as if this was a great burden. "And this land—Fenway Park—has so many secrets, but not ones any of us ever could have predicted."

"I'd love to know the secrets of Fenway Park," Oscar said, thinking of his own birthday, which was only a day away.

"You'd love to know what?" Auntie Oonagh asked Oscar, fitting the funnel to her ear. "Speak up! Speak up!"

“I’d love to know the secrets of Fenway Park!” he shouted.

“No, you wouldn’t, Oscar. Trust me,” his father said.

“And what do you do with your gift? Nothing! It’s worthless,” Auntie Fedelma snorted. “We’re here, forever. And we may as well just get used to it!”

“Stuck here? Forever?” Oscar said.

At this Auntie Oonagh started to cry. “Oh, no, no, no,” she muttered. “Oh, no. Don’t, don’t say it! Speak of it not! Don’t say the word!”

Auntie Fedelma leaned in close to Auntie Oonagh. Her face turned red. “Cursed!” she hissed.

Oscar thought of the sign he’d seen that afternoon on the exit ramp: REVERSE CURSE. He wanted to ask his father if curses were real. He didn’t believe in them. He glanced at his father, whose eyes had gone wet and jittery; and Oscar knew this was real. There was a curse. Did they share it with the Red Sox? “What kind of curse?” Oscar asked. “The same one that . . .”

His father didn’t let him finish. He nodded. “We’re all in it.”

And that’s when Auntie Fedelma said, “I want to see this Other of yours, this Outside World

Obligation, more closely."

"His name is Oscar," Oscar's father said.

"Yes, yes. Bring him to me."

"Why?" Oscar's father asked. "What does it matter?"

Auntie Fedelma's mouth twisted into a smile. "I want to see your *Oscar*. That's all. I'm an old, old woman. I'm nearly blind. I want a closer look."

Oscar's father nudged him. "Go ahead," he said.

And so Oscar walked over. Auntie Fedelma grabbed him by the arm, so brusquely that he dropped what was left of his pretzel. She leaned in so close that he could smell her. It was that medicinal scent that Oscar had first picked up on when he came in, but now he recognized it: linseed and neat's-foot—oils he'd used to condition his glove the year before. It was mixed with the stench of pine tar too. She looked at him sharply. Her eyes were shrunken by her thick glasses so much so that they seemed to be skittering around like beetles. She stared into his eyes, stared at the top of his head, at his face. He reined in his lips without even thinking about it. She pulled his arm up close to her face and then dropped it. She pushed him away and then motioned for Oscar's father to come to her.

His father stood his ground. "What is it?"

"He's a . . . he's a—you know. He's a Robinson!" She whispered it, but loudly enough for Oscar to hear.

"A what?" his father asked.

Oonagh leaned in close to hear, but Auntie Gormley didn't. She sat back and rocked in her chair, ignoring the fuss.

"He's a Robinson. A . . . a Mays, an Aaron," Auntie Fedelma said.

Oscar's father pretended not to understand her; but Oscar knew what she meant, naming all of the old baseball legends with dark skin. She was saying that he was black. Oscar stepped farther away; but his foot hit the edge of a throw rug made of grasslike indoor-outdoor carpeting, and he stumbled a bit.

Auntie Fedelma went on. "He's . . ." And then she finally blurted it, "He's from the Negro Leagues!"

"I don't know what you're talking about!" Oscar's father said to Auntie Fedelma, and then he leaned in closer. "I've shown you pictures all along."

"But the pictures were so small!"

"It doesn't matter anyway! It's not like that anymore," Oscar's father said. "None of that matters."

Oscar agreed. In the world of baseball, there were plenty of players of color. His head was flooded with names: David Ortiz, Manny Ramirez, Pokey Reese. Not to mention Robinson and Mays and Aaron. He wasn't sure how or why, but he knew that the color of his skin was important. He didn't want to be treated badly because of it, but he didn't want it ignored, either. All of these thoughts were clanging loudly in his head and didn't help him feel much better. Oscar didn't want to say anything, but he muttered, "Ortiz, Martinez . . ."

"What's that?" Auntie Fedelma asked. "Speak up there."

"David Ortiz," Oscar said again. "Martinez . . ."

"And how have they helped us?" Auntie Fedelma spat. "Ortiz and Martinez! They'll never set us free! We are a people of a Grand Tradition. We are now imprisoned. And if Old Boy had had a son of his own and not just an Outside World Obligation, then, well, that boy may have helped us. He may have been the one who got the gift that would set us free. But you are of no use to us. . . ."

"Stop it!" Oscar's father shouted. "Stop!"

But Auntie Fedelma didn't stop. "I'm just explaining to the Other what the situation is exactly. He isn't going to save us. He isn't the one we've been waiting for."

Save us? Oscar remembered that this was the

phrase his father had used in the pizza shop, but he still didn't know what it meant.

"He's of no use," Auntie Fedelma went on.

"Maybe things have changed! Maybe the person to break the Curse doesn't have to be Born of the Curse!"

Auntie Gormley nodded vigorously in agreement.

"He should know his place!" Auntie Fedelma shouted. "He shouldn't get ideas in his head! He's of no use!"

And then there was a great whistle. It was loud and high. Everyone froze and turned to Auntie Gormley. Oscar hadn't noticed the gap between her two front teeth, but there it was; and the shrill note pushed from it filled the small room. When she'd let all of the air out of her lungs, the room felt silent. Auntie Fedelma crossed her arms and closed her eyes.

Auntie Gormley then looked at Oscar. The whistle had exhausted her. She'd lost all of her air and now gasped a bit. Then she nodded at Oscar as if to say, *I like you, and I hope that you stay.*

Oscar nodded back. His father patted his shoulder, and Auntie Oonagh let out a nervous giggle.

Oscar looked around the cluttered room. He was in the underbelly of Fenway Park. He could barely believe it. He was here, with his father, and the Cursed Creatures. He looked up and saw a ladder sticking up into a rectangular hole in the ceiling. Where was the pitcher's mound exactly? he wondered. Was it right overhead?

He pointed to the ladder. "What does that lead to?"

CHAPTER FIVE

Under the Pitcher's Mound

OSCAR FOLLOWED HIS FATHER UP the rickety ladder through the hole into a small room—not much more than a crawl space, really. It wasn't possible to stand upright. Oscar's father was nearly bent in half. Even Oscar had to hunch. It was dusty, and at first the only light was shining up through the knotholes in the wooden floor. There was a trunk in one corner, some shelves built into one wall that were filled with neatly folded clothes, and a pallet made of thick, square, cloth-covered bases on the floor. A quilt of stitched-together Red Sox jerseys sat folded at the foot of the pallet. Oscar's father put his duffel bag down in the corner and pulled the string on a bare bulb that was screwed into a simple fixture lodged in the wall.

That's when Oscar noticed that the ceiling was just dirt, and he realized that this was really it: the underside of the pitcher's mound. It was rounded outward; and at the center of the dome there was the rubber, the spot where the pitchers stood. Oscar imagined all of the greats who'd taken their places on the other side: Babe Ruth, Luis Tiant, Lefty Grove, Cy Young, Roger Clemens, Mel Parnell, Curt Schilling, and Pedro Martinez.

"This is it, isn't it?" Oscar asked.

Oscar's father nodded.

Oscar shuffled a few steps forward so that he was under the rubber. He touched the dirt, holding the palm of his hand flat against it. It was cool and soft. "Is this your bedroom? Where you sleep?" he asked.

"It is," his father said, opening the trunk. "I thought you'd sleep here, too." He pulled out a rolled-up pallet and a quilt.

"I'd like that," Oscar said, wondering how he would be able to fall asleep knowing he was lying just under the pitcher's mound in Fenway Park.

Down below, Auntie Oonagh said, "It's almost time for Radio to talk to us! Turn them up! Louder, louder!"

Auntie Fedelma shouted, "Radio, our one true voice! God bless him."

"Who's Radio?" Oscar asked his father.

"They mean the voices that come out of the radio, really. But mainly, most of all, the AM sports radio station." He laid out the pallet and then shook out the quilt above it, letting it billow and then fall.

Oscar peered down on the aunties. Auntie Oonagh was snapping on each radio, all tuned to the same talk station; and with each click one voice got louder. Right now, a loud shock jock was hosting a visitor to the show: Dan Shaughnessy, a local sportswriter and the author of *The Curse of the Bambino*. Oscar had gotten the book out of the library, had read Shaughnessy's columns, and had heard him on the radio before, too. Shaughnessy had lots of opinions and plenty of stats and liked to talk up the Curse; each flub in the field, each loss, each player trade seemed to lead him back to it. Oscar didn't like him. At this very moment he was complaining about Schilling's injured ankle, and how that was just another sign of the Curse.

Auntie Fedelma closed her eyes tight and listened fiercely. "So true, Radio! That's right!" she'd call out. "You tell 'em, Radio!"

Oscar couldn't stand to listen to Shaughnessy

bad-mouth Schilling. He was one of the best pitchers in the whole league, and his injured ankle seemed like a cruel joke. Oscar had watched Schilling lose the first game in the series against the Yankees because he wasn't able to plant his foot and his pitches were thrown off by the pain. It made Oscar's heart ache in his chest.

"Why does Shaughnessy have to trash-talk the Sox all the time?" Oscar said.

"He just wants to sell books," his father said. "I don't take him seriously, but Auntie Fedelma worships him," Oscar's father said. "She isn't that bad, down deep. You should just ignore her. And Auntie Oonagh is truly sweet and kindhearted. She can be flighty, but she means well."

"And Auntie Gormley?" Oscar was most curious about her.

"She's mysterious in a way but wise in her silence. You can trust her."

Oscar looked down at her white hair, the twist of her bun. Auntie Gormley, as if sensing she was being watched, looked up. She gave a frail wave, and Oscar waved back.

"Can I ask you something?" Oscar said to his father.

"What is it?" His father took a seat on his pallet

and stretched out his legs in front of him.

"How come you never brought me here before? Did you think I wouldn't understand? Or that I wouldn't care or something? Or that I'd get scared?"

His father looked at Oscar intently. "Here's the thing, Oscar. We're stuck here," he said. "Now that you know that we exist, now that you've seen all of this, you're stuck here, too," Oscar's father said. "It's that way with humans when they cross over into our realm."

"'Realm'?" Oscar said. "What are you talking about?"

"You can go up above like I do," Oscar's father said. "But you can't stay up too long or you'll weaken. That's why I didn't want you to stay with me, to ever see where I lived. And then I was all muddled while waiting for your mother. I got to thinking that maybe you were, well, that you'd be the one to break the Curse, to set us free, that it was fate. But now I don't know." He wrung his hands and then looked at Oscar hopefully. "And I was thinking, too, that maybe you wouldn't think it was so bad to be here with your dad. We've wasted so much time. I could have been a great father all along—if it weren't for this Curse!" His father rubbed his forehead roughly. "What was I thinking? This is terrible. This is the worst mistake of my life, bringing you here!"

Oscar wasn't sure what to say. He sat there for a minute, stunned by it all. "But what if I break the Curse?"

"Then we'd all be free, all of the Cursed Creatures," his father said. "The Red Sox would even be able to win a World Series."

"You mean that I could really help the Red Sox win a World Series?" Oscar asked.

"And much more than that . . . but it's too much pressure to put on you. You're just a boy."

"I'd like to try to help," Oscar said. "There's nothing in the world I'd like better."

"It's too late. I mean, the Sox are already down two games to the Yankees in the playoffs. Too late." His eyes were shining with tears. "This curse has been on the Red Sox for eighty-six years. Eighty-six years!"

Oscar had been wanting something from his father, a bond; and although this wasn't the one he'd have chosen—being stuck here together—it was one nonetheless. "How did you end up here?" he asked.

His father sighed, and his voice took on a

different tone, as if he were reciting a fairy tale. "It's a long story."

"A long, good story or a long, bad story?"

"Both."

"Well, then, how about the part of the story where you met Mom?"

"I didn't do it very well—balancing both lives. I met your mother here in Fenway Park. She was the most beautiful girl I'd ever seen, and we went to games together—that was the dating part. And then I asked her to marry me here in the park. And then we got a place together, not far away." He was staring off, as if seeing it all in his head. He closed his eyes, soaking in the memory.

"And did she know all about you?" Oscar asked.

"The wings were hard to explain," he said. And Oscar could tell that his father didn't like that part of himself: his wings. Oscar knew what he meant. Oscar didn't like looking different from everyone else either.

"What did you tell Mom about your wings?"

"She took them as some strange abnormality. Some people have webbed toes, you know. I wasn't completely honest."

"Why did you adopt me?"

"We both wanted to take in a child who didn't

have a home, and then you showed up and you were perfect. But I was sickly by then, barely able to get out of bed—fevered and weak all the time. And I thought I might die. And your mother was tired. I was a drain on her. She had to take care of a baby and me. And so I came back here."

That was the reason he'd left? Oscar'd always thought that maybe his father had left because Oscar's skin had turned darker, his hair kinky. But it wasn't that at all, was it? His father had been sick. Oscar smiled. He couldn't help it.

"What?" his father asked. "Why are you smiling?"

"Nothing," Oscar said. He changed the subject. "So you take care of the grounds?"

"Yep, it's my gift."

"What are their gifts?" Oscar asked, pointing downstairs.

"Auntie Fedelma got the gift of deep belief. But she got all the wrong beliefs to believe in." He paused. "You know that, right? I don't have to tell you that she's wrong, that she's an old fool?"

Oscar shook his head. "I know people like her," he said, thinking of Drew Sizemore.

"Auntie Gormley got the gift of dreaming her soul elsewhere. She can dream that she's a cat if she wants; and while her body is sleeping, she lives inside of that cat."

"Wow," Oscar said.

"Yes, it's very wow; but it hasn't ever been very useful. She calls it her parlor trick."

"Auntie Oonagh got the gift of the future and the past. She has the Key to the Past, but she doesn't go through the doorway anymore. She says the key was stolen from her once and the Door to the Past was broken into, which is a serious crime of trespassing."

Oscar wasn't sure what a Door to the Past would look like. It had to be grand, though, perhaps made of gold?

His father went on. "She locked the door after her father disappeared, as the Curse settled upon us. She told me once that she was afraid that she would slip into the past, if she let herself, and never come back out."

"Mom talks about the past. She's read books about how to get rid of the past."

"Has she?" His father spoke in his broken voice, and Oscar realized he hadn't sounded like that since they'd left Pizzeria Uno. Oscar regretted bringing up his mother.

"You're tired, I bet," Oscar's father mumbled. "You should get some rest."

"Okay," Oscar said.

His father pulled some pajamas off of a shelf. He looked around the little room. "I guess I'll go downstairs to change. Give you some privacy to do the same." His father climbed down the ladder. The radio was still on. The loud, slurry voice of a caller was rambling on, obviously inspired by what Shaughnessy had been saying about *The Curse of the Bambino*. "Shoulda never sold Babe Ruth," the fan was saying. "The Bambino. 1919. That's when we went wrong."

Oscar had heard this before. Everybody had. Now that he was close to the Curse, he wondered if trading Babe Ruth was really tied up in it. The Curse seemed ancient. What if Oscar couldn't break the Curse? What if his father was right and it was too big of a job?

Oscar lay back on his pallet and stared up at the dirt ceiling. He felt a million miles away from the apartment over Dependable Cleaners. He pictured it in his mind: the little, old-fashioned bell and weather vane at the top; the moist heat rising up; the smell of soiled clothes, sweat, starch, and perc—the acidic chemical that got out the stains. And then, sometimes, his mother would lift her finger in the middle of doing something ordinary—paying bills or washing dishes—and she'd say, "There it is. Do you smell that?" And Oscar would walk to wherever she was standing and inhale a waft from the bagel shop next door completely unexpected: yeasty dough and cinnamon. He missed his mother all of a sudden.

Would he really have to live here forever? It started to sink in: stuck. Hadn't he felt stuck in his old life, too?

Oscar unzipped his suitcase to get his pajamas. He flipped open the plaid lid, and there on top of his neatly folded clothes was a small, rectangular present wrapped in blue tissue paper. A gift that his mother must have slipped in his suitcase.

Oscar picked it up.

It was thin. It only held one baseball card—he could tell. His mother had always gotten him bulk packs of cards from the dollar store that never had a great card in them. He had enough Allan Embrees and Mike Stantons to start wallpapering his room. But he'd always begged her for just one good card instead of bulk. Maybe his mother had listened this year. Maybe this was a Yaz card, finally, at last. His hands started shaking. He slipped off the ribbon and popped off the tape. And then he let out a sigh.

It was a mint-condition Ripken. But not Cal. It was Cal's brother Billy, who'd blipped onto the scene and then off again. His mother had probably thought Ripken and just assumed she'd got the right one. The other problem, of course, was that it was the Orioles. The *Baltimore* Orioles. There was a little slip of paper inside with his mother's handwriting on it. It read:

Oscar—my prince!

Happy birthday! Don't forget about me here in Baltimore!

Love, Mom

P.S. Maybe you'll be an Orioles fan one day!!!

And then there was a smiley face. Oscar hated the smiley face most of all.

An Orioles fan? Was she saying that he'd live in Baltimore one day when he was the Prince of Condos? Was she saying that he'd have to give up the Red Sox? Did his mother know him at all? He couldn't ever be an Orioles fan. He was a Red Sox fan. Forever.

And now he was more than a Red Sox fan. He was one of the Cursed Creatures of Fenway Park. It almost felt good to know he was really cursed instead of just having a hunch. He shoved the card in the back of his suitcase. He didn't want to be an Orioles fan or the future Condo Prince of Baltimore. He wanted to be the Prince of Fenway Park.

Tomorrow was his birthday, but he couldn't imagine that it would really feel like his birthday here. Would he tour the park? He could feel it hovering above him. If he had been one of them, with fairy blood, would he have gotten a gift, a powerful gift? He closed his eyes and imagined the Red Sox playing a game in Fenway. He wondered what that would be like.

His father reappeared, and as he climbed into bed, Oscar could see the small rises on the back of his father's pajamas—two lumps that twitched ever so slightly. His wings.

Oscar stared up at the ceiling. "I know you don't go to the games," he said. "But do you ever lie here during a real game?"

He looked over at Oscar and smiled. "You can hear their cleats scraping in the dirt."

CHAPTER SIX

The First Birthday Gift

OSCAR DREAMED OF HIS MOTHER. She was dancing in the stands of Fenway Park with a man Oscar knew was Marty Glib—even though Oscar had never seen Marty Glib. Oscar was standing on the pitcher's mound in his old Rockets' uniform from the summer before. His father was in the dugout. "Go on," he said. "Show 'em what you got, Oscar!"

Oscar had a ball in his hand, and suddenly there was a batter up to the plate. It was Weasel-man with the leashes of his noisily chirping weasels tied to his belt loop. The three aunties were in the stands, too. Auntie Fedelma had her hands over her eyes. Auntie Oonagh had her hands over her ears, and Auntie Gormley had her hands over her mouth.

"Go on," his father said again. "Show 'em what you got!"

And so Oscar pitched the ball with all of his might, and it came back at him—not just one ball but many. All of the balls were on wires now, and the wires were connected to Oscar's body. The balls were coming at him hard. He took off running away from them, ripping off each wire as each ball on it rocketed toward him.

"Go, Oscar!" his father cheered.

Oscar didn't want to be cheered, though. He wanted everyone to realize that the game was fake, that nothing was real. He wanted help. He called out, "Mom! Mom!"

But Marty Glib and his mother were suddenly great dancers. They were leaping ten, fifteen bleachers at a time and spinning wildly up in the air. They couldn't hear him.

The metal placards of the scoreboard kept clacking. Weasel-man was winning by ten runs, then a hundred, then a thousand. Finally, Oscar had ripped all of the wires loose. He tilted his head back to catch his breath. It started to rain. The drops pattered down on his face.

He opened his eyes, and bits of dirt were crumbling off the ceiling. Oscar sputtered awake. The dirt stopped crumbling.

It was still somewhat dark in the room. His father was snoring on the other side of the crawl space. Oscar knew it was still night. He heard feet on the ladder. He crawled over to the hole and looked down. It was Auntie Gormley. She was tottering across the living room to her bleacher seat. She sat down exhausted, breathing hard. She closed her eyes, folded her hands in her lap. What had she been doing up here? Oscar wondered.

The other aunties weren't in sight. Oscar could hear them talking in the kitchen. The radios were all still tuned to the AM talk radio sports station. But not all of the sounds that Oscar heard were coming from below. On the other side of the pitcher's mound, there was some strange thudding and a horrible laugh, like lonesome braying. And then he heard hooves clomping away from the mound. A set of hooves. Oscar's heart was thumping loudly. He could hear it in his ears.

Oscar looked around the little space. His father's alarm clock read 12:04. At the foot of Oscar's pallet in the red glow of the clock there sat a box with red shoelaces on top of it, all bound together into a makeshift bow. It was a gift, maybe a birthday gift. It *was* officially Oscar's birthday.

He crawled out from under his quilt and down to the foot of the pallet. Oscar untied the bow and opened the box. Inside of it, there was a model of a ball field, with yellow foul poles and a green wall, brown dirt, and white bases; it was, of course, Fenway Park. There was an old-fashioned scoreboard and batting cages and small, wooden figures—ballplayers made of wood. They wore tiny gloves made of real leather. More ballplayers—in jerseys from every era, and not just Red Sox jerseys—lined the edges of the field. Oscar saw Dodgers, Yankees, Braves—both Atlanta Braves and old Boston Braves—Chicago White Sox, and Cubs, too. The park was surrounded by stands filled with faces of fans painted onto the walls. There was writing on the side of the box: the date 09, 05, 1918. And there was only one player on the field: the pitcher standing on the mound—a lefty in a Red Sox uniform. Was it Babe Ruth? When he was traded to the Yankees, he was a pitcher, and the date fit.

But then the park was also modern. There was the Green Monster and its contemporary scoreboard. Oscar noticed that there was something strange about the scoreboard. All ten innings and the slots for runs, hits, and errors were lined up on the far wall. It was wrong. It was wrong, and yet it sort of made sense to Oscar. In fact, it seemed to be in a kind of code. Oscar had never been good at codes. His teacher from the year before had used them in math class, but they never made much sense to Oscar. This one, however, made perfect sense.

HE99E8ER7HOEE

Normally this would just look like a very strange score: H meaning Hits; E meaning Errors; R meaning Runs. They never got mixed in with the score; and the score never had blank spots, either, as if an inning had been missed. Usually an inning has only one number and one tally at the end: three digits—runs, hits, errors. Oscar knew it was wrong, that it wasn't meant to be the score of an actual game at all. But what surprised him was that he read it immediately, without really even thinking about it. He could barely explain his own thought process, it had been so quick. It was a five-letter word and an eight-letter word separated by a space; that had been obvious. The Es represented vowels, any old vowels. The Hs were Hs. The R was an R. The 9s were Ps, as Ps look like 9s: circles on sticks. The 8 was a B with its one circlish bump on top of another. And if the slant of a 7 was straighten up it would be a T. The second H helped, as repetitions do in code breaking; and if an O was shored up with a stiff back, it became a D.

It read: HAPPY BIRTHDAY.

He tried to explain the weird way his brain had just worked by the fact that it was his birthday, technically speaking. It was after midnight. He was twelve years old. He'd wondered if anyone would remember. And someone had.

He crawled over to the ladder again and peered down at Auntie Gormley. Is that what she'd been up to in the crawl space while he was dreaming? Had she been giving him his gift with its scoreboard message? What made her think he'd even notice it? And, if he did, why did she think he'd be able to figure it out? And why had he been able to figure it out?

He peered down into the small parlor again. The other two aunties were sleeping soundly. This time when he looked at Auntie Gormley, her eyes opened immediately and locked onto his. She smiled, and then she began to blink. It was a complicated series of blinks that would look like someone having a fit . . . except that it didn't look that way to Oscar.

No. It seemed as if she was spelling out words—another code—and the words made sense.

The first zigzag eye movement and half blink with the left eye was the letter Y. Rolling her eyes with a half blink meant O. A smile motion and a half blink meant U. A full blink meant a new word. She'd spelled Y-O-U. The rest of the sentence was easy to understand: H-A-V-E full blink G-I-F-T.

"I do?" Oscar whispered down over the distant racket of pans in the kitchen.

She blinked once for Yes.

"Did you give it to me?"

She blinked once again.

"But I didn't think you could. I didn't think any of you could. I don't belong here. I'm not of any use."

She rolled her eyes as if to say *Nonsense!*

"Do you think I can help?"

She blinked.

"Do you think I'm the one who can save us?"

She blinked.

Oscar couldn't quite believe it. He wondered what his father would say—and Auntie Fedelma.

"What is my gift?" Oscar asked.

She only looked at him knowingly.

"It's that," he said, pointing at the scoreboard.

"It's the ability to, well, break codes? To understand without being spoken to? It's the gift of, um, of . . . Am I close? It's the gift of . . ."

And then Auntie Gormley spelled out: R-E-A-D-I-N-G S-I-G-N-S.

"Oh," he said, a little confused and disappointed. What good would that do? He needed the gift of toughness and bravery and strength. Sure, he'd be able to understand Auntie Gormley better, but what good would this do him in breaking the Curse?

He sat back on his heels for a moment, trying to process it all. He looked over at his father, still asleep, then again at the message: Happy Birthday.

Auntie Gormley knew it was his birthday. She'd given him a gift. He hadn't expected anything. He leaned over the edge and whispered, "Thank you."

Auntie Gormley nodded and closed her eyes.

CHAPTER SEVEN

The Curse

OSCAR REALIZED THAT HE'D DOZED off when he was woken by a thudding noise. He opened his eyes to see his father on his knees, wearing his orange safety vest, knocking on the rubber of the pitcher's mound with the end of a baseball bat.

"Glad you're up, Oscar!" his father said.

"You woke me up," Oscar said. His father's clock read 1:05 a.m. "Are they awake?" Oscar asked, looking down through a knothole. The living room was still lit, the radios on.

"Oh, they nap sometimes, but they may still be listening to the recaps. It's like the middle of the day for us, you know. We're nocturnal. We're on the opposite clock as those up there." He pointed overhead. "Easier for everyone that way."

"Oh," Oscar said.

"Well, it's a good thing you're up. You can come along and help me with my work."

And with that he gave one last hard jolt to the rubber atop the mound. It popped out of place. A bit of moonlight streamed down, filling the crawl space.

Oscar could barely speak. He could see a rectangle of dark sky. "Is that . . ."

"It is," his father said. "I need to check the field conditions. See if there are any problems." He pulled a brass periscope out of the trunk and then flipped a switch on the wall that Oscar hadn't seen before. A bank of field lights turned on overhead, and the rectangular hole grew brighter. Oscar's father fitted the periscope's wide eye up through the hole. He fiddled with the focus and pinched his own eye shut to have a look.

"What kind of problems?"

"The Pooka of Fenway Park. He sometimes gallops through the field around midnight. He can ruin the infield dirt, making grounders impossible to read, or put divots in a baseline that'll cause a ball to pop foul and holes in the outfield that'll cause a ballplayer to twist an ankle. Almost as bad as the Bossards made Comiskey Park."

"The Bossards?"

"Gene Bossard was the big daddy of grounds-keeper cheats—worked for the White Sox. They wrote it all up in his obituary even. You know Fenway was built on a swamp; well, Bossard kept Comiskey Park that way for the sinker ball pitchers, and he watered down first base when the base stealers were in town. He moved the portable fences back for the Yankees. He kept the baselines raised, too, for Nellie Fox's bunts—so they stayed fair. The Bossards invented frozen baseballs; and their nastiest trick was putting baseballs in an old room with a humidifier forever on full tilt so the balls would get heavy with water. Some say the pitchers had to wipe the mildew off them." He shook his head.

"Are you that kind of groundskeeper?" Oscar asked.

"Nope. My skills are used for the good of the game. I repair what the Pooka destroys."

Oscar's father peered across the field one last time. "The Pooka must be restless tonight. There's work to be done. Have a look." He tipped the periscope toward Oscar. Oscar shut one eye and peered through the lens.

It was a glorious sight. The floodlights made

the grass so green, it had a yellow undershine to it. Oscar's eye roved over the powdered white lines, the giant scoreboard and the towering stadium, the rows and rows of seats.

"It's amazing!"

"Yep, a real mess all right."

"What?" Oscar said. "I don't see any problems."

"Look at the grounds, Oscar. Look closely."

At first Oscar was too astonished to see anything wrong; but he stared as hard as he could, and then the pockmarks and divots became clear. "Oh," he said. "I see them now."

He lowered his voice. "The truth is, Oscar, not everyone wants the Curse to be reversed."

"Really?" Oscar asked, looking at his father.

"Some depend on it." He took the periscope from Oscar and put it back in the trunk.

"How?" Oscar said.

His father reached his arm up and out of the rectangular hole, patted around, laid his hand on the rubber, and pulled it back into place, plugging the hole. He whispered, "The Curse is what made them who they are." He glanced at his duffel bag sitting in the corner. "Do you want to read it?"

"Read what?"

"The Curse."

Oscar glanced at the duffel bag too. "Is it in there?"

"I keep it with me at all times."

Oscar thought of the dusty, golden, locked box. He wanted to come clean with his father, tell him that he'd peeked in the duffel bag when his father had been in the bathroom at Pizzeria Uno, but even more importantly now, he needed to tell his father about his gift. But he wasn't sure if his father would believe him or not. How would he put it? I am the one who can save us. It's me after all. But Oscar could barely believe it himself.

Oscar's father was crawling to the duffel bag, pulling it toward Oscar. Oscar spoke very softly. "I got a gift," he said.

His father shook his head. "Oh, that's right! It's your birthday! Happy birthday, Oscar. I have to rewrap your gift. Maybe we'll have a little party later."

"No," Oscar said. "I got a gift." He lunged to the foot of his pallet and picked up the Fenway Park model, and then he paused and looked at his father. "And I got a *real* gift. I'm twelve now."

His father froze. "But, but, you're . . . you're not . . ."

"I know," Oscar said. "But Auntie Gormley gave it to me, and it's stuck."

Oscar's father looked down through the square hole leading to the living room. Oscar did too. The three aunties were fast asleep. "It stuck?" he asked.

"I can read signs."

"What kind of signs?"

"Well, I'm not sure what kind yet. But so far I can read Auntie Gormley's blinks, and I read that." He pointed to the scoreboard on the model.

"That's no score at all."

"It says 'Happy Birthday.' "

"It does?"

"Yep."

His father stared at the scoreboard. He was disappointed, Oscar could tell. And Oscar was embarrassed. It wasn't a gift at all. He'd broken one code, and he'd been able to understand an old lady. Big deal.

His father said, "Oh, well, that's all good, Oscar. I'm glad that Auntie Gormley gave you a gift." And this seemed worst of all, that his father was faking being pleased about it. He was holding the duffel bag. "Do you want to read the Curse?"

Oscar nodded, even though he didn't really feel like it anymore. What good would it do?

His father took out the dusty golden box. He pulled a key chain out of his back pocket and stuck one of the keys into the lock. The lock gave a click, and the box popped open. Inside was a long, narrow scroll of paper. Oscar's father pulled it out. "Have to be careful with it. It's so old."

"How old?" Oscar asked.

"Written in 1919."

This was the year that Babe Ruth had been traded. "So the Curse has everything to do with Babe Ruth, doesn't it?"

"Only in part. Only in part. Here," he said, handing him the scroll. "Read it to yourself. The beginning of it doesn't make much sense. No one's ever been able to make sense of it. And the rest, well, we understand it all too well. I can't bear to hear it again."

Oscar unrolled the tiny scroll and started to read silently.

The Curse and Its Three Unbreakable Rules

We are each an orphan, a big-handed boy learning to stitch seams. We try hard to find a place called home. Tough hearts, baseball tough, lodged in our chests, are more bruised than you can know. Use your eyes to see Babe there . . . an unloved

boy in a tailor shop. His heart can break, like all of ours, into a wide green field filled with a need to be loved—a roaring crowd of love. And now I will curse you on the blood moon, the hunter's moon—because who are you, Red Sox, to sell a soul, to call it names and cast it out?
Sincerely,
Keeffe Egg

May you be cursed, Fenway Park.
May horned creatures reign the dark.
May a Pooka roost in your hill.
May the Banshee cry and keen at will.
May weasels nest
and nettles infest.
May herds of mice swarm
and evil managers do harm.
May you be close enough to taste the win
but always, truly, lose before you even begin.
And now the Three Unbreakable Rules:

1. *No one can explain anything to the Breaker of the Curse beyond the words writ here.*
2. *Every Cursed Creature has a Position to Play.*
3. *There can be only one Breaker of the Curse. Once he sets his mind to breaking the Curse, he must succeed or no one ever will.*

* * *

As Oscar rolled up the Curse, his hands were shaking. His heart felt jittery, as if it were kicking around in his chest. "Who is Keeffe?" he asked.

"The Aunties' father, my grandfather."

"What about your father? Who was he?" Oscar asked.

"Never mind him either. He didn't get on the ship. He was fully human. He abandoned us. Keeffe was my father figure. But then he cursed us and left us."

"Oh," Oscar said. "I'm sorry."

"I know; I should be forgiving. My grandfather had failings. He never got over being cast out of Ireland. And he was heartbroken at the time, too. My grandmother was sickly on the ship. She didn't make it over."

"His wife died?" Oscar asked.

"People died on ships back then. I wasn't born yet. I never knew her."

"And your father had already left you."

"Yes," his father said, a little frustrated. "What's your point?"

"It's just that you're kind of an orphan, almost, half. And the aunties are orphans too, in a way. We're all a long line of orphans. It's strange. . . ."

Oscar looked down at the rolled-up scroll in his hands. He felt a little breathless, as if he were being chased.

"But I have the aunties, and you have your mother and me."

"That's right," Oscar said. "But still, if you're an orphan once, you always are, in some way. There's always somebody—maybe a stranger you'll never even meet—who you've got to forgive."

"I know I'm supposed to forgive Keeffe. But the fact is, he ran off. Got out while the getting was still good, before his curse had time to take."

"But," Oscar said, his heart thudding loudly now, "there's a message inside of the note to the reader of the Curse."

"A message?"

"And I think it was written to me."

CHAPTER EIGHT

The Message Inside of the Curse

IT WAS EASY FOR OSCAR. He saw it right away. He read it as clearly as if it were the only thing the Curse had to say.

"In the first paragraph—the part you said doesn't make much sense—well, at the beginning of each sentence, I counted letters until I came to the twelfth letter," he said.

"Why did you do that?" his father asked.

"I don't know. I mean, twelve is an important number—you know, for me, well, today. But I can't explain why I did it. I just did. I kind of crossed out the first eleven letters and concentrated on the twelfth in my mind, and then I read each word that started with those twelfth letters."

His father took the Curse from him and did what Oscar said. He said the words slowly just one at a time. "Cross out the first eleven letters: 'We are each an' . . . and you're left with the word 'orphan.'"

"That's me," Oscar said.

His father went on. "Cross out: 'We try hard to,' and you've got the word 'find.' "

"Mmhm," said Oscar. "Go on."

"Okay, okay, I'm going. Cross out: 'Tough hearts,' and you've got 'baseball.' "

"And so it reads, 'Orphan, find baseball.' Go on."

"All right. Cross out 'Use your eyes,' " and you've got the word 'to.' And then cross out 'His heart can,' and you've got the word 'break.' And then cross out 'And now I will,' and you've got the word 'curse.' "

"That's the message," Oscar said. " 'Orphan, find baseball to break curse.' "

His father was still holding the narrow scroll of paper. " 'Orphan,' " he repeated in a whisper, " 'find baseball to break curse.' " He gazed up at Oscar. "It's been there all along. I just couldn't see it." He raised his fist in the air—as high as it could go in the crawl space. "You've done it, Oscar! 'Find baseball to break curse'!" he shouted, and then he grabbed Oscar by the shoulders and pulled him to his chest, giving him a huge hug.

Oscar wasn't used to being hugged by his father like this. He closed his eyes. He drank it in. He knew what the Curse had been saying about being an orphan and having a heart as tough as a baseball but bruised, too.

His father leaned over the ladder hole and shouted to the aunties, "The boy has done it!"

The aunties snorted awake. "What's that?" "Who?" "Come again!"

"Oscar," he shouted, "has broken a code in the Curse. We've just got to find a baseball!"

"He did what?" Auntie Fedelma growled.

"Auntie Gormley gave him a gift! He's twelve! And it worked!"

"You gave him a gift?" Auntie Fedelma shouted at Auntie Gormley.

Oscar scurried to the edge of the ladder hole to look down and see Auntie Gormley's answer. Would she stick up for him?

She pointed up at Oscar and shook her fist in a kind of victory.

"He's the one who can save us!" his father shouted.

"He is not!" Auntie Fedelma shouted back.

"Is he?" asked Auntie Oonagh, pointing the funnel in her ear from one person to the next, hoping for a clear answer.

"Maybe we won't be saved by someone Born of the Curse but by someone who has *Lived* the Curse," Oscar's father said joyfully. "And the boy is cursed! He feels as cursed as the Red Sox! Don't you?"

Oscar had never seen it as a good thing before. "I guess so," he said.

"That's what he said," Oscar's father shouted down. "It just might be him! Don't you get it?"

"Humph," Auntie Fedelma muttered angrily. "Radio knows that you can't break the Curse. Shaughnessy knows it! Everyone knows that you can't break the Curse. Plus, the Sox are already losing to the Yankees. Down two! They'll never come back. Never!"

Auntie Oonagh ignored Auntie Fedelma. She clapped her hands. "Hooray! A baseball! That won't be hard to find! We live in a ballpark!"

There was more shouting among Auntie Fedelma and Oscar's father and Auntie Oonagh. But Oscar was no longer following the conversation. He felt dazed, light-headed. He pulled on his father's sleeve. "Not just any baseball," he said. "It has to be *the* baseball. The one he used for the Curse. And how are we going to find *that*?"

His father crossed his arms and blinked. "I have no idea."

Oscar stared down at the aunties blankly. "A hunt," he said.

"A hunt," his father said, sitting back, staring at the model of Fenway Park.

"Why even look? You'll never find it!" Auntie Fedelma shouted to them. "Mark my words, Old Boy, you're setting yourself up for a terrible disappointment. Remember 1948? 1967? 1975? 1986? Not to mention just last year, 2003?"

Auntie Gormley rocked in her bleacher seat and softly whistled "Take Me Out to the Ball Game."

Oscar and his father sat there in the crawl space for a moment, dazed by it all.

"What did Keeffe mean by 'a big-handed boy learning to stitch seams'?" Oscar asked.

"Ruth. His parents handed him over to an orphanage when he was little. St. Mary's Industrial School for Boys. He wasn't technically an orphan, I suppose, but he was abandoned, an orphan in the larger sense—the kind we understand in this family."

Oscar nodded. Of course.

Auntie Fedelma was still shouting. "Mark my words! Failure! Loss!"

Auntie Oonagh was trying to shush her but sounded as if she was simply losing air.

"St. Mary's was big on baseball and little else. Most of the boys were taught a skill and were sent out to work instead of to school. Ruth worked for a tailor."

Oscar stared up at the mound's rubber. He thought of the look he'd gotten through the periscope. "I wish I could fit up through the pitcher's mound," Oscar said more to himself than to his father. "Squeeze myself right up through that hole."

"I don't know why you'd want to do that," his father said.

"So that I could see the field!" Oscar said. "The way the greatest pitchers of all time have seen it. Right from the mound."

"I mean, why would you want to shove yourself up through the hole when you can just use the door."

"The door?"

"Sure, the seamless trapdoor," his father said. "By the spigot. There." He pointed to the underside of a pipe. "Works the same way as the rubber on the pitcher's mound but it's a bit bulkier. May as well start the hunt right there." He pushed up on the dirt ceiling halfway between the pitcher's mound, and the spigot. The earth trembled a bit.

"Good-bye, Aunties!" he shouted down to the living room. He picked up a sack marked SEED from the built-in shelf. "We're off!"

"Hooray!" shouted Auntie Oonagh.

"You'll regret this, Old Boy. You and the Other will only be terribly disappointed!" Auntie Fedelma called out.

"My name is Oscar," Oscar said.

His father smiled at him, and Oscar smiled back. "Follow me quickly," he said.

His father pushed hard on the dirt ceiling, which was on an angle. In an instant, the dirt turned into a door, just as the door to their house had appeared in the tunnel wall covered in barbed ivy and nettle bushes. The door swung open and hit the ground with a thud. His father popped out, grabbed Oscar by the hand, and pulled him out too. As Oscar emerged from the opening into the crisp night air, Fenway seemed to rise up all around him, glowing in the floodlights.

He walked to the top of the pitcher's mound. At

first he could only stare at his shoes on the rubber. He knew exactly where he was.

His father flipped the door back, and it fell a little hastily and a bit crookedly. And then he stood next to Oscar and said, "Pedro Martinez, Curt Schilling, Keith Foulke."

"I know," Oscar said quietly.

"Roger Clemens, Oil Can Boyd, Luis Tiant," his father went on.

Oscar's voice was caught in his throat now. He could only nod.

"Cy Young and Babe Ruth. All of them stood here, too. Probably even stared at their shoes in the dirt."

Oscar could feel his eyes fill up with tears, but not the same kind as under the awning at Pizzeria Uno. The greats had all stood here, and new greats were coming. Game 3 of the playoffs was just a day away. Oscar tried to imagine standing here with the whole team around him. It was too much.

"It's okay," his father said. "I feel that way too, sometimes, still." He patted him on the shoulder. "Take a look."

Oscar slowly lifted his eyes. There was a low green wall, red seats rising to blue seats in the grandstands. It was all much closer than he'd imagined, much closer than it seemed on television.

There was a small green box, open-air, suspended above the grandstands behind home plate like the carriage under a blimp—the broadcast booth from which Joe Castiglione and Jerry Trupiano announced the games. Above it stretched a huge bank of windows—the .406 Club, where the organist played during the games. And then, in red letters on a white board: FENWAY PARK. The sign towered over him. Oscar looked down at the circle of dirt on which he was standing, and another in front of him, and, within that one, home plate.

"David Ortiz," Oscar said. "Manny Ramirez."

"Mo Vaughn, Rice, and Yastrzemski," his father said.

"Ted Williams," Oscar said.

"Yes, yes, Williams."

Oscar had revered these players all of his life, and now, reciting their names felt like a prayer whispered in a quiet cathedral. Without these names, Fenway Park would be empty, barren. But these names made it alive and holy.

He glanced at the Red Sox dugout, the empty seats hovering above, and looked down the first baseline. Oscar peered out into right field. Across the grass there was the warning track and the bull pens. There was Pesky's Pole—the only place old Johnny Pesky could hit a homer.

Oscar looked toward second base and right field. His head was flooded with more names: Griffin, Doyle, and Walker.

His father pointed to right field. "Evans, Nixon."

Above the green center field wall, a triangle of blue seats tapered toward a giant television screen that was blank. He looked out to center field and shortstop. "Lynn, Burke."

"Burleson and Aparicio," his father said.

And here Oscar hesitated. He knew that if he turned left, the Green Monster would be there—the massive, historic wall. He pivoted slowly, feeling humble.

It was enormous, stretching from the red seats rising to the left field foul pole, where Carlton Fisk had hit a home run to win Game 6 of the 1975 World Series, all the way out to the flagpole in center. It was broad and tall, and seemed almost to tilt forward, over the field.

Oscar's eyes rounded third—Petrocelli, Boggs, Hobson—and headed home. Pena and Fisk. He drew in a deep breath, feeling very small. He glanced back at the doorway through which they'd come. The square of grass was still visible, but then his father bent down and ruffled the grass, and the seams disappeared.

"I thought I'd never get to share all of this with you. It's a magical place. But there's so much sadness here, too." His father walked over to the divots in the infield grass. "Hoof marks," he said, "take a look. The Pooka." His father took a handful of seed from the tin and sprinkled it on the pocks. Oscar thought of the third rule of the Curse. They had already crossed the point of no return—success, or the Curse will last forever. It made him feel cold. "This dirt has absorbed a lot of sorrow, and that's what makes it so soft."

"Sorrow?" Oscar asked.

"It started with Babe Ruth, but the Curse would have starved if it hadn't been fed. And it was surely fed."

"Who fed it?"

"Too many to list. You know what they said to Jackie Robinson when he tried out?" Oscar knew. He'd read all about Red Sox history. "Not Red Sox type, right? And they said Willie Mays wasn't ready. We know what they meant." He threw more seed on a hoof mark. "Because they were black, they weren't good enough for the Boston Red Sox. This is the worst team in the history of baseball on race. You know that, though, don't you?" His father knelt down to eye the field at ground level.

"I know it," Oscar said. "I just didn't know that you knew." His father never talked about race—not Oscar's and not anybody else's either, for that matter. Maybe this was part of the reason why. Oscar could tell that his father was uncomfortable.

"Race shouldn't mean anything. It shouldn't be important. It shouldn't matter." Oscar's father stood up and wiped his hands on his pants.

Oscar wanted to say that it did matter and that it was important, but he wasn't sure how he'd explain it if his father asked him *why* or *how*, and so he kept quiet.

"Nasty sportswriters did their share, too." His father pointed to the dugout. "And sometimes there was ugliness in *there*. Player against player."

"The players went against each other?" Oscar asked.

"It's a long season, and losing can make players lash out," his father said, gazing around at the stands. "And don't forget about them."

"The fans?" Oscar asked. "Not them."

"Some of them have kept the Red Sox going—

their love is like an engine. But others . . . well, we all know Buckner deserves to be in the Hall of Fame. Who do you think runs him down? Fans do! And after all the great things he did for the Red Sox and for the game!" He shook his head. "You should hear the ugly things some of those fans have shouted over the years, jeering and booing. Do you think that kind of meanness just evaporates into the air? It doesn't. It's all fed the Curse, Oscar." He sighed. "Some people in the outside world have gotten close to understanding the Curse. Shaughnessy got a little of it in *The Curse of the Bambino*, but he's really only fed the Curse too, with all of his cynicism and ugliness—more sorrow. And Bill Lee . . ."

"The left-handed pitcher? Spaceman?"

"Yeah, he gets part of it in that philosophical, kind of poetic, other way of thinking that he has. And Howard Bryant wrote about it the best in that book of his called *Shut Out*. He's come the closest. But no one has ever understood the whole thing. No one has ever discovered us. Even if they tear this place down and the land turns back to swamp, we'll be the swamp creatures stuck in it. Unless we can reverse it. Unless *you* can, Oscar."

"But how?" Oscar said. "Where will we find the baseball?" He looked up and let his eyes rove around the stands. There was a light on in the broadcast booth that he hadn't noticed before. Had it just come on? He could see three figures huddled together, leaning toward the field. And, above them, in the .406 Club, a strange clump of glowing dots lit a gaunt face. The dots grew brighter and brighter, and then the face was lost in a whirl of smoke. "Someone's watching us," Oscar whispered.

"The Cursed Creatures. Yes," his father said. "Up there." He pointed to the broadcast booth. "The Bobs and Stickler." He pointed to the .406 Club. "And in there, Smoker, the horned organist. But worst of all . . ." He turned and pointed to one of the slits in the Green Monster. It was lit up too, shining fiercely. "The Pooka."

"'Every Cursed Creature has a Position to Play,' " Oscar said, remembering Rule 2 of the Curse.

"And . . . 'There can be only one Breaker of the Curse. Once he sets his mind to breaking the Curse, he must succeed or no one ever will,' " his father said, repeating the third and final rule. "Have you set your mind to it?"

Oscar looked for the divots and pocks, but they had smoothed to nothingness. The glossy grass had filled them in. He was scared, but there was a stirring in his chest like his heart was a revving engine.

He closed his eyes for a moment and took a deep breath. “Yes,” he said. “I’ve set my mind to it.”

“Good,” his father said. “You know, some things are easy to fix. But sorrow isn’t one of them. This is going to be harder than either of us can imagine. Are you sure?”

“I’m sure,” Oscar said.

The air was cold. Oscar and his father stood there a moment. Everything was quiet, their breaths clouding and then disappearing in the night. A rough breeze kicked up and whipped through the stands. It gusted into a sharp wind and seemed to find its way over the grooves and reeds of the bleacher seats until it formed its voice; and in that breeze, Oscar heard a breath, and then a whisper—a voice that said, “Welcome. . . .”

The voice seemed as if it had come from every direction at once. It was a voice made of wind, but filled with emotion too. It was a voice that seemed to want something.

In the next rush of wind, it said, “Home.”

“Did you hear that?” Oscar asked.

“Hear what?” his father said. “That crying moan? It was the Banshee—the Lost Soul of the Lost and Found.”

“But did you hear what she said?” Oscar asked.

"What?" his father asked. "She doesn't speak. She only cries."

"I guess it was nothing then," Oscar said, though he knew, deep down, what he'd heard. "Let's go."

"Where?" his father asked.

"To meet the Cursed Creatures," Oscar said. "It's what the Curse said. They each have a position to play, don't they?"

CHAPTER NINE

Auntie Gormley Dreams Her Soul Elsewhere

WHILE THE VOICES OF OLD Boy and Oscar were muffled by the trapdoor, Fedelma stood up and marched in a tight circle.

"What is it?" Oonagh asked.

Fedelma grabbed her purse off of a side table and said, "I'm going out. I've got an appointment."

Gormley squinted at Fedelma suspiciously.

Oonagh said, "But you haven't gone out in ages! None of us has."

"Well, I am going out. I have to meet someone." She tightened the frail wings on her back and shrugged on a heavy woolen coat—something retrieved from the Lost and Found in the 1940s.

It was moth bitten and a bit short in the sleeves. “Have my arms gotten longer?” she said to herself.

“Don’t go out there!” Oonagh shouted, suddenly all a-dither. “It’s too brutish!”

“I must do what I must.”

“You could be snatched by the Pooka!” Oonagh started to blubber then.

Gormley simply kept a steely gaze.

“Why are you looking at me like that, Gormley?” Fedelma asked.

Gormley stared at her in a way that seemed to say: You’re up to no good, and I know it. She mouthed “Who?”

Fedelma said, “Who what? Who am I meeting?”

Gormley nodded.

“It’s none of your business.”

Fedelma took a deep breath and opened the door. She paused, but only for a second, and then walked out the doorway, shutting the door behind her.

Oonagh started up with a nervous case of the hiccups—pacing and twittering and hiccupping. “That Fedelma! Why would she go out? What is she thinking? It isn’t safe! *Hic*!” She stopped and blushed and apologized. “Excuse me. My!” And then started over with her worries. “That Fedelma!”

Oonagh made it difficult for Gormley to fall asleep, but Gormley knew that she had to if she was going to find out what Fedelma was up to. Gormley took deep breaths, swelling up her chest with air and then letting it go, ever so slowly. She thought of quiet things: the days before they came to Fenway Park, before they were kicked out of Ireland with a false promise. The Great Famine was over, and the potatoes had been pushing their heads up from the soil again—the soil surrounded by green grass. The soft rains. She thought of the time when she was in love. Her human was so kind and gentle, but not brave. No, not brave enough to be in her world with her. She shook her head. No, she didn't want to think of the human leaving her and her boy. She thought instead of her father with his strong wings, her mother so beautiful but so fragile in her humanness.

And Gormley no longer heard her sister's anxious babbling and hiccupping. She could see only the tunnels, and Weasel-man working to untangle leashes. Bodiless, her soul was growing cold. She had to act quickly. She was hovering above the weasels, trying to look for one that seemed healthy and quick. They were hard to keep track of, and

Weasel-man was so massive that it wasn't easy to see around his girth. And then she heard her sister's voice: Fedelma shouting for Weasel-man.

Weasel-man dropped his work. "Fedelma?" he whispered. "Could it be?"

Gormley saw a weasel with warm eyes, a gentle expression, and a muscular body. She dived into the weasel's small form quickly. She felt her way into the new, wiry shape. She enjoyed the way the weasel darted amid the others, the tussle, the reach of her paws, the lengthening of her back, the kick of her hind legs. She kept her new weasel eyes on the heels of Weasel-man. Her soul warmed.

Weasel-man's eyes were wide-open. He tugged the leashes anxiously. "Come, come," he said. "It's my Fedelma, calling for me!" He took off running, and Gormley kept pace with the rest of the weasels. Her weasel body was young. It had no arthritic soreness, no creaking of bones. She felt lithe and agile and quick. She stayed at the head of the pack, rounding the twists and turns of the tunnels. The other weasels were yapping and calling out. Gormley followed suit. She yapped and yapped, the breeze tunneling through her ears.

Her sister called out again, sharply and urgently. "Weasel-man? Weasel-man!"

Finally, they turned the last corner, and she saw her sister standing right next to the front door. Gormley knew that her sister was afraid that if she were to wander too far from home, she might not be able to find her way back, what with the winding halls and her weak and clouded eyesight. She watched her sister step away from the door, toward the sound of yapping. "Weasel-man?" Fedelma said. She took fifteen steps—only fifteen—counting them carefully.

Weasel-man was so breathless from running that he could barely speak. He bent down, putting his hands on his knees for a moment to catch his breath, and then he rose up—my, my, the enormous bulk of the man! "Fedelma!" he said. "You've come out! You've come out to see me! To thank me for the cooler! It was a gift. I can get you anything you want from Concessions, just ask! I was going to stop in today—drop off a fresh box of hot dogs; but here you are! Here you are!"

"Hush, Weasel-man." Fedelma was blushing, but she spoke in a scolding tone. "I need you to do something for me."

"Anything," Weasel-man said tenderly, leaning in close. "You know that."

The other weasels were jumping around the hem of Fedelma's skirt. Gormley situated herself between their shoes. "Rein them in, would you?" Fedelma said.

"Of course, it's just that they get excited. They love you so!" He tightened the leashes by wrapping them around one meaty fist. Gormley was choked back and now had a less-than-perfect view from between Weasel-man's frayed pant legs.

"I need you to take a message to the Pooka."

"The Pooka?" Weasel-man was alarmed. Gormley was too. She knew her sister was up to no good—but this? "Why would you want to do that? No, no, not a good idea!"

"Don't tell me my business!" Fedelma said. "Just do what I tell you."

"But the Pooka?" Weasel-man's eyes glazed over. "I saw him once with my own eyes. His shaggy horse head, his glowing eyes, his enormous legs, and—worst of all I tell you, worst of all—his hefty pink hands, just like a young man's. It was awful to behold. And how he didn't say a word, just raked his hoof in the dirt and stared at me."

"Are you too scared? What kind of man are you?"

"It's just that most of those he's snatched never came back. Remember the Cursed Creature with the lazy eye? And that one with the nasty cough? One day there. Next day not."

"You said you'd do anything for me! Anything! Did you lie to me?"

Gormley tried to make out Weasel-man's expression, but she only had a view up his nostrils. He shook his head. "No, no, of course not. I wouldn't lie to you."

Fedelma rummaged in her pocketbook, pulled out her small date book—from 1912—and tore an unused page from the back. She found a pen and started writing. "This here," she said. "I want him to get the message. Do you hear me?" She spoke through gritted teeth, almost as if she were grinding her words. "That boy thinks he's going to break the Curse!"

"That boy? The one I saw with Old Boy?"

"Yes, that one! He's up to no good."

"Do you think he can—," Weasel-man started to say.

"No, of course he can't! He'll only make it permanent. He's useless."

"But what if he can . . . ," Weasel-man said, a bit dreamily.

"He can't. But mark my words, Weasel-man: We know this awful life. And what we know is better than what we don't know. Trust me. As a girl in Ireland, I thought we were going to live in the promised land. And what did we get? Worthlessness. You can't trust change."

"Well, I don't know. What if . . ."

"Weasel-man!" She grabbed him by his shirt. The weasels surrounding Gormley hunkered down and began to growl. Gormley joined in. It felt good to growl at Fedelma at this moment. Fedelma hadn't always been this way—so bitter, so fearful. Why had she changed so?

Fedelma loosened her grip and patted Weasel-man's buttons, but didn't change her tone. "You exist because of the Curse. Who knows what would happen to you? You could simply disappear! Horns and all! And we'd never see you ever again. Just like . . ."

". . . your father, the one who'd done the cursing? Keeffe?"

Fedelma shook her head. "Look, just get this message to the Pooka. Understand?"

Weasel-man nodded. "I will," he said, his voice cracking with a mix of love and fear, already weighted with regret.

Fedelma nodded her sharp chin; and Gormley watched her turn around, count her fifteen steps, and, soon enough, disappear through the nettle- and vine-covered door.

Weasel-man sighed deeply. He looked over the pack of weasels at his feet and fiddled with Fedelma's note in his large hands. "One of you will have to do me a favor," he said. "I can't go to the Pooka. I can't look him in his shining eyes." A shiver ran through his body.

This was Gormley's chance. She had to know what was written on that slip of paper. Some of the weasels started to dance over one another and preen, but Gormley didn't. She stood still and stuck her weasel chin up high.

"You, there," he said, pointing to a weasel with a boxy head.

No, no, thought Gormley.

She shuffled quickly over to the boxy-headed weasel, and while Weasel-man was rummaging through his pockets for something, Gormley slapped the boxy-headed weasel on the back as if he were choking and she was just trying to help.

Weasel-man looked up just as the boxy-headed

weasel started to yap at Gormley and, oddly enough, the banging on his back induced some coughing. "Oh, my, well there," Weasel-man said. "You okay?"

The boxy-headed weasel nodded; but his eyes were watering, and he didn't look good.

"You should take a rest," Weasel-man said. He pointed to Gormley. "How about you?" She nodded brightly and sprinted to his shoes. "So, go through the tunnels toward left field, take the tunnel that leads into the Green Monster. Find the Pooka in the scorekeeper's room in the wall. No game today, so the Pooka will be there. Give him this message. And wait for a response."

Weasel-man handed her the piece of paper, which Gormley clamped in her teeth. Weasel-man gave her a nudge, and she ran off as swiftly as she could.

Gormley was terrified. Her tiny weasel heart was rattling in her chest while she made her way through the tunnels under the field, but eventually she felt a safe enough distance from Weasel-man to pause and read the note.

She unfolded it with her paws and spread it out on the dirt floor.

Dear Pooka,

With deep respect, I bring to your knowledge the presence of a no-good boy living amongst us. My Old Boy calls him by the name Oscar. He is clearly an Other from the Outside World—an orphan, if truth be told. He has proclaimed that he is going to try to break the Curse. You must take him for a ride and deposit him far, far away, perhaps in a deep, dark wood. I throw myself at your mercy.

Sincerely,

Fedelma, Humble Daughter of the Curse

This was worse than Gormley thought. She knew that Fedelma thought the boy might fail, but she didn't know that she wanted him to disappear—for good. Why would her sister want the Curse to be permanent? Gormley rolled up the note with her shaking paws. She could make the note disappear. She could chew it up with her weasel teeth and swallow it. She paused, sitting on her haunches. She thought for a moment. She knew that she had to go forward. She had to get the note to the Pooka. She had to allow things to take their course. Oscar was their only hope. He was the boy who could break the Curse. Everyone had to play his or her position. It was in the rules.

She placed the note in her mouth and scampered on. The tunnel sloped quickly below the roots of the wall. She skittered her way up a zigzagging ramp to the scorekeeper's room.

She didn't enter through the Pooka's door. She shoved herself through a hole next to some pipes instead. The room was dark and musty, concrete and steel. It seemed empty. Gormley's small nostrils tensed. She could smell sneakers and, most of all, horse. She ran along a low step, past a row of white placards, and darted around the legs of two chairs and a step stool. Now she could see the field lights peeking in through the slots in the wall. She stayed to the dark edges.

In the far corner, the Pooka lifted his heavy horse head. His nostrils flared. He then stood up clumsily and shook his mane. "Who is there?" he asked.

Gormley stepped out of hiding and stood before him. She was frozen now. The Pooka didn't smell of fear or anger. He smelled of loss and sadness that glowed up from his stomach through the holes of his vacant eyes on either side of his horse head.

He walked toward her, his strong human hands hanging at the sides of his furred haunches. "What's this?" he grunted. "You come for a tour, weasel?

Want to see the signatures of the greats, or would you prefer a ride of terror?" He lunged at her.

Gormley flinched, shut her eyes, and then slowly opened one and then the other.

"You've come here with a purpose," the Pooka said, leaning over her.

She dropped the note at his hooves.

"Is this for me?" he asked. He picked up the note and read it, his horse lips moving ever so slightly. Then he clattered quickly to one of the slits in the wall. He stared out over the field. "He's here? He's among us?" He pulled a pen off of the scorekeeper's chair, flipped over the note, and wrote on the other side. Obviously, he wasn't used to writing. He held the pen awkwardly in his hand and spoke the words as he scrawled. "Dear boy by the name of Oscar," he said. "Meet me under home plate tomorrow night at the stroke of twelve. I have words for you and for you alone. The Pooka." He then rolled up the note and held it up to the weasel's mouth. She took it.

And although the thought of Oscar taking a ride through the night skies on the Pooka's back made her stomach churn with worry, Gormley knew that Oscar had to take the ride. It was inevitable. Things were clicking together, making a new shape.

"Take this to the boy named Oscar. If you lose it, misery will follow you all of your days. Trust me, I know misery."

And suddenly, Gormley wasn't afraid of the Pooka. She felt sorry for him. He was cursed. They weren't so different. She snapped her teeth and gave a nod.

"Be quick," the Pooka said.

And this struck the weasel. "Be quick," she said to herself. It felt familiar somehow. She stared at the Pooka, not wanting to leave him just yet.

"Go!" the Pooka said angrily.

Gormley turned, scampered to the hole, and, in an instant, was padding and clawing down the tunnels, retracing her own scent. She was haunted by the Pooka's hollow, glowing eyes; and each time she blinked, they appeared like torches in her mind.

Then she heard the Banshee—the Lost Soul of the Lost and Found—moaning off in the distance. Weasel-man didn't like the Banshee. No one did. He would run from her, and so would his weasels. So Gormley headed off in the opposite direction. She smelled popcorn and deep fryer fat and, most of all, other weasels. She followed the scent. The yips grew louder until finally she turned a corner, and there he was: Weasel-man, hunched over a delivery of sodas and beer.

She gave a loud chirp. The other weasels grew quiet, and Weasel-man turned. He looked at her, saw the note. She could smell his rising fear.

"Did you meet him? Eye to eye?" Weasel-man asked.

The Pooka's eyes—oh, how they glowed! Gormley nodded.

"Did he take you for a ride?" Weasel-man went on.

There was no time for questions. She skittered through the crowd of weasels to his pant hem and dropped the note. He bent down with a grunt and picked it up. He wasn't delicate; plus, his hands were shaking. Trying to open the note, he nearly ripped it in two. He read it to himself, and then he let out a great gust of air.

"Better him than me!" he said. "Oh, but still . . . too bad. I mean, poor kid. I wonder if he'll survive it. I wonder if he'll be strong enough. Hard to tell. Hard to say. Probably not, though. I'll bring it to the boy myself." He looked down at Gormley. "But won't Fedelma be pleased with me!" He reached into his pocket and threw a bit of old pretzel to Gormley. She backed away and let the other weasels fight over it. She was thinking of the Pooka:

the way he'd struggled with the pen; his lingering scent of loss; his empty, luminescent eyes—how he wasn't what the legends made him out to be, not really.

CHAPTER TEN

Oh, the Cursed Creatures!

AS OSCAR STEPPED OFF OF the pitcher's mound and followed his father to the backstop, he was wondering how they were going to enlist the help of the other Cursed Creatures. Every Cursed Creature has a position to play? Even the Pooka? "What's the Pooka like?" Oscar asked.

His father paused at the on-deck circle. His jaw tightened. He closed his eyes for a moment and then said, "I suppose you need to know. Pookas have lived in Ireland for centuries. Sometimes they're hairy beasts, sometimes goats. Our pooka took the shape of a third kind: a horse walking upright, with glowing eyes and the hands of an ordinary man." Oscar met his father's eyes; they were glassy with fear. He pulled open a door just beyond the on-deck circle. They both stepped inside. "A long time ago, there was no wall in left field, no Green Monster," his father went on.

"I know," Oscar said. "It was just a hill. People used to sit on it and watch the game. Called it Duffy's Cliff, because Duffy was so good at playing bounces off of it."

"Right. And pookas live in hills. So when Keeffe summoned a pooka in the Curse, it took up residence in the hill itself. And when the hill was leveled in 1934 and the Green Monster was built, the Pooka just took up residence in the small room within the wall."

Oscar's father took off his orange vest and clipped an old, laminated card with his faded picture on it. The words PRESS PASS were written across the top of the card. They made their way to the ramps behind the Concession booths and headed up.

"The Pooka is a Cursed Creature," Oscar's father said wearily. "He once was a man, but he brought about his own ruin and was turned into a pooka. As a form of punishment, the Pooka always has a task he must perform—a thankless, endless task. I don't know what his task is exactly. And pookas lose all their earthly goods when they change over: their food, clothing, shelter—their old lives. And like the other Cursed Creatures of Fenway Park, the Pooka shares his room with a human. During games, the scorekeeper sits in a room in the Green Monster itself. Chris Elias is in there these days. He looks out through a slit, which is like a rectangular mail slot in the wall. You saw it earlier, lit up by the Pooka's eyes. When there is no game and no scorekeeper, the room belongs to the Pooka." His father sighed mightily and put a trembling hand on Oscar's shoulder. "I want to keep you away from the Pooka," he said. "But I don't think it's going to be possible. He's protective of the Curse. Who knows what's in store?" He let his hand fall to his side. "That's enough talking about the Pooka now."

Oscar could tell that his father was shaken. Oscar had more questions—about the Pooka's night rides through the sky—but he knew not to press.

They went through a green door and down a hallway covered with framed pictures of former Red Sox players, and then entered the .406 Club. It was a yawning, humming space filled with cushy stadium seats that overlooked the park from behind home plate. An organ stood in one corner. The club was named, Oscar knew, after Ted Williams's batting average during the 1941 season—the last time any player in the major leagues had hit over .400. No one was there. Nailed to the wall just above the organ was a No Smoking sign.

They sat on the organ bench. Fenway Park stretched out before them like an exhibit at the Boston Aquarium. The field and the stadium had its own life, separated from them by the glass wall. Oscar stared out at the field, the glowing white lines, the vast green.

"The official organist's name is Josh Kantor."

"He'll be here tomorrow night, right?"

"He wouldn't miss a playoff game. He's a good guy. But he has no idea that he shares his work space with Smoker."

"Why do you call him Smoker?"

"Is it obvious why Weasel-man is called Weasel-man?"

"Yep," Oscar said.

"This will be too."

And as if on cue, the door creaked open, streamers of smoke blew in, and Smoker swaggered out of a gray cloud like a magician. "Hello, good people!" he said graciously in a voice so low and gruff it was barely audible. He was smoking four cigarettes, two out of each corner of his mouth. He wore a Red Sox baseball cap much like Weasel-man's, hiding his horns. He was bony and tough, his skin leathery. "Have you come for a little light music?" he asked hopefully. And then he groaned. "Or are you in the mood to get a chant going?" He waved his hand at Oscar and his father. "Get off the bench! Get up!"

Oscar and his father slid off the bench and let Smoker take over. As soon as he sat down, the cloud of smoke caught up with him and hovered, giving the impression that Smoker was caught inside of a crystal ball. He leaned forward out of the cloud when he spoke. Oscar got little peeks at the knot in the bridge of his nose, his pointy chin, and his craggy, gray skin. "This here is a Yamaha AR100 Electone electronic organ," Smoker said. "The best of the best. Or as the French say, the cream of the cream." And then he played a gorgeous classical snippet of trilling notes that slowly turned into the national anthem, as if a game were just about to start. "Who is this child?" he asked, stabbing the butt of a cigarette in Oscar's direction. "Is he yours?"

"Yep," Oscar's father said. "This is Oscar."

"Charmed," Smoker said, though he didn't offer his hand for shaking. "What brings you?"

"Well," Oscar's father said, "Oscar is going to try to break the Curse."

The organ's notes smeared and then came to a sudden stop as if Smoker's hands had slid off of the keys. There was a silent moment, and then he played three ominous chords, reaching down into the low notes. "Does he know what's at stake? Does he know the rules? Does he know about the Pooka? The Pooka doesn't like people sniffing around the Curse. Does he know that?"

"I do," Oscar said.

"Well, then," Smoker said. "Good luck to you." And he played a short, jaunty tune that sounded a bit like "Sweet Caroline," the song that was always played in Fenway during the seventh-inning stretch. "Let me know how it all goes. Off you go!"

"Not so fast," Oscar's father said. "We may need you.

"The second rule says that each Cursed Creature has a position to play. We don't know what that means, but it could mean that you might help us somehow.

"For example, you haven't ever come across a misplaced baseball—an old-looking one from, say, 1919 or so?"

Smoker played a quiz show theme song, a tick-tock rhythm. "Hmm," he said, and then chased his fingers up the keyboard and stopped. "I can't help you."

"Any ideas? At all?"

Smoker stood up and folded his arms across his chest. "You know what I want?"

"You're changing the subject," Oscar's father said.

Smoker ignored him. "I want to make my own music heard. I'm tired of chants and hoo-ha." He picked up the sheet music sitting atop the organ, rifled through it. "Junk!"

"What do you mean?" Oscar asked.

"Everything I try to play becomes some sort of baseball hoo-ha," Smoker said, his low voice warbling with sadness. "I can be quite classical, but 'Take Me Out to the Ball Game' is always lurking underneath! Do you know how that feels? But," he said with a bit of hope, "if I could just have a true audience for my compositions, if I had a true purpose for my art, I could play like one of the greats. I know it."

"If we could arrange that—a true audience—would you help us?" Oscar asked.

Smoker popped out of his cloud joyfully. "You could do that?"

Oscar's father poked Oscar with an elbow. "I don't know how we could. I mean, Josh Kantor is the one who has the booth when there's an audience. I mean . . ."

Smoker's face crumbled. He retreated into his cloud.

"But if we could somehow?" Oscar said. "Let's just say . . . if we could, would you help us?"

There was silence.

"Are you in there?" Oscar asked.

A few muffled sobs.

"Are you okay?" Oscar's father asked.

The smoky cloud began to swell. Oscar and his father had to back up as it grew to envelop the organ, filling the entire .406 Club. They started to wheeze and cough.

"Smoker," Oscar's father gasped. "We need you."

Then, finally, Smoker emerged from the cloud for a moment. His mouth was stretched wide, it was so filled with cigarettes. It was a wonder he could still speak clearly at all. But he did. With perfect enunciation he said, "If you can help me, I will help you. I will give my true gift—music!" He then darted back into his cloud, which drifted across the room. The door opened and closed. Smoker was gone.

Oscar and his father headed out of the .406 Club and walked back to the ramp. Wisps of smoke still lingered in the hall.

They dipped through a doorway to the Hall of Fame Club, a restaurant nestled under the .406 Club.

"Smoker and his gift of music," Oscar's father muttered as they wound their way around the empty tables. "How is that going to help us?"

Oscar shrugged. "It's better than nothing, I guess."

His father nodded in agreement and then waved his arm around the restaurant. "These days, the radio and TV people pack into the cushy roosts next to the .406. But once upon a time, the old Red Sox announcers used to sit here—with an open-air look at the field—Ned Martin and Jim Woods."

Oscar's father opened the door of a supply closet. It was filled with boxes of napkins, straws, canned sodas, and ice buckets. There was a door in the floor propped open by a mop. Faint light drifted up, along with the sound of a ball game on a radio. "Here we are," his father said, as if reporting terrible news.

Oscar leaned over, looking down through the opening at a steep ladder.

"Down there?"

His father nodded. "But I have to warn you," he said. "Stickler likes to make fun of me. He never lets up! And the Bobs! They're always getting in the middle of things with their stupid play-by-plays." He balled up his fists and shoved them into his pockets.

"Can't we stand up to them together?" Oscar said nervously, thinking of Drew Sizemore.

His father smiled then, a soft, gentle smile. "I'm glad you're here. You know that?"

Oscar nodded, feeling a little shy for a moment. "I'll go first," he said, and then he started down the ladder, his father shuffling behind.

The broadcast booth was small and fairly dark. The air smelled sour and stale, and overwhelmingly of burned coffee. A two-headed, horned creature with a single massive back covered in a mix of fur and tweed sat in a chair in front of them. The heads turned in unison.

"The Bobs," his father said. "Mustache Bob and Jowly Bob."

One had a mustache and pop eyes; the other was jowly, his chins wobbling slightly as he gazed at Oscar wide-eyed. Instead of baseball caps to hide their horns, they wore gray fedoras and shared an old-fashioned mic—silver and fat, with an RCA label. They sat on two rolling wooden chairs shoved together. They were conjoined somewhere in their beefy torso. They terrified Oscar. He stumbled backward into his father's chest.

But they weren't alone. They muttered, "What's this? What's this now?" and leaned in for a closer look at Oscar. This exposed a third horned creature slouched in the seat behind them. The third horned creature didn't have a mic. He'd been leaning way back in his chair with his feet propped up on the desk, but popped forward and stood in one swift motion. He was a wiry, anxious guy with a flattened nose, as if he'd been in a fight; and he had a restless angriness, as if he were looking for another one. He wore a baseball mitt on his left hand and kept socking it with his right fist.

"Stickler," his father hissed under his breath.

Jowly Bob said, "It's a beautiful night for baseball and thanks for joining us. Joining me in the booth tonight is as always, my partner, Bob. Bob?" There were no speakers in the room. The mic was unplugged and useless, but still Jowly Bob had a raspy radio voice—full of static, full of distance and echo, as if it were being broadcast through an old, badly tuned radio. Oscar wasn't sure how he did it.

Mustache Bob pulled the mic away from Jowly Bob. "Actually, I think we're expecting rain, as a thick layer of clouds is hurrying in from the southeast. We'll be lucky to get this one in tonight, Bob, as the Red Sox look to break an eighty-six-year skid against the stalwart defense and punishing power of . . ." And here, Mustache Bob made some static noises with his mouth and faded out.

"There isn't a game tonight," Oscar said timidly.

"There isn't always a game, but there's always a battle," Jowly Bob said. "And joining us in the booth tonight is the slim right-hander, Malachi Egg, and what looks to be a mouthy rookie just up from the minors."

"This is Oscar," Oscar's father said.

"We don't offer half-priced tickets for kids. Red Sox policy," Stickler said in a gruff voice. "You'll have to pay full price for him, or are you broke, Egg? Not getting enough allowance from your aunties?"

The Bobs spun the casters on their chairs, wheeling closer to the action in the booth.

"Egg's had a real shaky season, a weak arm. Let's see if he bobbles this one. I smell Buckner!" Mustache Bob said.

"Hey, that's not funny," Oscar said, knowing his dad's love for Buckner.

Oscar's father mumbled. "The boy is one of us. He doesn't have to buy a ticket."

"I live here," Oscar said.

"Egg fields it cleanly, shovels over to the rookie," Jowly Bob reported with a hint of disappointment. "Handy teamwork."

Stickler glared at him. "What do you want here, anyway, Egg?"

"Well," Oscar's father said quietly, "um, see. Well . . ."

"I'm going to break the Curse," Oscar said.

Everything went silent in the booth except for the pounding of Stickler's fist into his glove. Then Stickler roared with laughter, and the Bobs followed suit.

"There's a little comic relief, my friends," Mustache Bob said.

Oscar's father shuffled back to the ladder. "C'mon," he said. "Forget them. Let's go."

Oscar shook his head, and once the laughter died down he said, "The second rule of the Curse says that each of the Cursed Creatures has a position to play. So, I take it that, in baseball lingo, this means each of you has to play your part. If I'm going to be able to break the Curse, that is."

"Listen, kid, you aren't going to break no curse." Stickler turned to Oscar's father. "What's this supposed to be—your son or something? What are you, seeing impaired, Egg? Do you need a large-print program?"

"I don't know what you're talking about," Oscar's father said sternly.

"Hate to say it," Stickler went on, "but he ain't yours. You just got stuck with the bill, if you know what I mean!"

"There's a drive toward the Monster," Jowly Bob roared.

"This one is way back," Mustache Bob said. "Looks like Egg is going to miss it. . . ."

"You talk like you think my father's afraid of you. He isn't," Oscar said. "And he doesn't care what you have to say about me." Oscar wasn't even sure what he was saying. His knees were shaking.

"But the rookie shows up out of nowhere, and it pops into his glove. A sliding catch right under the old man!" Mustache Bob said.

Stickler started pounding the glove with his fist a little more angrily. "This ball field is cursed. The Curse can't be broken. Not by anybody and not by you, that's for sure."

"You talk tough," Oscar said. "So why haven't you been able to break the Curse, huh? You've been here long enough. You really aren't all that tough, are you?"

"Looks like the teams are engaged in a little trash talking," Mustache Bob added solemnly.

"Why don't you come a little closer and say that to my face," Stickler said.

Oscar glanced at his father, whose expression was a mix of pride and shock. Oscar took a step forward. "You really aren't all that tough, are you?"

Stickler lunged at Oscar, picking him up off the floor and pushing him against the narrow, built-in table under the window. Oscar's head was at such an angle that he could see the field, could feel the cold breeze on his face. He was pinned, but there was now a tussle above him. He could hear his father shouting, "Get off him, Stickler!" There was grunting and shoving, and the two Bobs were still calling the play-by-play.

Oscar, stuck in his spot, looked out at the field through the window. "Cursed"—the word came back to him. That's how he felt. He felt like Drew Sizemore was chanting "Who's your daddy." He felt stuck, like he had back at home. The world was rotten all over. He let his eyes blur, and that's when he picked up on something in the stands above right field. The seats. Some were folded up. Some weren't. And the ones that weren't folded up were in patterns: rows and lines. The seats spelled something.

Oscar still couldn't turn around, but he didn't want to, anyway. The first letter Oscar could make out was a P and above it a T and above it a K. He followed all of those letters to find three words stacked on top of one another:

KNOW

THE

PAST

Who had put that message up for him to see?

Stickler lost his grip, and Oscar fell to the floor. His father was wrestling Stickler into the back corner. He had an elbow against his neck. "Don't ever touch my son again," his father said, his wings rattling against the back of his shirt.

Stickler nodded, his eyes bulging.

Oscar's father eased up slowly and then let him go. He turned to the Bobs. "What?" he said. "What happened to the play-by-play? Anything to say now?"

The Bobs, stunned, were completely silent. They shook their heads. Jowly Bob's chin swung back and forth. Mustache Bob's mustache sank at the edges, anchored by his frown.

And Stickler? Oscar realized he'd played his position, without even knowing it. He'd shoved Oscar into a spot where he saw a sign: KNOW THE PAST. As Oscar followed his father up the ladder, he glanced back over his shoulder. "Thanks, Stickler," he said.

Stickler glared at him. "Whatever, kid," he said, then pounded his fist into his glove and folded himself into his seat.

CHAPTER ELEVEN

The Pooka and the Banshee

ON THEIR WAY BACK THROUGH the empty restaurant and down the ramps, Oscar's father slapped him on the shoulder. "Did you see Stickler's face there at the end?" his father said, beaming. "And the Bobs? They were speechless!"

"It was great," Oscar said, his chest warm, his heart still pounding. It *had* been great. His father had stuck up for him, and Oscar was proud that he'd spoken up, too.

Half jogging down the ramps, his father actually let out a hoot, and Oscar hooted too.

They made their way back to the field and soon enough found themselves sitting on the bench in the dugout, breathless, waiting for the Banshee. A fine mist started coming down, with a sharp rising wind. Their victorious mood left over from the dugout seemed to disappear quickly as if carried off by the bitter wind.

"When is the Banshee supposed to get here?" Oscar asked, shivering.

"She'll show. She's always looking for someone she's supposed to meet—another lost soul," Oscar's father told him. "But she's always alone."

"What is a banshee?" Oscar asked. It dawned on him that he wasn't sure exactly what he should be looking for.

"A banshee is a kind of ghost who warns that a death is coming by crying in this awful howl so full of hopelessness that you can feel it inside of you. It rattles you to your very bones." He shuddered. "When she's not out here, she floats around the Lost and Found—which seems to be her home, in a way. Like all banshees, she howls and keens when death approaches, but she also cries each year as the World Series gets closer. We wait and listen; and then we hear the shrill rise of her voice, and we know. We know."

Oscar told his father what had happened to him while Stickler had held him down against the table in the broadcast booth. "He played his position," Oscar said. "He led me to the next sign."

"And he didn't even mean to help," his father said, one side of his mouth curling up into a smile. "I like that."

"But I don't know enough yet," Oscar said. "What made Keeffe curse the Red Sox like that anyway? How do curses work?"

"Well, you make a curse, and then it hardens like concrete. Keeffe took off before it was set in stone. He didn't tell anyone. He just disappeared, and then the Cursed Creatures were conjured up, the weasels, the mice, the Pooka."

"And the Banshee?"

"Her too," Oscar's father said. "She showed up with the rest of them.

"My grandfather wanted what he thought he deserved: lush new land in America. He was a farmer. He wanted this great piece he was promised: land on the Emerald Necklace. But he got this swamp and then the ball field. Right? And he was angry about being thought of as different, tired of being the half-blooded orphan; and he had no stomach for injustice. And so Ruth getting traded; well, it hurt him in the same way he'd been hurt before."

"I get that," Oscar said. "I understand."

"But he was wrong. What he did was wrong! He

cursed all of us in the process."

"Speak for yourself!" said an oily voice behind them. Oscar knew before he even turned around that it was Weasel-man. He could hear the yipping now and smell the dirty weasels from where he sat. "Do I look cursed to you? I'm a model of American prosperity!" Weasel-man popped off his cap. "What're a few horns among friends?"

"Weasel-man," Oscar's father said. "Fancy meeting you here."

"Are you going to ask me where the baseball is?"

"How do you know about that?" Oscar asked.

"I know everything. That's how I know."

"Well? Do you know where it is? Seen anything like it?" Oscar's father asked.

"Finding the ball, that's how you think you're going to break the Curse? Don't you know that the Pooka won't let that happen?" He handed Oscar the slip of paper, which was nibbled on one corner and slightly ripped.

Oscar read it aloud: "Dear boy by the name of Oscar: Meet me under home plate tomorrow night at the stroke of twelve. I have words for you and for you alone. The Pooka."

"Be sure to pack lightly. I think you're in for a bumpy ride!"

"No, he isn't!" Oscar's father said, standing up and pacing. "I won't let him go! It's too dangerous. He could fall off while they're up in the sky. No, no, no. Absolutely not." Oscar wasn't listening. He was staring at the note, looking for a message to decode. He let his eyes go soft and blurry. He looked at it sideways from one direction, then the other. But there was nothing at all.

"He's got to go," Weasel-man said. "The Pooka will only hunt him down. Does he want that?"

His father continued to stomp and fume. "He can't go!" his father kept saying, while Weasel-man shouted back, "He has to!"

Oscar flipped over the piece of paper, hoping to see a message if he looked at it from the other side. But instead he found Fedelma's note to the Pooka. He read it. He knew she didn't like him, but she'd *betrayed* him? She'd sent the Pooka after him? He balled up the note and shoved it in his pocket.

Oscar looked out into center field. His father and Weasel-man were still fighting. The sun was coming up. The stadium took on a dusty glow. The mist was still coming down, but now it had a glistening shine. And that's when he saw the Banshee, dancing in the outfield, her long skirt drifting over the grass, her bare feet, her pale hands and cheeks. Beads of rain made her hair look jeweled. Her arms carved letters out of the rain, and the letters formed words.

Go to the Pooka, she danced with the loose cursive of her body. *You need to know his secrets.*

Oscar looked across the field at the Green Monster, where the Pooka probably was at that very moment. Four slits in the wall brightened. They burned golden yellow. Oscar thought of the Pooka's eyes, how he'd heard that they glowed.

And then the Banshee let out a moan, a soft cry. This got the attention of Weasel-man and Oscar's father. The three of them now looked at the Banshee as she faded into the mist. Oscar recognized the sadness of the cry. The Banshee had been the one who'd spoken to him through the wind, and probably the one who'd left a message in the bleacher seats, too. Oscar glanced back to the slits in the wall. The glow dimmed.

Oscar looked at his father and Weasel-man, their faces softly lit by the sun.

"You aren't going," his father said. "That's final."

Oscar nodded, but he knew that Weasel-man was right and that he would have to disobey his father. *I'm going,* he thought. *I have no choice.*

CHAPTER TWELVE

The Birthday Party—More Gifts

AUNTIE OONAGH WAS SMILING SO hard that her cheeks seemed to have risen up her face—bulbous, pink, and taut. She clapped her hands loudly to make sure she had everyone's attention. Even Auntie Fedelma, who'd been scowling at the floor, looked up. "I've a surprise for Oscar!" Auntie Oonagh announced.

She walked to the counter and picked up a platter domed with a silver top. The dishes all seemed to have been made of metal plates with numbers from the scoreboard. The drying rack was made of the protective wiring in a catcher's mask. The place mats and trivets matched the rubber home plates that tiled the floor. The kitchen was small and cramped; and everyone was squished in, trying to pretend he or she was comfortable—except Auntie Fedelma, who would occasionally curse the small space.

Auntie Oonagh lifted the top of the platter. "For you, Oscar," she said. "I made it myself." Auntie Gormley raised her gnarled finger. "With Auntie Gormley's advice," Auntie Oonagh added. She had molded cotton candy into the shape of a round birthday cake with Cracker Jack trim.

"What's it say on it there?" Auntie Fedelma asked. "I can't see it, Oonagh! Why did you write it so small like that?"

"It had to fit on the cake!" Auntie Oonagh said.

Oscar's father read it: "Happy Birthday, Oscar!" The words were spelled out in M&M'S. Oscar hadn't had a birthday party since he was little—maybe seven or so. That time, his mother had invited some of the people from the dry cleaners up to their apartment for cake. A soggy, store-bought cake—it had gotten mixed up with someone else's and read HAPPY RETIREMENT, MRS. COONIG. Oscar's mother had been really angry about the cake. "I wanted it to be special!" she said to Oscar. The folks from the dry cleaners were uncomfortable. They left early, and his mother felt bad about that too. So, the following year, Oscar asked that they not really do anything. That had been fine with him. Birthdays weren't his mother's thing; her own made her cry for a day or two. And his father's gifts had always been disappointing. In fact, the gift that Oscar had first seen in Pizzeria Uno was sitting on the table behind the cake. His father had rewrapped it in fresh newsprint. But it seemed less awful now that he understood his father's world. He'd been making the best of what he had all of these years.

He was surprised by how happy he was about Auntie Oonagh's silly, homemade cake. It was lopsided, and the lettering was uneven. And even though Oscar loved sweets, it seemed as if it would be way too sweet for anyone to eat a whole piece.

"Where are some candles?" Auntie Oonagh asked, clattering through the cupboards, her tiny wings pulsing nervously on her back. "I don't know where they could be!"

His father had decided not to tell the aunties about the message from the Pooka. Why disturb them? Plus, his father was convinced that the matter was closed, that Oscar wasn't going. But Oscar's mind kept flashing on the note: the odd scrawl of the Pooka on one side and Auntie Fedelma's betrayal on the other. Every time he thought of the note, he remembered his father's face as he told him about the Pooka's eyes and hands, and the terrifying rides across the night sky.

"Here," Oscar's father said, pushing his gift toward Oscar. "While she's searching for candles, go ahead; open it."

Oscar looked over at Auntie Oonagh.

"Go ahead," she said.

And so Oscar tore off the paper to reveal a mitt. It was shiny and new, the tag still on it. "How did you . . ."

"Oh, quarters here and there that fall out of people's pockets," Oscar's father said. "Happens all the time. Amazing what people leave behind."

"It must have taken you forever," Oscar said.

"Do you like it?" his father asked.

"I love it," Oscar said.

"You never know when you might need it," his father said.

"Ha! He'll never use it. When was the last time any of us played a game here?" Auntie Fedelma said.

"I'd love to see a game one day," Oscar said. "And use this to catch a foul ball."

"Oh, don't watch!" Auntie Oonagh said. "It's too

painful. It will hurt too much."

The aunties shook their heads.

"One day when you've been through as much suffering as we have, you'll understand," Auntie Fedelma said.

"Well, I don't have any candles," Auntie Oonagh announced. "But I have a gift." She pulled an oddly shaped gift wrapped in newsprint out of her apron pocket and put it on the table, where it clunked down heavily.

"No, no," Oscar's father said, already knowing what it was. "You can't. It was *your* gift, Auntie Oonagh."

"What is it?" Auntie Fedelma said with grave irritation. "What's there? I can't make it out!"

Oscar looked at Auntie Gormley, who was blinking joyfully, as if a wish of her own had come true.

"It's for you," Auntie Oonagh said to Oscar.

Oscar picked it up, peeled back the paper, and there was a key: a gray, wrought iron skeleton key on a faded golden ribbon. Oscar pinched the ribbon and watched the key spin in front of his eyes.

"What is it? Tell me!" Auntie Fedelma said, leaning into the key. "Is he holding something by its tail?"

"It's the Key to the Past," Oscar's father announced.

"The Key to the Past?" Oscar asked, imagining again a grand door—gold and maybe arched with fat columns—that this key might unlock.

"That's not right!" Auntie Fedelma shouted, pushing her chair away from the table and crossing her arms.

Oscar's father stood up and paced in a small, nervous circle. "You can't hand down your gift. What if the boy doesn't succeed? It's too much pressure."

"Oh, but what if he succeeds!" Auntie Gormley signed.

"Too much pressure?" Auntie Oonagh said anxiously, lifting her funnel to her ear. "Is that what you said? Have I done something wrong?"

"No, no," Oscar said. "It's got to help. Where's the door?"

They all turned and pointed to a very short, square door built into the kitchen wall. It looked more like a cabinet with a small black wrought iron keyhole.

"*That's* the Door to the Past?" Oscar asked doubtfully.

"Yes," Oscar's father said. "It'll take you anywhere, any time."

"You have to make up a rhyme about where you want to go and when," Auntie Oonagh said. "I never could think of a good rhyme! What rhymes with *Borneo*?"

Auntie Gormley signed, "You'll need it." And then she looked at him very seriously. Was she trying to tell him something more?

"You have to be careful with that key," Oscar's father said. "Use it wisely."

"And always, always, always lock the door behind you," Auntie Oonagh said.

Oscar slipped the key into his pocket. "I will," he said.

Then there was a small moment of quiet. Everyone was trying to figure out what he or she had forgotten. Auntie Gormley had given Oscar the gift of reading signs. His father had given him the mitt, and Auntie Oonagh had given him the Key to the Past. Suddenly, in unison, they all turned their attention to Auntie Fedelma.

"Fedelma, do you have something for Oscar?" Auntie Oonagh asked.

Auntie Fedelma took a moment to ponder, and

then she said, "Yes, I do." She smirked. "I have a promise to give him."

Oscar didn't want to hear the promise; but she was leaning forward, as if she was going to whisper into his ear. He didn't want her to get that close, so he reared back, forcing her to say it aloud.

"Dear boy, dear, dear boy," she said, "life is going to reach out to you and offer you an adventure. Take its hand. Take the adventure." She stared into Oscar's eyes. Her own were cloudy and gray. "And if your grip on adventure gets loose, just let go. I promise you I will be there to catch you when you fall."

"That's not true," Oscar said. "You want me to fail. You're lying."

"What?" Auntie Fedelma shrieked. "You little ingrate! *You* are the liar!"

Oscar turned to the others. "She wants me to go for a ride on the Pooka, to lose my grip and fall. *That's* what she's saying! But she won't be there to catch me."

"Oh, Oscar," Auntie Oonagh said gently. "Auntie Fedelma is kindhearted. Truly. You don't really know her yet."

"She's right, Oscar," his father said.

"I know she wrote the Pooka a note," Oscar

said, heat rising in his cheeks.

Everyone turned and stared at her.

"Did you do that?" Oscar's father asked.

"No! Of course not," she sputtered. "That's ridiculous!"

Oscar reached into his pocket and pulled out the wrinkled, bitten, torn note, slapped it down on the kitchen table. Auntie Oonagh and Oscar's father leaned in to read it. His father said, " 'Deposit him far, far away? Perhaps in a deep, dark wood?' "

Auntie Oonagh closed her eyes. She hummed a bit too, to make sure that she couldn't hear a thing. This was too much for her to bear. Oscar's father covered his eyes with his hand. Auntie Gormley was the only one who didn't seem surprised. She only glared at Auntie Fedelma, shaking her head.

"I meant that the Pooka would save him by depositing him far away from any *dangers* in the *safety* of a deep, dark wood. So, so, so he could get away from all of this curse-breaking business once and for all. I only want to, to, to *save* him—and all of us—from his certain failure!" Auntie Fedelma stammered. "You must believe me! My promise to Oscar is that I won't stop trying to protect him! I won't stop! It is my mission." She looked at Oscar with her milky, nearly blind eyes. "Trust me, Oscar.

Mark my words," she said. "I will *never* stop."

She was trying to comfort him, but the coldness of her voice sent a chill down Oscar's spine. He tried to look tough, locked in a cold stare with Auntie Fedelma.

Auntie Oonagh clapped her hands and said, "Well, now, I'm glad that's all cleared up!"

"It isn't really all cleared up. The Pooka wrote me a note back," Oscar said. "He wants me to meet him at midnight under home plate."

"Oh, dear, dear," said Auntie Oonagh.

"Well, you have to go, I guess," said Auntie Fedelma. "You can't ignore a request from the Pooka."

"Oscar isn't going for a ride on the Pooka," his father said. "We've already discussed it."

"He has to," Auntie Fedelma said, pounding her gnarled fist on the table. "We can't anger the Pooka!"

"Oh, dear, dear," Auntie Oonagh said again, grabbing hold of Auntie Gormley's hand. Auntie Gormley was the only one in the room who seemed calm.

"It doesn't matter. It's decided. He isn't going," his father said with finality.

Auntie Fedelma gave a snort and turned toward the wall.

The room fell into an awkward silence. And then Auntie Gormley raised her hands in the air as if getting ready to conduct a marching band.

"Oh, yes, let's sing!" Auntie Oonagh said.

And so they did—Auntie Oonagh and Oscar's father were boisterous. Auntie Gormley mouthed it with joyful exaggeration. While Oscar was distracted by the song, looking down at the cake, Auntie Fedelma reached onto the table with her gnarled hand, inched over to the note, covered it with her hand, and then closed her fist and stuck the note in her pocket.

When the song was over, Oscar's father said, "You should make a wish even without candles!"

Auntie Gormley nodded firmly.

"Go on, Oscar," Auntie Oonagh said.

"Be careful," said Auntie Fedelma with a fake smile. "Choose very wisely. You need all the wishes you can get."

"I only have one wish," Oscar said.

"Oh, we all know what that is!" Auntie Fedelma said. "Now, I'm just trying to protect you, Oscar. And my advice is this: Don't waste a wish on this curse-breaking business!"

"I don't think you do know my one wish," Oscar said, because Auntie Fedelma had been wrong. He wasn't going to wish to break the Curse. "I don't need to make a wish for that to come true!" He smiled at his father, and his father smiled back, though a little nervously.

"Go ahead and wish, Oscar," Auntie Oonagh said.

"For whatever you want," his father said.

Oscar closed his eyes. He could feel the bulky key in his pocket. He patted it with one hand to make sure it was really there, and he made his wish: that for his birthday next year they would all be together just like now, but with his mother there, too. He kept his eyes closed. "Should I blow on the cake like if there were candles?"

"Sure," his father said.

And so Oscar blew, but for a second he was scared to open his eyes. He was afraid that if he opened them, he might find that this was just some kind of dream. But he had to and so he did; and everyone was still there, and he was relieved to see them all—even Auntie Fedelma with her scowl.

Auntie Oonagh gave him the first slice. He put a forkful of cotton candy cake in his mouth, but he didn't chew it. He just let it melt on his tongue.

CHAPTER THIRTEEN

The Past

OSCAR LAY DOWN ON HIS pallet of bases in the crawl space under the bulb attached to the wall. He could hear machinery overhead: the official grounds crew. It was morning, and so for the Cursed Creatures and for Oscar, it was time for bed. He'd been awake all night. He could hear some faint snores drifting up from the aunties' hammocks below; and his father had tinkered for a while, sorting through various satchels of grass seed, but now was sound asleep.

Oscar was exhausted but couldn't drift off. He picked up the miniature Fenway Park model and stared into the minifield, the cramped dugout. Game 3 was coming. Later that very day, the Red Sox players would be filling the real Fenway Park—

the Yankees, too. It was almost time. The thought of the game itself going on as he'd be nestled below was almost too much to comprehend. The Red Sox, he thought, they need me, even though they don't know that I exist.

He had to get to the Pooka at the spot below home plate at midnight. But how? How in the world would he be able to slip away from his father at just that hour without his father noticing and stopping him?

His mind felt blurry and useless. Before getting into bed, he'd slipped the Key to the Past into his new mitt and shoved the mitt under his pillow. Now he slipped his hand into the mitt just to make sure the key was still there.

The Key to the Past. He closed his eyes and let his mind float a bit. And that's when the idea came to him: that the present is just a flimsy door between the past and future, and how quickly the future is pulled through that door to become the past. His father would be watching over him at midnight. But *after* midnight? The key, he thought, I can use the key to meet the Pooka once that moment is in the past. Is that what Auntie Gormley had meant when she'd signed that he would need the key, and looked at him so seriously?

He leaned over the edge of his pallet and looked down through the ceiling knotholes; and just as he expected, she was poised there, her chin up, her eyes waiting to meet his. She gave a smile. He smiled back.

She signed with her eyes: "You will come back to us in one piece. You're going to save us."

So she knew.

Now he could roll over and sleep.

Oscar woke up to the tinny sound of a phone ringing. He was on a nocturnal body clock now like everyone else here. It was evening. He'd slept the day away.

His father was downstairs, calling him. "It's your mother! Hurry up!"

Oscar crawled quickly to the ladder and jumped most of the rungs. She hadn't forgotten his birthday after all. He ran to the receiver his father was holding out to him. It was an old, red, rotary phone. He'd never noticed it before. He supposed it might have been a dugout phone a couple decades back.

"Hello?"

"Happy birthday!" his mother said. "I'm so sorry I missed the day. I was working. I got a job here helping Marty out in the office. It's exciting.

Real estate! So much more exciting than handling someone's delicates. How are you?"

"I'm fine," Oscar said. He felt shy suddenly, not sure where to start. He didn't talk on phones much.

"Did you have a good birthday?"

"Yes."

"Do you like it there?"

Oscar scanned the room—the row of aunties in their toe-curled cleats, eating their breakfast at dinnertime; the floor tiled in home plates; the newspaper clippings taped to the walls; the stacks of radios. "Mhmm. Yeah."

"Do you miss me?"

"Mhmm," he said, but it wasn't a hearty response. He was still mad at her for leaving him like that. He wasn't sure how to tell her. He didn't want her to cry, and she sounded happy enough. Why ruin it?

"Things are looking really good here. I think I'll be sending for you sooner than I thought."

"Sending for me?" Oscar whispered. His father was lingering in the kitchen not far off, reading the newspaper. Oscar hadn't known that being "sent for" was part of the plan. Not that his mother even had a plan.

“Yes! I mean, it’s great here! You want to be with me, don’t you?”

He was stuck here. He couldn’t go to Baltimore. And even if he broke the Curse, he didn’t want to go to Baltimore. He felt a flash of anger. It wasn’t fair for her to jerk him around from one place to the next. “Why?” Oscar said. “So I can become an Orioles fan?”

She hesitated. “No, no, you can stay a Sox fan if that’s important to you. Let’s not talk about it. The future is the future. Let’s live in the present.”

“I don’t understand how you can live in the present,” Oscar said. He wanted to know the past. He wanted to have hope in the future.

His mother sighed, and she sounded suddenly worn out.

Oscar changed the subject. He really wanted to tell her about the Curse, the Pooka, all of it; but instead he said, “The Red Sox play tonight. They could turn the playoffs around.”

“I hope they do,” she said, sounding as if she was going to cry. And then Oscar wondered whether things were as good as she’d been saying.

“Gotta go, hon,” she said.

“Okay.”

“I love you.”

“I love you, too.”

Oscar hung up. His father lowered the newspaper. “Wasn’t it good to hear her voice,” he said, though it was more of a statement than a question.

“I guess so,” he said.

His father leaned toward him. “Looks like rain. The Sox might not play tonight. It would give us more time to find that baseball.” He gave a big smile. “I’m going to chart a new course. Make a new plan. Divvy up the park so that we can hunt most effectively. What do you say?”

A hunt with his father for a missing baseball through Fenway Park—today it made perfect sense, but it was something Oscar couldn’t have even dreamed of a few days before. He felt lucky to be here with his father, finally, in his home. It was like some old ache had lifted away, and something in Oscar’s chest rippled like a pennant caught by a sudden wind.

CHAPTER FOURTEEN

The Door to the Past

THE RAIN STARTED TO COME down hard, bouncing off of the tarp covering the field. The dugouts were full. Both teams were there, waiting for it to ease up, and the fans were still pouring in. Oscar could feel the quaking energy overhead. He imagined them all in slickers, huddled under umbrellas.

There was no piped-in organ music. Smoker had given up the .406 Club to Josh Kantor. The Bobs and Stickler had abandoned the broadcast booth. The Pooka had disappeared from the scorekeeper's room by now, surely, and had burrowed in his dugout home under the Monster. Oscar and his father joined the aunties stationed in the living room among the radios, all tuned to the same station—the

AM talk radio sports station—for news on whether the game would be called off or not. The aunties sat in their bleacher seats, and Oscar was sitting on the edge of one of the hammocks made of netting, trying to look casual; but he shifted restlessly, jiggling his knees. His father was laboring over a sketch of a map of the underbelly of Fenway Park. It was on a large piece of paper stretched out on the floor.

At one point Oscar leaned forward and whispered, "And we have to get Smoker and the Bobs to play their positions. Don't forget."

"I'll get to that," his father said. "I will."

But that was about all Oscar could help with at this point. He was fixed on the game. Brown was supposed to pitch for the Yankees. Oscar thought of Brown's pitching hand. He'd broken it by punching a wall in September. He wondered if it would ache in the rain. He thought of Schilling, too, who, according to the AM talk radio sports station, had shown up in the Sox bull pen for a fifteen-minute warm-up wearing a high-top sneaker on the foot with his bad ankle. He wasn't pitching at top speed, but he was there; and Oscar felt a jolt of joy. We can win, he thought, but the momentum came and went. Fourteen minutes before the game was to start, it was canceled. The tarp would stay in place.

There was nothing between Oscar and his meeting with the Pooka now but time. And Oscar's plan was to let the time go. He didn't need the present. He had the Key to the Past. He wished that Auntie Gormley would glance at him, give him an encouraging sign; but she was dozing in her bleacher seat: her lids heavy, her cheeks slack, her breathing punctuated by little rattling snores.

Oscar was listening to the broadcaster drone on. His father was scribbling and erasing and muttering under his breath. Auntie Oonagh was knitting. But Auntie Fedelma was growing squirrelly. Her eyes started to do some mad twitching. She kept staring at the clock and then at Oscar.

As the night ticked slowly closer to midnight, the room took on a new antsiness. Auntie Oonagh's knitting needles clicked more rapidly. Oscar's father scribbled more fiercely. Even Auntie Gormley's snores picked up speed. Everyone knew that the Pooka would be lumbering to the meeting place, that he'd be waiting, that he'd grow angry. Would he come after Oscar? Would he take it out on someone else? Oscar would have to be patient. By midnight Auntie Fedelma was fuming. She couldn't take it anymore.

"The Pooka will be after us but good now. Won't be surprised if he sets fire to this place with a glance of his fire eyes. We're doomed. All because of that boy."

"My name is Oscar," Oscar said.

His father shouted, "You wrote to the Pooka and got him involved in the first place! This is your fault!"

"Oh, dear me, I can't take it, can't hear another word," Auntie Oonagh said, sitting back and humming to herself.

Auntie Fedelma screeched and fussed and fumed and hissed and pouted and stomped her cleats on the floor. Auntie Gormley slept through it all.

At around ten minutes after twelve, Oscar's father said, "Well, that's over. I'm going up to the crawl space, work on my new plan." He rolled up his map and clomped toward the ladder.

"I could make popcorn," Oscar said. "I'm hungry."

"Okay, then," Oscar's father said. "Bring it on up when it's ready."

Oscar said, "Sure," and headed into the kitchen. He turned on the popcorn machine, filling the metal canister with kernels. Once the popping racket set in, he checked on the aunties. He wanted Auntie Gormley to give him another sign, but she was snoring softly. Auntie Oonagh was still knitting, more calmly now. Auntie Fedelma was listening to the latest theory of the Curse on the radio. But when Oscar spied on her, she could sense it. Her head snapped to the kitchen doorway, but Oscar dodged away; and with her bad eyesight, he didn't think she saw him.

He pulled the key from his pocket, already feeling sick with guilt. He was breaking his father's trust, and they'd just begun to get along so well together: the way they'd handled Stickler in the broadcast booth, the shiny mitt that his father had worked so hard for, the new map his father was making to go with his new plan. He even thought of the way his father had said that it was nice to hear his mother's voice.

But he had to meet the Pooka. He had to do what he had to do. And Auntie Gormley understood.

He squatted down in front of the cabinet, slipped the key into the hole, and unlocked the door. It was cold inside. Oscar could feel a draft. His puffy yellow vest was slung over the back of one of the kitchen chairs; and since he didn't know where he'd end up tonight—on the back of the Pooka or worse—he put it on. He got down on his knees and looked through the door to a small passageway, unlit, earthen. He crawled in and shut the door behind him, making sure it was locked.

He crawled quickly. The dirt was a little moist. He could feel the wetness seep through the knees of his pants. This tunnel had as many twists as the passageways full of nettles and barbed ivy. He was trying to think of the perfect rhyme to describe whatever was beneath home plate and something about midnight. He thought and thought, but his mind always wandered to the power he had. He could say anything about *any* time and place. Where did he really want to go? What did he really want to see? The past would always be in the past. He could always catch up with the Pooka, couldn't he?

He slowed down. What would it hurt if he went to just one place first? Just one? This was such a huge gift. Finally he blurted out the one thing that was on his mind: "To tell the truth, I want to meet Babe Ruth."

And it rhymed. He hadn't said it very loudly. In fact, his voice sounded small and weak in the tight tunnel, muffled by the earth all around him.

There was no grand transformation. Nothing. Maybe this was just another passageway. Maybe this didn't lead anywhere. Or not for him. Maybe it only worked for those with fairy blood. He thought about turning around. He'd probably get in trouble, big trouble, for sneaking out like this. He already felt horrible about it. And he was going to turn back—he was just about to—when he saw a long, rectangular window of light in the distance.

When he reached the window, he slipped his hand into what seemed like a closet. There he found jerseys. Red Sox jerseys—old-fashioned ones. They were coarse. He pulled one, stretching the back of it wide. It was a broad jersey—no name, no number. It buttoned down the front and had RED SOX stitched on it.

There was a space to climb down, and Oscar did—into a narrow closet. No, Oscar corrected himself, a locker. It was wooden and doorless. He recognized the fungal stink.

He stepped out of it into a large, dark room.

But then ceiling lights flipped on overhead and a voice said, "Hey, kid, what are you doing in here?"

The man was tall and broad and ruddy. He was wearing a suit and a long coat and a hat with a black band. He was holding a cigar, but it wasn't lit. His face was wide, and his nose, too. He had shiny black eyes. He was, of course, Babe Ruth, but so much bigger than Oscar had ever imagined. He said, "You one of Bossy's kids?"

"Bossy?"

"You lost?"

Oscar looked around the locker room—at the wooden benches, the old overhead lights, the players' lockers with wool uniforms on hangers, the potbellied stove in the middle of the room. "No," he said. "I'm not lost."

"What you got on there? A life jacket?"

Oscar looked down at his puffy yellow vest. He wasn't sure what to say. "It's a costume."

"Close enough to Halloween, I guess."

"What year is it?"

"What *year*, kid? Don't you know? You bang your head or something?" Ruth had a big, wide smile.

"I'd just like you to tell me. That's all."

"C'mon, kid. It's 1919."

"And you're still here with the Red Sox?"

"Where else would I be?"

"Nowhere," Oscar said. "It's just . . ."

"Just what?"

"Frazee."

"You don't know what year it is, and you want to talk management all of a sudden?"

Oscar could hear voices off in the distance. He

didn't have much time. "Frazee might say some mean things about you one day, but you'll go down in history as the best of the best. No one will ever forgive him for the bad things he's going to do and say to you."

"You think he's a bad guy, huh?"

"I do."

Ruth stared at Oscar then, taking a step forward, tilting his head. "Do you know something about bad guys? Bullies and stuff like that?"

Oscar nodded.

"You know, when I was little, I lived in a place called St. Mary's—it was a school for wayward boys, no-goods, like me. And you know what the kids called me at that place?"

Oscar shook his head.

"They called me Nigger Lips."

Oscar didn't move. He just looked at Ruth, and it seemed as if Ruth knew what it was to be Oscar in a way that no other adult had ever seemed to.

"You think people still call me things like that?" Ruth asked.

"No," Oscar said. "You're famous."

"You're wrong. They still do. The difference is that when I was a kid, like you, I thought it was because there was something wrong with me. But now I know it's that something is wrong with them."

Oscar nodded.

"No matter what Frazee says, I'll keep on swinging with everything I've got. I'll sometimes hit them big, and I'll sometimes miss them big. But I'll always be living as big as I possibly can. You can't beat the person who never gives up."

"I won't give up then," Oscar said.

Someone down the hall shouted for Ruth. "I gotta go," he said. "You sure you're okay?"

"Yeah, I'm just waiting for my dad. He'll be here soon."

"You look kinda familiar. We met before, you and me?"

Oscar shook his head.

Babe walked over then and held up a piece of hard yellow candy wrapped in plastic. "Here," he said. "A little early for Halloween, but I like your costume. You're a survivor, right? Of a shipwreck? Like the *Titanic*?"

Oscar nodded and took the candy. "Um, and one more thing," Oscar said.

"What is it?"

"You were talking about swinging big and hitting big. I know you're a pitcher now, mostly, but maybe . . ." He suddenly felt flustered. This was Babe Ruth. His cheeks felt flushed.

"Go on," Ruth said. "Go on, kid."

"Um, well, maybe you should hit more. I mean, pitchers only get up to bat once every five or so games, but hitters can get up to bat five times in one game."

Babe looked at him seriously and then smiled. "I'll keep that in mind, kid," he said; then he looked at his vest one more time. "A survivor. I like it." And he walked to the door of the locker room and tipped his hat, then he was gone.

CHAPTER FIFTEEN

Meeting the Pooka—Face-to-Face, Eye to Glowing Eye

BACK IN THE SMALL TUNNEL, Oscar heard distant voices, muffled by the locked door, echoing dimly through the small tunnel.

"Is he in there?" It was Auntie Oonagh.

"I told you that boy couldn't be trusted!" Auntie Fedelma said victoriously. "Do you believe me now?"

"I just don't think he'd do this," his father said. "I really don't."

His father's faith in him made Oscar feel awful. He'd disobeyed, and on something pretty important too. Oscar knew he should probably turn back, confess, not go to the Pooka. But he wanted to do what Babe had suggested—either hit big or miss big—and he at least needed to really try. He didn't have much time to think. He kept crawling as quickly as he could. He whispered, "I need to meet the Pooka at this past midnight and I can't be late. Take me to the tunnels that will lead me just below home plate."

This time the change took place quickly, so quickly that the floor disappeared and Oscar landed with a thud in the larger tunnels. Looking around, it dawned on him how very much the tunnels all looked the same: ivy, barbed nettles, cement, wires. They all smelled the same too: burned coffee, buttered popcorn, hot dogs, mouse turds, and the oily fur of weasels. He realized pretty quickly that he was lost. He didn't know how to get to the space beneath home plate or back home. He broke into a run, hoping to get to one or the other faster. But panicking would only get him more lost.

And so he stopped and told himself to calm down and think.

That's when he heard the panting behind him and the scrabble of nails skidding to a stop. He looked back, and there was a weasel, all by herself. She looked frightened, caught.

"Are you following me?" Oscar asked.

The weasel nodded.

"Well, I'm lost, so you can stop."

The weasel looked as if she wasn't sure what to do next. She cocked her head and snapped her teeth.

Oscar read the snaps, just as he did Auntie Gormley's language of darting eyes and blinks. "Where do you want to go?"

Oscar was astonished. He said, "Can you help me? You know these tunnels, right?"

The weasel gave a chirp and nodded.

"I want to go to the place under home plate. Can you take me?"

"To the Pooka?" The weasel's teeth snapped out a little code. "Are you sure?"

"How did you know?"

She didn't answer.

"Yes," Oscar said. "I'm sure."

"Okay then," the weasel snapped, "but only if you let me come with you for the pooka ride."

Oscar paused. "How did you know about that too?" he asked.

She just blinked at him.

Oscar didn't want to take a weasel with him, but he had no choice. He wasn't in a good negotiating spot. He nodded grudgingly. "Yeah, okay, sure."

"Okay," the weasel snapped. "Follow me."

The weasel scampered ahead, and Oscar followed. They both were sprinting through the tunnels now this way and that. Oscar had always wanted a dog. The landlord didn't allow them, though. Weirdly enough, this was as close as he'd ever come: boy and weasel running through the underground passageways of Fenway Park to meet a pooka. He was having fun. He wasn't as scared as he had been. He loved to run. He'd been the fastest base runner on his team last year.

The weasel stopped dead in her tracks. She lifted her nose in the air, pulsed her tiny nostrils. "Mice," she snapped.

And then Oscar could hear them, too—a wave of them, just like before, with his father. "No!" he shouted. "Run!" But it was too late. The mice were upon them, a rising tide lifting them up. Oscar and the weasel bobbed swiftly this way and that, speeding down the twists and turns. Oscar was terrified. Where would they end up? Surely he'd miss the meeting with the Pooka now, and he'd have to find a way somehow to get back to the Door to the Past and start all over again!

The mice took a hard turn to the left. Oscar and the weasel slammed into a wall and fell to the ground. The wave of mice continued on without them down another darkened tunnel.

Oscar rubbed his shoulder. “What are we going to do now?” he asked the weasel.

But much to his surprise, she snapped, “It’s just around that corner there.”

“What is?”

“The spot beneath home plate,” she snapped. “The mice dropped us right where we need to be!”

Oscar paused a moment. Had the mice played their position just like the Curse said? He decided they had. The echo of their scrabbling claws grew quieter and quieter in the distance.

The weasel snapped, “Pick me up. Put me in your pocket.”

Oscar scooped up the rodent and shoved her in his jacket pocket. “Okay, ready?” He was asking himself more than he was the weasel, but the weasel gave a snap of approval. Oscar was glad now that the weasel was coming. He wanted the company.

He turned the final corner. It was dark at first, and all he could see were two flames floating like lamps. But then he saw that the lamps lit a large, dark muzzle and nostrils, and that they weren’t two flames at all but eyes. The whole horse face turned, and the Pooka examined Oscar with only one of his glowing eyes. Oscar could see his gleaming coat, his triangular ears, his broad chest, and the mane running down the middle of his back. The Pooka took two steps forward on his hooves, and then he reached out his hand. A man's hand—pale and strong.

Oscar went to shake it, but that wasn't what the Pooka had in mind. He grabbed Oscar's hand; and with amazing strength, he hurled Oscar on his back. "Let's go!" he shouted. Oscar barely had time to grab the Pooka's mane before he took off at a gallop.

The Pooka wove his way, hurtling down the tunnels so fast that Oscar's eyes teared in the wind. The weasel in Oscar's jacket pocket nestled down low, with only the tip of her head peeking out. The Pooka didn't slow down as the tunnel rose toward the ceiling. He simply rammed his horse head into the dirt, and another trapdoor flew open at the edge of the outfield, peeling back the tarp. He stopped without warning, used his back hooves to kick the trapdoor back into place, and then galloped on a bit more until they were no longer on the ground but leaping with such force that it seemed as if they were flying up the stands, climbing higher and higher toward the final row.

Stinging rain slashed Oscar's cheeks, but that was the least of his problems.

"Watch out!" Oscar shouted. "Slow down! There aren't any more seats!"

The Pooka kept on, though. He wasn't listening, only striding higher; and at the final row of seats, Oscar shut his eyes. The Pooka leaped, and they were stalled in midair, falling. Oscar screamed. But then the Pooka's hooves began to churn, and they were galloping again—on nothing more than the cold wind—the Pooka's glowing eyes lighting the way.

The city lights bobbed below. Oscar could see Boston Harbor, its polished black surface reflecting the tall buildings of downtown Boston, and the boat lights and the planes landing on the strip of land that jutted into the harbor. At first Oscar found himself swallowing the cold air in gulps, tensing at the slaps of rain. The wind was so strong it filled his lungs as if they were a pair of bagpipes. He tried to speak, but his voice just squeaked. He could barely breathe. So he closed his mouth, shut his eyes, and took shallow breaths through his nose. The weasel had burrowed down in Oscar's pocket and was curled into a trembling knot.

Once Oscar caught his breath, he asked, "Where are you taking me?"

The Pooka didn't answer.

Oscar kept frantically weaving his fingers into

the Pooka's mane more and more tightly. The ride was jarring, not rhythmic like a horse ride. Oscar clung to the Pooka's back, trying to stay as close as possible. The air was colder up here. It stung his face and hands until they went numb. His shoulders were wet. He sneezed and blew his nose into his sleeve.

"Where are you taking me?" he asked again.

The Pooka went faster. The lights of Boston were long gone now, and there was only ocean off to the left—the occasional lights of a ship, the pulsing red blips of a passing airplane. The water below was a dark sheet. And to the right there were clusters of lights—cities—with more lights stringing them together. "Don't drop me," Oscar said.

They rode on for what seemed like an hour or more, and now Oscar felt as if his runny nose had turned into a chest cold. He felt a little fevered. There was more ocean, more cities. The Pooka was slowing down. He had a wheeze in his lungs as well.

"Are we going down? Tell me where you're taking me!"

Finally the Pooka said, "I'm taking you where your heart wants to be."

"My heart?" Oscar said. "What do you mean? My heart?"

The Pooka circled over a city, and then a certain spot within the city. He circled and descended as if galloping down a huge spiral staircase, and finally landed, quite precisely, on the landing of a fire escape. He stood on his hind legs. Oscar let go of his mane, though his hands were cramped from holding on so tightly. And he slid down the Pooka's back, landing on the cold metal. He felt weak. He coughed and coughed and then, finally, caught his breath. The Pooka looked tired. The glow in his eyes was dimming. The weasel looked sickly, too. Her eyes were red, her lids droopy. She jumped out of Oscar's pocket, bobbed around on the landing, and then threw up over the edge. Oscar thought of his father in Pizzeria Uno, how pale and sickly he always looked. And, for the first time, Oscar understood that he was truly cursed.

"So this is how you make people disappear?" Oscar said. "You either drop them from the sky or you just leave them in the middle of nowhere."

The Pooka shook his horse head, his mane flipped on his back. He looked at Oscar with his softly glowing eyes. "No," he said. "I've never made anyone disappear."

"Not true," the weasel snapped. "Two Cursed Creatures went for a ride with him and didn't come back. Scalper, who lingered on Yawkey Way and lived under Concourse B, and Ticket Taker, who was sickly."

"What about Scalper and Ticket Taker?" Oscar asked.

"Sometimes the Cursed Creatures want to go. They come to me, and I help them. You'll die eventually if you leave the ballpark for too long. They both wanted to see Ireland again. And so I took them. They refused to go back."

Oscar looked around. "Are we in Ireland?"

The Pooka shook his head. "Does your heart want to go to Ireland?"

"I don't think so," Oscar said.

"Well, then, think. Where does your heart want to go?"

Oscar sat there and thought. He'd already met Babe Ruth—and it wasn't really his heart that had wanted to meet Babe. Not really. His heart? What was his heart missing? Well, his mother, of course. He thought of the phone call, and his chest ached. It hadn't gone well. He still felt sore about it. "My mother," Oscar said finally. "I guess my heart wants to at least see my mother."

The Pooka nodded to the window near the fire escape.

With great effort, Oscar stood up and looked inside. There was a kitchen with a shiny stove, a microwave, and a fridge. It was simply an empty kitchen. And then a figure walked in. Oscar's mother. She was wearing her bathrobe, the one from home that she always wore. She was alone. She opened the fridge, got out a carton of milk, and poured a glass.

"She drinks milk when she can't sleep," Oscar said.

His mother leaned on the sink, her back facing him. Her shoulders started to shake. He knew she was crying. "I don't understand," Oscar said.

"She misses you. She thinks she's made a mess of things."

"Why did you bring me here?" Oscar was angry now. He didn't want to see his mother crying. He'd seen that all his life. "You were supposed to help me with the Curse. You're supposed to help me find the baseball."

"I can't talk about any of that," the Pooka said. "The rules."

"Yes, I know," Oscar said, remembering Rule #1; "but I was hoping you could give me a sign, a message. I can read signs. It's my gift."

"How does the Curse go?"

"Um, I don't know. I don't have it memorized,"

Oscar said. His mother was crying harder now. It was distracting. He wanted to go in and comfort her, but he knew he couldn't. He knew that an action such as that would be breaking a rule, too.

"How does it start?" the Pooka urged him.

The weasel tugged on Oscar's pant leg. "How does it start?" she snapped. "Think."

"It starts out about how we're all orphans," Oscar said.

"Yes, and then . . ."

"It talks about Babe Ruth when he was a boy learning a trade."

"What trade?"

"A tailor."

"And what did he do at the tailor shop?"

"I don't know," Oscar said, frustrated. He felt swimmy headed and flushed. "He made shirts?"

"That he did. That he did."

"So?" Oscar said. "So what?"

"It takes an orphan to understand an orphan."

"Are you asking me if I understand Babe Ruth?"

"Not really Ruth, no."

"Then who?"

"We're all orphans."

"I know that. It's in the Curse. But we aren't

ALL orphans! Ruth and I were abandoned. We understand it, but—"

"Who else has felt abandoned? Who else felt cast out?"

Oscar wasn't sure what kind of answer the Pooka was digging for, but he knew that the Pooka was deeply anxious. His human hands were shaking. Oscar was shaking, too. He looked at his mother through the window. She'd calmed down some. She was sitting at the kitchen table, looking at the picture of herself and Oscar taken at the water park. She blew her nose in a tissue. She was wearing her necklace, but she wasn't fiddling with the beads. What did it all mean?

The weasel tugged urgently on Oscar's pants again. "Lift me up," she snapped. And Oscar did. He could feel her ribs rising and falling quickly—she was breathless. The weasel leaned forward toward the Pooka and stared at him intently. Her eyes were glassy. Oscar thought of the Pooka's questions again: *Who else has felt abandoned? Who else felt cast out?* Like the weasel, Oscar now stared into one of the Pooka's eyes. He looked directly into its center—the pupil, the dark middle—and in it he saw another eye, small and brown and filled with longing. "Are you . . . ," Oscar began. "Are you who

I think you are?" Was this Keeffe? Could it be?

The weasel started to tremble then. She let out a quiet whimper.

"I can't answer any questions," the Pooka said. "It's against the rules."

"You know where the baseball is, don't you?" Oscar asked.

The Pooka held out his hand. "I've got to get back home quickly. I have something I have to do," he said. "No more questions."

The weasel sobbed and turned away. Oscar wasn't sure why she was so upset, but he held her to his chest and stroked her head. He looked in through the window one last time. His mother was shuffling across the kitchen. She turned out the light. The Pooka had both hands on the fire escape railing and was looking up at the sky, checking out conditions.

Oscar said, "It's you. It's *been* you all along, all of these years!"

The weasel seemed stricken by this—weak and sobbing—as if it were all too much to take. She nosed her way back into the pocket while the Pooka looked at Oscar with faked innocence. "I don't know what you're talking about."

"Why did you make that curse?"

"I don't know what you're talking about," he said weakly.

"They all think you've abandoned them, that you got out while the getting was good."

The Pooka hung his head low, covered his glowing eyes with his hands. "I don't know what you're talking about."

"Why did you do it?"

The Pooka looked at Oscar. "Do you think I'm happy? Look at me."

Oscar couldn't. He was ashamed that he'd gotten so angry with the Pooka. He hadn't just cursed Fenway Park and left. He'd cursed himself, too. There was more to the story than Oscar knew right now, but the Pooka couldn't tell it. The Curse had rules; and if Oscar was going to break the Curse, the Pooka had to be careful about what he said or the Curse would become permanent.

"I'm sorry," Oscar said.

"It's okay," the Pooka said. He grabbed Oscar by the shoulder and gave him a gentle rattle. "That weasel would make a good spy. Do you understand?"

"Not really," Oscar said, patting the weasel in his pocket. Why had she reacted so strongly to the Pooka? She seemed to have gone limp.

"You will."

The Pooka held out his hand and looked at Oscar gravely. “Tell no one about our conversation. Do you promise? No one.”

Oscar said, “I promise.”

He grabbed the Pooka’s hand, and the Pooka swung him onto his back. “That tailor shop where Babe Ruth learned his trade used to be not very far from here,” the Pooka said, trying to sound casual. “I’d take you there, but it doesn’t exist anymore.”

“You’ve been to that tailor shop before?” Oscar asked.

“Once,” the Pooka said. “Just once. Let’s go home now. Let’s go home.” He climbed the railing, gave a leap, and galloped up into the dark clouds.

CHAPTER SIXTEEN

The Weasel Spy

THE RIDE BACK TO BOSTON was even more jarring than the ride to Baltimore. The Pooka was frantic. He kept repeating, "I have to hurry. I've got to go faster!"

Oscar was clamped to the Pooka's back, hands wrapped in the mane; the weasel curled in a ball deep in Oscar's vest pocket. He got the wind kicked out of him each time the Pooka leaped unexpectedly.

"Why are you going so fast?" Oscar shouted.

"I have a task. I must do it or I won't see her."

"Who?"

"No one," the Pooka said. "No one at all."

The Pooka clamored over the stadium wall and

galloped across the field to home plate. Steam pouring from his wide nostrils, he kicked open the seamless trapdoor near home plate and jumped through the opening, with Oscar still on his back. Then he reached up and pulled the door down after him.

The tunnel grew dark. Oscar slid to the ground. His legs and arms felt rubbery and loose in the joints.

"I've got to run. You'll find your way back," the Pooka said.

"Wait," Oscar said. "There's more to the story, and I have to understand it if I'm going to find the baseball and break the Curse. You have to tell me what I need to know. Send me a message somehow. Promise?"

"You know," the Pooka said, pointing to the weasel in Oscar's pocket, "that what we need first of all is a spy."

The weasel poked her head out. She couldn't take her eyes off of the Pooka's hands. It was as if she was trying to memorize them. Oscar stared at the weasel; and when he looked back up, the Pooka was already a blur in the distance.

Oscar stood there for a moment. He didn't know how to sort anything out: Babe Ruth, the Pooka, his own mother at the kitchen sink. The weasel broke his concentration. She snapped her teeth.

"What?" Oscar said. "What is it?"

She snapped, "I'm going to follow him."

"What?" Oscar said.

"I would make a good spy. He said it twice. He wants me to spy on him."

Oscar picked the weasel up out of his pocket and set her on the floor. "Okay then. Are you all right?"

The weasel nodded, but she wasn't convincing. "I have to keep my head and find out what he's got to do, why he was in such a hurry."

"Right," Oscar said. "Go, hurry!"

The weasel ran off—a quick scamper—and Oscar was alone in the tunnels again with no idea which direction to turn.

Oscar wandered for what seemed like a long time. He was exhausted and thirsty; but now that he was back in Fenway Park, he no longer felt sickly. Just a little sad. He kept thinking of his mother crying at the sink. He missed her; and being lost in the underbelly of Fenway Park among the nettles, keeping an ear out for a wave of mice—none of this helped any. If he failed now, the Curse would be permanent. He would be stuck here forever. This made him miss his mother even more sharply. He felt like sitting down. He could feel the tears welling up just behind his eyelids.

He came to a stop and released a huffing sob; but before the crying could really start, he heard voices in the tunnel, calling his name. "Oscar! Where are you? You down here?" It was a gravelly voice, low and deep. Smoker?

Oscar saw the cloud first. It was gathering speed, headed right for him. He could see the glowing tips of Smoker's cigarettes and hear him saying, "You're in big trouble. Everybody's been looking for you! I was called away from my precious work!"

And then Oscar was swallowed whole by a cloud of smoke. He could barely see. Luckily the horned organist, with cigarettes dangling from both corners of his mouth, had his arm around Oscar like a protective wing. "Do you know how worried everyone's been?" he said. "They say you went through the doorway of the Door to the Past. They say you went on a ride with the Pooka. Is it true?"

"Yes." Oscar coughed.

"Oscar!" His father's voice was echoing through the tunnels. "Oscar!"

"And you survived!" Smoker said, his gravelly voice rumbling with excitement. "They say you're going to break the Curse. Is it true?"

"I don't know," Oscar said. He felt a little dizzy from the ride or the smoke or both. Was he going to be able to break the Curse? How was the Pooka going to be able to let Oscar know where the ball was without violating the Curse? Oscar then heard his father's voice close by. "Oscar? Are you in there?" His father's face poked into the smoky cloud—cheeks red and hardened by anger, lips stiff. Oscar was suddenly terrified, even more so than he'd been on the back of the Pooka.

But his father's anger suddenly melted. He grabbed Oscar, lifted him off the ground, and said, "You're alive! You're safe. You're home."

Soon enough, Oscar found himself at the kitchen table again, the faces all pressed in. It was strange how big and flushed and eager everyone was, all poised to hear what he had to say. It was warm in the kitchen, which reminded him of the moist heat of the dry cleaners—how it would fill the apartment, warming the bathroom tiles, making the windows sweat. The faces were ones he knew well by now; but this close, they seemed to ring around him like giant, fleshy beads on a necklace. Auntie Oonagh's head tilting so that her good ear was closest; Auntie

Fedelma, her overcast eyes—those milky beetles—darting behind her thick glasses; Auntie Gormley, whose pruned lips were puffing and whinnying as she snored, sleeping soundly; and Oscar's father, his face still creased with leftover worry but also proud—all cheeks and eyes.

"What was he like up close?" Oscar's father asked. "Did he talk to you?"

"Um . . . ," Oscar said.

"Was it very scary?" Auntie Oonagh asked. "Where did you go?"

Oscar nodded. "It was a hard ride, and cold, too."

"Did he try to pitch you off?" Auntie Fedelma asked.

"He didn't try to pitch me off. He isn't like that. He's, well . . ." Oscar wasn't sure what to say. He couldn't tell them what he wanted desperately to say, which was that the Pooka was Keeffe. They hadn't been abandoned. Keeffe had cursed himself as well, and he was stuck and heartbroken, too. "He's actually good. He's actually trying to help."

"To help?" Auntie Fedelma snorted.

"No, no, no," Oscar's father said. "The Pooka can't be good. He can't. You could have died. He's made people disappear."

"They wanted to," Oscar said.

"Wanted to disappear?" Oscar's father asked.

Oscar nodded. "They missed their homes."

"Are you saying that you're friends with the Pooka now? Going to have him over for dinner?" Auntie Fedelma said.

"I'm not having him over for dinner," Oscar said. "I don't think he's the type that would come if you invited him."

"You shouldn't have snuck out," Auntie Fedelma said. "Are we punishing him? Shouldn't he be grounded?"

"I'm not sure what to do," Oscar's father said.

"Flog him!" Auntie Fedelma shouted.

Oscar knew that he deserved to be punished somehow. He'd disobeyed his father. But he didn't want to lose any ground. What about the clues from the Pooka? Would the weasel have news for him? Did she get to the Pooka in time to spy on him? "I still have to try to break the Curse," Oscar said. "I want to make it up to you all."

Auntie Fedelma was glaring at Oscar. "You aren't GOING to BREAK THE CURSE! How many times do I have to tell you?"

Everyone stared at her, shocked.

"Don't you all know that it's better to know the future even if it is bad than it is to *not* know? What has not knowing gotten us? A swamp! And then a ball field! And then a curse! At least we can rely on the Curse. We *know* the Curse! Why do something and risk making it worse?"

Oscar stared at Auntie Fedelma. He wanted to call her crazy, but there was something about what she was saying that didn't sound crazy at all. Hadn't he put up with Drew Sizemore? He never tried to change that. He knew that Drew Sizemore wanted to make his life miserable, and all Oscar did was try to be invisible. But now that Auntie Fedelma was saying it out loud, Oscar knew it was wrong. What if people such as Jackie Robinson had just put up with the way things were? "We have to at least hope for something better, at least try," Oscar said.

Auntie Fedelma wasn't listening. "I'm saying this for your own good."

Oscar let out a forceful sigh. He looked at Auntie Gormley, who must have been in the middle of a vivid dream. Her eyebrows knitted together. Her eyes shut more tightly. It was almost as if she were trying to explain something very important to some-one in her dream. Oscar wondered what she would tell him now if she were awake. Would she tell him to be strong, to have hope? Oscar said, "You've got to have faith! The Curse *can* be broken. I know it."

At this Auntie Fedelma stood up stiffly. "I'm going out! I have an appointment!"

This time, no one said a word. Fedelma hobbled out of the kitchen, her wings rustling behind her. She put on her moth-bitten coat and walked out the front door, into the tunnels.

"She's up to no good," Auntie Oonagh said.

But that's when it dawned on Oscar that Auntie Fedelma, who was surely up to no good, actually thought he *could* break the Curse. She saw him as a real threat. Oscar said, "But she believes in me more than any of you."

"That's not true," Oscar's father said.

"It is true," Oscar said, "and I think you know it's true, deep down."

Oscar stood up too. He walked out of the kitchen and climbed the ladder up to the crawl space. He lay down on his bedding. This was it. Regardless of whether his father really believed in him or not, they were closer than they'd ever been before to breaking the Curse. He couldn't wait for the weasel to come with news. He jiggled his feet and tapped his hands on his chest in rhythm to his fast-paced heart. He felt electric.

Aboveground, on the flip side of the dirt ceiling, the wet grass was being aired for that night's game. Ortiz, Damon, Martinez, Bellhorn, Lowe—all of the Red Sox were somewhere in Boston, thinking their own thoughts, maybe praying, maybe running through their own pregame mantras. The field's soil was sorrowful; the Curse had hunkered down here, deep in the bones and bowels of Fenway Park. These were the Boston Red Sox, who had the weight and momentum of eighty-six years of losing. But things were different this time. Oscar knew he could help. He remembered that Babe Ruth had told him, "You can't beat the person who never gives up."

CHAPTER SEVENTEEN

Teams

THE WEASEL FOLLOWED THE POOKA through the passageways, up the tunnel inside of the Green Monster. When the Pooka had opened the door to the scorekeeper's room, he'd left it open a crack—just enough for a weasel to pass through without making the door squeak. Which is just what she did.

The Pooka pushed open a small, cabinetlike door near the floor of the scorekeeper's room, under the scoring table. It was undetectable until the Pooka pushed it, and then it revealed a small cupboard with a cardboard box inside. The Pooka moved quickly. He put the box on the table and rummaged through it. He pulled out a bunch of wool yarn, then a handful of thin string, and then a small, tough, rubber ball. He began winding the wool around the rubber ball, keeping an eye on the dark outside of the slit in the wall and on the clock. His hands were a blur of motion. When the wool was wound tightly, he started in on the string. He wound and wound at a demonic pace, his hands orbiting the ball in superfast motion. None of this made any sense to the weasel until the Pooka had run out of string and was holding something the size and shape of a baseball.

Finally the Pooka reached inside of the box again and pulled out two pale leather skins—hourglass shaped. The weasel knew that this was it: the cursed ball, the one that Oscar was looking for in order to break the Curse. The weasel waited for the Pooka's next move: to stitch the leather skins together with red thread.

But the Pooka didn't reach into the box for anything else. He simply held the ball in his cupped hands, and he began to weep. A few bright tears ran from his eyes, down his horse cheeks, and onto the score table. He looked up at the clock. It was five a.m. Soon it would be light outside. He held the ball in his hands and looked out of the slit. Off in the distance there was organ music—something classical overrun by an inevitable rally song—Smoker at the bench. The Pooka kept staring out of the slot; and then, suddenly, he drew in his breath.

"There she is," he said softly, as if he were speaking to the weasel now. "Dancing."

The Banshee? Dancing at dawn? It had to be her. Gormley didn't quite understand why her father would want her to see the Banshee. Gormley's soul felt ragged with sadness. She couldn't take her weasel eyes off of the Pooka, her father. His hands—she had remembered them well: muscular and strong, the knuckles a bit tough. His true old eyes in the center of his horse eyes—she recognized them from the way he used to look at her when he was singing ballads.

The Pooka stood there holding the ball for a while, and then sunlight started creeping into the scorekeeper's room. He pulled away from the slit. The organ music came to an abrupt end, as if Smoker had been suddenly called away.

"Smoker," the Pooka said, tilting his horse head as if struck by an idea. "Music. Coded messages!"

He put the skins back into the box, and then he sighed heavily. He dropped the ball; and holding on to the end of the string, he let the ball unwind and roll to a corner, where it kicked around as the Pooka undid all of his work.

* * *

Auntie Fedelma took her usual fifteen steps and waited for Weasel-man. He arrived breathless, late. The weasels were sprinting beside him, twisting their leashes. He was jangled and wrung his hands nervously. "What's happened? Did they find the boy? I haven't heard a thing."

"We lost that game, Weasel-man. Failure! Loss!"

"He's alive?"

She nodded. "He's alive and well and seems as if he's made a friend."

"A friend?"

"The Pooka himself!"

"Oh," Weasel-man said. He was stunned. He stared down at the weasels bounding over one another. "I didn't expect that."

"No, I bet you didn't. So, now what?"

"I don't know," Weasel-man said.

"You're of no use. I need . . . I need . . ." Her eyes glistened; a smile curled across her face. "I need a team of my own! Where are Stickler and the Bobs?"

"In the training room, I bet," Weasel-man answered, confused. "Stickler likes to take a soak."

"Take me there!"

"Why do you want them?" he asked.

"Just take me there!"

Weasel-man obliged. He held out his arm and let Fedelma grab hold. He led her through the tunnels. It was still very early in the morning. Fedelma held tight to Weasel-man's arm. They took the twisting routes underground: right and then left, and then Fedelma stopped in her tracks.

"Wait. Hush," she said to Weasel-man. Over the occasional chirps of weasels, she heard something in the distance: a rhythmic clomping. "Hear that?"

"What?"

Then there was a whinny. "That," she said. "The Pooka! Let's hurry! What if he's after us?"

Weasel-man sped up, giving the weasels' leashes a giddyap; but Fedelma started losing her footing. "No," she said, "you'll have to carry me!"

Weasel-man bent down, and she climbed onto his back. She looked down one of the passages and saw a faint glow. "The other way!" she whispered loudly. "Hurry!"

Weasel-man took off in the opposite direction.

She struck his shoulder again and again. "Faster!" she said. "He's here somewhere with us! Faster!"

Finally they came to an unmarked spot among

the barbed vines and nettle bushes.

"Here it is," Weasel-man said, easing Fedelma off of his back to the ground. Her cleats hit the ground and she wobbled a bit, her heart rattling in her frail chest. She listened for the hooves, for a stray whinny; but there was nothing. "Let's go," she said.

Weasel-man gave a knock on the unmarked spot.

"Just us chickens!" someone yelled.

Weasel-man shoved on the wall, using the heft of his weight. The wall gave way, and he helped Fedelma through the opening, the weasels following quickly behind, and then he closed it. The door faded into the wall again, disappearing from view.

The training room was bright. It smelled of alcohol swabs and sweat and menthol and chlorine. Stickler was waist deep in a single-person hot tub. The Bobs were sitting on a massage table, as if they were waiting for a trainer to tape them up—or, in their case, untape them. Radio was playing in the background—the AM talk radio sports station—in fact, blaring away.

"Fedelma? What are you doing here?" Stickler said, sitting up straight in the foggy steam of the tub.

Auntie Fedelma ignored Stickler. She was still jangled from the run through the tunnels. She walked to the center of the room, squinting all around. Everyone was uneasy. Jowly Bob turned off Radio, and he never did that. But the room still felt as if it were full of static.

"Seriously, Fedelma. When's the last time you were out here?" Jowly Bob said. His face looked pale and wobbly, like uncooked dough.

"What's brought you?" Mustache Bob added, tugging on his mustache nervously.

Auntie Fedelma stood there. She stared at Weasel-man, with the pack of weasels at his feet; the two Bobs; Stickler standing in the steaming tub, bare chested, flabby, and sweating. "This is my team," she muttered. "My lousy team." She clapped her hands in the air. "Listen up!" she said, walking to a dry erase board. She picked up a marker, popped off its cap. "We're going to band together. We're going to get that boy. Put a stop to him once and for all. Weasel-man, you'll help because you're loyal to me. Stickler, you'll help because you never liked Old Boy to begin with. And Bobs, you'll help because, well, this is the real thing. This isn't sitting in a booth when there is no game. This isn't sitting in any booth at all. This is getting in the game!" She glared into the eyes of Weasel-man, Stickler, the Bobs. "And we're going to win!"

* * *

Back in the underbelly tunnels of Fenway Park, the Pooka was still galloping. He had seen, for the briefest moment, Fedelma, his daughter; and now he couldn't shake the image. It had been such a long time. She looked older and wizened, so much so that at first he didn't recognize her. But then he caught the sharp angles of her face, the determined set of her jaw, the steely glint of her stare; and his heart broke all over again. His Fedelma, his little girl. For a moment his eyes had gone blurry with tears, and he felt even more breathless. He forgot what he was doing here, running through tunnels. Who was he looking for?

It came back to him: Smoker. He had to get a message to Smoker, who would code it and, hopefully, get it to the boy. He had faith in Oscar. He loved his bright eyes and his open expression. He was a sincere boy with a kind heart and a quick mind. He could do this; the Pooka knew it. He could break the Curse. He was the boy who the Pooka had dreamed of, once upon a time, the boy who would release Fenway Park from all of its suffering.

He regained his full gallop and flexed his nostrils in hopes of picking up a scent. Luckily, Smoker wasn't too difficult to sniff out; and after taking some winding turns, the Pooka caught a whiff of smoke and followed it until it bloomed around Smoker himself. The glow of the Pooka's eyes lit up the smoke so that it looked like a sunlit cloud.

"Who's there?" Smoker said, then coughed jaggedly.

"You know who it is," the Pooka said.

"No," Smoker said, still encased in smoke. "Don't take me! Don't hurt me!" he pleaded.

Shoving his hand into the cloud, the Pooka handed Smoker a note. "Read it. Do you understand?" the Pooka asked.

There was a short pause. "No," Smoker said.

"Good. That's the way it has to be. I can't tell anyone, not a soul. But I should be allowed to hand you what you take for nonsense, and you should be able to play it as nonsense, and Oscar should be able to hear it as something else. And in the end, technically, I haven't told anyone. See what I mean?"

"Not really, no," Smoker said.

"Well, you don't have to. I want you to take these words and play them, somehow, in your music. Play it so that Oscar can hear it."

"Well, I don't know. I mean, I'm not really that

good at composing. . . . I mean . . .”

“I’m relying on you,” the Pooka said, flaring his nostrils and clomping one mighty hoof on the ground. “We all are.”

“Okay then,” Smoker said. “I’ll try.”

“And hopefully we’ll make history,” the Pooka said. “The quiet kind of history that is invisible, that runs beneath the surface of world events. The history of *our* kind.”

Oscar heard distant scratching, but it wasn’t coming from overhead. It wasn’t the sound of cleats scraping the rubber. It was coming from the wall beside his head, and it sounded like tiny, clawing paws.

The noise coming from deep inside of the dirt wall beside Oscar’s bed began as a small scratching but grew louder quickly. He sat up and watched as the dirt in one spot began to crumble, leaving behind a little hole. He saw sharp teeth and a small, furry muzzle emerge from the hole, and then the weasel heaved herself out with her small paws. Her fur was rumpled and dirt caked, and a little mud was packed into the thin gap between her front teeth—but she was smiling.

“What is it?” Oscar asked.

She started snapping so quickly that his decoding skill couldn't keep up. He had to stop her. "Start over," he said. "Go slower."

She snapped, "The Pooka has the baseball. It's hidden in a box in a cabinet in the wall." She explained everything that she saw: the rubber center ball, the winding of wool and then string. "And then he put the skins around the ball and held it in his hands and cried."

"Wait," Oscar said. "Where was the red stitching? The two red threads that lace up the skins?"

The weasel shrugged and then went on. She described how the Pooka went to the slit and peered out, saying, "There she is!" And he was gazing at the Banshee. The Banshee! The weasel stopped speaking. Her eyes went glassy, but then she pressed on. "The sun came up. He ducked inside and then undid all of his work, put the wool and string and skins back in the box, back in the cabinet."

Just at that moment, the door flew open and a very huffy Auntie Fedelma charged in, threw off her coat, and slumped in her bleacher seat. Oscar and the weasel could hear Auntie Oonagh and Oscar's father ask a flurry of questions, but Auntie Fedelma said, "I'm going to sleep. I need to shut my eyes and think!"

Everything went silent then. Oscar and the weasel started again.

"He was looking at the Banshee," Oscar said. "I saw her dancing once in the outfield, and the slit in the wall was glowing. . . . She's waiting for someone to meet her, isn't she? She's waiting for him." Oscar tapped his temple, thinking.

The weasel snapped, "On the ride back to Fenway Park, he was in a hurry. He worried that he wouldn't be able to see her. Remember?"

"I asked him about it. I asked who. And he said no one. But it's her. It's the Banshee. And he has an endless task—just like all pookas must. His is to wind the baseball, but he's missing the final thing."

"The red threads," the weasel snapped.

"He could break the Curse himself, maybe, if he had those threads. Where are they?" Oscar asked the weasel.

"He should know," she snapped. "He's the one who made the Curse in the first place." The weasel shook dirt from her fur.

"But would he turn himself into that pooka?" Oscar asked.

And then another voice sounded in the crawl space—Oscar's father. "He didn't mean for that to happen. No one expects to turn into a pooka, I guess." He appeared at the top of the ladder, his face puffy. There was a quiver to his lips. He looked about to cry. "All these years he's been so close. . . ."

The weasel burrowed quickly under Oscar's blanket before Oscar's father spotted her.

"How long have you been standing there?" Oscar asked.

"Long enough," his father said. "Long enough." He looked behind him at the two aunties in their bleacher seats. "They don't know. Only me."

"You aren't supposed to know."

"It's okay, Oscar. You didn't break the rules. I found out on my own." Then Oscar's father stammered a bit before he could come out with it. "Listen, Oscar. You're right. I have to have more faith in you. But you have to have more faith in me, too. I guess." He let out a gusty breath that rattled his chest. "The Curse has to be broken. The Red Sox have to win. Do I know everything now? Really, come clean."

"Well, there is this," Oscar said. He threw back the quilt, and there was the dirty weasel.

"Oh," he said. "I thought you were just talking to yourself. Is that one of Weasel-man's weasels?"

Oscar nodded. "I think she's my weasel now, or I'm her boy," Oscar said. "I mean, we're friends."

The weasel smiled bashfully.

"Hello," Oscar's father said. "Okay, let's start at the beginning."

Oscar told his father all about disobeying him, going through the doorway of the Door to the Past and meeting Babe Ruth. And then the weasel took over and started snapping out her part, about meeting Oscar in the tunnels to get him to the Pooka.

"I don't speak weasel," Oscar's father said.

"I'll translate," Oscar said, and he did. He translated everything as the weasel went on, ending just at the part where the Pooka didn't have the red threads but that Oscar hoped that he might send a message somehow.

Oscar's father was quiet, sorting it all out, running over it all in his mind. "So, let's make a game plan," his father said with some real conviction in his voice. "We'll find the red threads and put the baseball together once and for all. Let's reverse the Curse."

"Yes!" Oscar said, relieved that he wasn't in terrible trouble.

"But I have only one requirement," he said.

"What's that?" Oscar asked.

"That we work as a team, okay?" Oscar's father put out his hand, palm down.

"Yep," Oscar said, putting his hand on top of his father's.

"Yip," yipped the weasel, putting her paw on top of Oscar's.

They threw their hands (and one dirty paw) up in the air. A team.

CHAPTER EIGHTEEN

A New Coded Message

OSCAR AND HIS FATHER CRAWLED onto their pallets. The weasel curled up near Oscar's feet.

Oscar tried to sleep but was fitful. He was so bruised and sore from the Pooka's ride that it was hard to find a comfortable position to try to fall asleep. He stared at his Fenway Park model and wondered what would happen in the real Fenway Park the next day. Would the Red Sox be able to turn it around? His stomach churned with nerves. He closed his eyes and listened to his father snore and the weasel purr and two aunties rustle occasionally like birds in eaves and the third auntie occasionally blurt out something evil ("May your souvenirs turn to balls of fire that destroy all you know!"). The night kept racing through Oscar's mind. Of all of the strange things that he'd seen, it was his father's face that kept coming back to him: weak and trembling when he learned that Keeffe was the Pooka, expectant and cheeky while he waited to hear of Oscar's ride, but mostly the way the anger melted away so quickly when he found Oscar in Smoker's cloud. *You're home.* That's what his father had said. *You're home. You're home.* And what was amazing to Oscar was that it felt true. He *was* home. *This* was home.

Oscar slept so deeply that when he woke up later that day, he barely remembered his dream. At first it was just a blur of blue sky, some clouds. He was on the back of the Pooka trying to stitch the clouds together with endlessly long pieces of red thread. It was one of those crazy dreams that was more a feeling in your body than images lingering in your head. He woke up a little disoriented.

It didn't help that the weasel was up and running in circles, and that the aunties had radios blaring and someone had scalded some hot cocoa and the room smelled of freshly burned chocolate.

Oscar had overslept. The weasel snapped, "The fans are already pouring in! The game is on! Skies clear!"

Oscar jumped up. "Really? The skies are clear?"

The weasel nodded.

Oscar scooped her up and climbed down the ladder.

Auntie Gormley was still sleeping. Auntie Fedelma was rocking in her bleacher seat. Auntie Oonagh was knitting an unevenly stitched afghan.

"Where's my father?" Oscar asked.

"Is the hot cocoa ready?" Auntie Oonagh shouted. Then she saw the weasel and screamed. "Oh, no! Infestation!"

Auntie Gormley tossed in her sleep.

"It's a weasel, a friend of mine!" Oscar said.

"Oh, so he's a thief too!" Auntie Fedelma shouted. "He stole that weasel from Weasel-man! Old Boy! Did you hear that?"

Oscar wished Auntie Gormley weren't still asleep. He needed her now. How could she sleep with all of this noise? Oscar's father ambled into the room from the kitchen. He was holding a steaming pot. "What is it?"

Auntie Fedelma ignored him and smiled sickeningly. "It's no matter."

Oscar didn't like the way she seemed to give up so easily. It wasn't like her and made him even more nervous.

Making matters worse, the radios were tuned to pregame chatter.

The weasel snapped her teeth in objection.

"She's right!" Auntie Oonagh cried. "We always lose like this!"

"No," Oscar said. "We don't have to if we work together as a team!"

"A team!" Auntie Fedelma snorted. "Ha!"

The radios were tuned to pregame chatter. "Looks like the Sox are in for an uphill battle. Down two games. This is the crucial game. No one's ever come back from a three-to-zero deficit in a playoff situation—no one in the history of the game. Never. If they lose this one, well . . ."

This was too much. Oscar couldn't take it anymore. "I'm sick of it!" he said. He turned to the nearest radio and twisted the knob. It went silent. He reached for another.

"What are you doing?" Auntie Oonagh said.

"The boy is wild!" Auntie Fedelma shouted. "Old Boy, can't you control him?"

Oscar turned off another radio and another. The room got a little quieter, and then a little quieter still.

"We never turn off the radios before a game!" Auntie Oonagh said anxiously.

"Are you going to do nothing, Old Boy?" Auntie Fedelma shouted.

Auntie Gormley gave a restless snore. The weasel snapped her teeth.

Oscar's father stood back and let Oscar turn off all of the radios, and soon the only thing they could hear was the organ music. It wasn't a chant. No. It was a haunting and beautiful song.

Oscar stood still. He listened to the tune. It was a sad song, filled with loss and longing. But the tune also felt trapped, confined; and, ever so softly in the background, Oscar could hear the Banshee singing in a lonesome cry.

"That's us," Oscar's father said. "That is the song of the Cursed Creatures."

Auntie Oonagh was the first to start crying; but then the weasel started up, and tears slipped down Oscar's father's cheeks. Auntie Fedelma pushed her tears off of her face quickly; and, oddly enough, Oscar even saw small tears on Auntie Gormley's sleeping face.

Oscar was the only one who didn't cry. He was too excited. The notes of the song were lining up. They made sense somehow. He said, "I don't even know how to read music. I only know what Mrs. Calendar taught me in music class. But there is something in the notes."

"There is?" Oscar's father asked.

"A message?" the weasel snapped.

"Yep," Oscar said.

"The Pooka's coded message: B, A, B, E. Those were the first four notes Smoker played. They spell, of course, 'Babe,'" Oscar said.

"Ruth," Oscar's father said. "Go on."

"Then it gets trickier: E, E, E . . . F, F, F . . . B, B . . . F, F, F . . . C . . . A, A . . . E . . . D."

"What does that mean?" the weasel asked.

The song had ended, and Oscar was thinking furiously. "Well, 'Babe' was easy because notes run A through G. And the first four letters are all found in the first seven letters of the alphabet. But then," Oscar said, pacing in a circle. "Smoker had to find a way to show the letters in the alphabet that come *after* G. Well . . ."

"Well?" Oscar's father asked.

"He started with double notes," Oscar explained, staring at the transistor radio in his hands. "H is two As played in a row. I is two Bs played in a row. J is two Cs played in a row. And when he got to O, he had to dip into triple notes. O is three As; P is three Bs. See?"

“Kind of,” snapped the weasel. Auntie Gormley snorted in her sleep.

“Not a bit, deary,” said Auntie Oonagh.

“Oh, just get on with it, smarty-pants!” Auntie Fedelma shouted.

“What does it spell out?” Oscar’s father asked.

“And then he played C—G, G, G—F—F—E, E, E.” Oscar held the weasel tight, turned to his dad. “Babe stitched cuffs!”

Oscar’s father’s face fell. “But, but that doesn’t help!”

The weasel snapped, “Oh, but it might!” She looked up at Oscar.

Just then there was a quick knock at the front door and it swung open wide. There stood Smoker, breathless. Oscar barely recognized him at first. He was only smoking one cigarette. Had the others fallen from his mouth on the jog there? The cloud was just a bit of gauze hovering over his head.

“Did you hear it?” he asked Oscar, wheezing. “Did it make sense?”

Oscar nodded. “You spelled out ‘Babe stitched cuffs.’ ”

“Am I allowed to say yes now that you’ve guessed it?”

"I think so," Oscar said.

"Well, then, yes! Right! I did it!" Smoker pulled the cigarette from his mouth, tamped it out in a Styrofoam coffee cup sitting on a table nearby. He cheered. "I did it. I don't know how I did it, really. I mean, I caused a diversion. Someone smelled smoke. Kantor rushed out of the .406. I rushed in, and, well, I played!"

"You played beautifully!" Oscar's father said. "It was perfect!"

"I felt some other presence there," Smoker said. "I can't explain it. Some other sad and lonesome presence."

"The Banshee," Oscar said.

"You're right," Smoker said. "It was the Banshee. I could feel her presence somehow." And then he stopped, pulled a new pack of smokes from his shirt pocket, suddenly anxious again. "But it still makes no sense. How will cuffs help you find the baseball?"

"Well, we aren't looking for a baseball. The Pooka has that. We're looking for the red threads to stitch it up."

"Oh, I have red thread," said Auntie Oonagh. "I'm quite a seamstress!" She pointed to her sewing basket sitting by her cleats.

"Not just any threads," Oscar's father said.

"No, not just any threads," Oscar said to Smoker. "We can figure this out." He reached up, plucking the pack of cigarettes from Smoker's hand and giving it to his father, who balled it up. "We can do this."

"Oh, can we?" Auntie Fedelma said venomously, flipping a radio back on. She pointed to the clock on the wall. "You're too late. Radio is announcing the first pitch." The fans were pounding their feet overhead. Auntie Fedelma was right. Over the pounding rhythm of the fans' feet on the bleachers, Jerry Trupiano was reporting, "And here come Dom DiMaggio, Bobby Doerr, and Johnny Pesky, heading out on the field to throw the first pitch of Game 3 of the 2004 American League Championship Series. . . ."

"Johnny Pesky," Oscar's father said sadly.

"The goat who held the ball? They got the goat to throw out the first pitch. He ruined it for us in forty-six!" Auntie Fedelma smiled nostalgically.

"It wasn't his fault the Series was lost," Oscar's father said. "Why won't you let that go?"

But Auntie Fedelma wasn't paying attention. "Listen. I hear her again."

Oscar heard a cry, but it wasn't the same cry that had accompanied Smoker's composition. No, this time it was high-pitched, anguished, grieving. He'd never heard anything so horrible before. It made his chest ache. The weasel heard it, too. She wriggled in Oscar's arms; and even Auntie Gormley, who'd slept through all of the earlier noise, couldn't sleep through this distant cry. She wrestled awake. Her eyes opened, and she sat up and stared at Oscar. The weasel jumped out of Oscar's arms and scurried to a corner, suddenly frightened.

"The Banshee," Auntie Gormley signed with her eyes, now fully awake.

"She's already mourning the loss!" Auntie Fedelma said. "And that's not all! My team is coming for you, boy. Do you hear that, too?"

The bass of footsteps were pounding in the tunnels, getting louder and louder, drowning out the Banshee's cry.

"My team isn't going to let you foul up the Curse! My team is going to put a stop to you, boy, once and for all!"

"Fedelma!" Auntie Oonagh cried.

"Have you lost your mind!" Oscar's father shouted. "No one is going to lay a finger on Oscar. Do you hear me?"

The door flew open again. This time Weasel-man shoved his broad body in, trailed by his weasels, Stickler, and the Bobs. The weasel in the corner bounded over, anxious to be back with her pack. Everyone started shouting at once—about Oscar, the Curse, the Red Sox, the awful unknown of the future. Stickler went right for Oscar's father and poked a finger in his chest. "Been waiting a long time for an opportunity to sock it to you," he said.

Oscar's father poked back. "Back off, Stickler. This isn't about us!"

Oscar stood in the middle of it all, awestruck.

He wasn't sure what to do, and then he felt a tug on his sleeve. It was Auntie Gormley, small and bent over. She pulled Oscar to the side of the living room; and in one swift motion, she scooped up the loose weasel. They slipped into the kitchen.

"What is it?" Oscar asked.

She pointed to the Door to the Past. Oscar pulled out the key on its long golden ribbon, and unlocked the door. Auntie Gormley shoved the weasel into his arms then. "Take this too," she signed, pulling a transistor radio off of the counter and putting it into his hands. "So you can keep up with the game." Oscar balanced the weasel and the transistor radio, bobbling them a bit.

"The weasel will know the plan," she signed. "As soon as I can find a place to drift off and dream again. My little parlor trick at work."

Oscar remembered that his father had told him that was what she called her gift: her little parlor trick. "It was you?" he asked. "You were inside of the weasel?"

"And I will be again," she signed.

Just then the rowdy crowd thundered into the kitchen. The Bobs negotiated the narrow doorway by sliding through sideways. Weasel-man ducked down.

And in the center of the ruckus, Auntie Fedelma roared, "Where is he?"

Stickler snatched Oscar up by the back of his shirt, jostling the radio from his hand. It clattered to the ground. "Here he is!" Stickler announced.

"Let him go!" Oscar's father roared.

Oscar kicked out as hard as he could, and Stickler caught Oscar by one ankle and then the other, holding him upside down.

Oscar's father rushed Stickler. "Leave him alone!"

His father started shoving Stickler, and an awkward scuffle broke out. The Key to the Past fell out of Oscar's pocket and skidded across the kitchen floor. Oscar's father got Stickler in a headlock, and Stickler lost his grip on Oscar. Oscar tumbled to the floor right next to the Door to the Past.

Auntie Oonagh trilled, "Stop! Stop! Don't!" and

started banging Weasel-man on the back with a pot. The Bobs tried to wrestle the pot from her. Auntie Fedelma was cheering wildly. And Auntie Gormley was gone!

Oscar got as low as he could, trying to find the key; but there were too many frantic feet. He had to go, even if he didn't have the key. The transistor radio was right there, the announcer calling the end of the first inning: the Yankees, 3, the Red Sox, 0. He grabbed it and crawled through the doorway of the Door to the Past. As he turned around to close the door, there was the weasel, scampering toward him. He knew immediately that it was Auntie Gormley.

"C'mon," he whispered. "Hurry!" His hand grabbed hold of the edge of the door. Auntie Gormley—the weasel—slipped through. But just as he started to close the door, a pair of eyes caught his—a pair of milky, nearly blind eyes. There was Auntie Fedelma on her hands and knees, staring at Oscar through the mayhem of scuffling legs. She smiled at him—a grim and evil smile—and ever so slowly lifted one hand to show him something: a gray, wrought iron skeleton key on a faded golden ribbon.

Oscar slammed the door.

CHAPTER NINETEEN

A Race Through Time

"AUNTIE FEDELMA HAS THE KEY," Oscar told Auntie Gormley in her weasel shape. They were crawling as quickly as they could down the dark tunnel on the other side of the Door to the Past.

"No!" snapped Gormley. "What do we do now?"

Oscar had been churning over the new clue. "'Babe stitched cuffs,'" he repeated to himself. "'Babe stitched cuffs.' Stitched. And what do you stitch things with? Thread."

Auntie Gormley snapped, "Is that where Keeffe hid the red threads?"

As Oscar's mind sped up, his crawling slowed down. "Maybe Keeffe got Babe to stitch cuffs to sleeves using the red threads?" He was breathless. He turned to Auntie Gormley, who was twitching her weasel nose.

"But," Auntie Gormley snapped, "in 1919 when the Sox traded Babe Ruth, he wasn't a tailor. He was a ballplayer. Keeffe couldn't have gotten him to stitch anything by then. Unless . . ."

"Unless he went through the Door to the Past, unless *he* was the one who stole Auntie Oonagh's key. And he found the young Babe Ruth, before he was Babe Ruth—back when he was just an orphan from St. Mary's learning a trade in a tailor shop instead of going to real school, back when he was . . . a big-handed boy learning to stitch seams. It's right there in the Curse!"

Oscar paused and pounded his fist in the dirt. "And where is the shirt now? Is that what we're looking for?"

"We can't look for the shirt," Auntie Gormley snapped. "It's gone. Pookas lose everything they own when they turn into pookas. The shirt disappeared!"

Then Oscar froze. He imagined the moment: Keeffe only feeling the change at first, maybe a stiffness in the bones of his feet as they hardened into hooves and a bristling on his skin as the fur began to inch up and cover him; his clothes becoming thin and then dusty and then disappearing altogether; and finally, his head probably growing heavy as his jaw lengthened, and his eyes being swallowed by the glowing holes in his giant horse head. Oscar shivered at the terrifying image. One thing was clear now. He turned to the weasel. "The shirt and the red threads were lost in the Curse! The Curse took the one thing that we need to break the Curse!"

Light flooded the tunnel. The Door to the Past had been opened. Oscar jumped forward. The weasel squeaked. "It's Auntie Fedelma!"

Oscar started crawling again, faster than before; and his thoughts kept up with him. "But we've already gone through the Door to the Past. If Keeffe visited the tailor shop once, like he said, just once, then we can, too. We can find the young Babe Ruth and get him to, get him to . . ."

Oscar could hear voices now. One of the Bobs shouted, "I can't fit!" Stickler said, "No, no. Let me in!" Weasel-man offered to give a shove. Auntie Fedelma was telling everyone to shut up and let her through. And Oscar's father was calling, "Oscar! Oscar!"

"We have to rhyme," Oscar said. "And fast. That's the only way out, really."

Auntie Gormley snapped, "We have to get to Babe *after* Keeffe's given him the threads but *before* he's started stitching."

"I can't think straight." Someone was crawling in the tunnel now. A shifting shape blocked the kitchen light through the door.

"Yes, you can!" the weasel snapped. "You're not a little boy anymore. We're relying on you!"

"Where is he?" Auntie Fedelma was shouting. "I can't see anything!"

Oscar grabbed the weasel and, with one hand, hustled forward. He needed a simple rhyme. "Um, um. We need to get to Ruth's tailor shop really fast, when Keeffe used the Door to the Past."

Auntie Fedelma called out. "Don't try to run away from me! I'm after you!"

Oscar closed his eyes tight, blocking her out. "Take us to the moment after Keeffe leaves. Before Ruth starts to stitch the sleeves!"

There was light ahead of them now. Oscar raced to it.

And soon enough, Oscar and the weasel popped out through a small panel of ductwork in the back room of a tailor shop.

It was after hours. The back room was barely lit. The shop seemed empty. There were rows of machines, shelves filled with bolts of cloth. Oscar could feel that cold coming on again. They were away from Fenway Park; they were already growing weak. He picked up Auntie Gormley, who already sounded wheezy in her small, weasel lungs.

"What if he's not here?" Oscar asked. "What if we can't find him? What if we've gotten it all wrong?"

But then they heard the hum of a small motor. They looked down the empty rows and saw the bulb of a sewing machine. A young man was curled over the machine, pumping the pedal while wedging material under the thrumming needle. In Oscar's hand, the transistor radio was still on. Trot Nixon homered, bringing Varitek in with him. Suddenly, back in the future, the Red Sox were only down by one.

"It's him," Oscar whispered. "It's Ruth."

Ruth didn't hear them coming—the machine was chugging too loudly. He didn't notice Oscar until he stopped hitting the pedal and the machine went quiet. Ruth looked up and was startled, almost knocking over his chair.

"Sorry," Oscar said. "I didn't mean to scare you."

"You nearly gave me a heart attack and kilt me," Ruth said. "Geez, kid."

Oscar thought it was funny that Ruth called him kid even though they looked to be the same age. He smiled a little.

"What's wrong with you? Should I punch that smile right off your face? What are you doing here, anyway? And what's that? Some kind a badger you got there?"

"It's a weasel," Oscar said. "It's a pet, kind of. Look, I can explain everything." But just then the transistor radio broke out into applause. The announcer was shouting the news. "Tie game!" Damon had gotten a single and Mueller had scored. The sound was tinny and echoed in the dusty room.

Ruth stared at Oscar, amazed. "What did you say?"

"That wasn't me," Oscar explained. He held up the radio. "It was the radio."

"A radio?" Ruth said. "It talks? Is it magic or something? A box that talks?"

"One day everyone will have these." He handed it to Ruth. "Take a look for yourself."

Ruth held it in his big hands. He fiddled with the dials, making the volume louder, then softer; losing the station, then bringing it back; turning the radio off, then back on. "That's really something," he said. "Where'd you get that?"

"Um, well, it's hard to say exactly," Oscar said with a sneeze. "I'm from the future."

"Ha!" Ruth laughed. "The future? Very funny, kid. Very funny."

"I am," Oscar said. "I know, for example, that you're going to become the most famous ballplayer of all time."

"Is that so?"

"Yes."

Auntie Gormley was watching everything, her narrow weasel head zipping back and forth between them.

"What kinds of numbers?"

Oscar had all of Ruth's stats memorized. He said, "Your career mark of 714 home runs will stand as the all-time record for thirty-nine years."

"Who's going to beat me?"

"Hank Aaron's going to hit his 715th on Opening Day of the 1974 season."

"It's hard to believe that it'll be 1974 one day. Will people wear space suits and fly around, you know, with rocket packs on their backs?"

"No," Oscar said. "But Aaron will seem like it, he'll be so fast. Everyone still talks about you as one of the all-time greats! I already read your life story three times—how your parents worked at that bar, and your father was rough on you."

Ruth looked down at his machine. "That's no good to print."

"There's good stuff, too. I know all about St. Mary's. And how you'll get discovered by the Orioles as a pitcher. All of that."

"Huh." Ruth stood up. He was tall for his age, a good bit taller than Oscar. He looked around the tailor shop. "I won't be a bum all my life."

"Nope, you sure won't. They'll call you the Sultan of Swat."

Ruth looked down at his hands. "That's not what they call me now," he said.

"I know what they call you now. I've been called stuff, too; but, you know what? One day I'm going to learn from you that it isn't something wrong with you. It's something wrong with them."

"Today just keeps getting stranger and stranger." Ruth sat down, wide-eyed.

Oscar felt dizzy, and grabbed the back of one of the sewing tables. "Was somebody else already here? A guy who wanted a special favor maybe?"

"Maybe," Ruth said defensively.

"Maybe it was a man named Keeffe, and he had some threads. Red threads, and he wanted you to stitch them into the cuffs of a shirt?"

"Maybe," Ruth said.

"I'd like you to use some other red thread," Oscar said. "I need the ones he brought in with him."

"We're in a tailor shop. We've got all colors of threads," Ruth said. "But why do you need those?"

"To break a curse, actually. To break a curse on the Red Sox."

"A curse?" Ruth asked, his head cocked. "What do you mean?"

"What's going to happen is, you're going to help the Red Sox win a World Series in 1918, and then they're going to trade you."

"Trade me? But you said I'm going to be the best!"

"Yeah, well, it's going to be a big mistake," Oscar said.

"It sure as hell will be," Ruth said.

"But after they sell you to the Yankees, you'll single-handedly out homer the entire Boston team in ten of the next twelve seasons."

"Okay then," Ruth said, hiking up his pants. "Well, okay. That's better."

"But see, right now the Red Sox haven't won a World Series since they sold you—eighty-six years ago."

"Serves them right."

"But—" Oscar started to cough again. The weasel sneezed.

"But what?"

"But there are people stuck in the Curse, too. Cursed Creatures of various kinds. Orphans, really, cursed along with the Curse."

"Orphans?"

"Yep."

Ruth walked to the window and looked down at the street. "Is my pop ever going to see me play in the big leagues?"

"Yep. He will. Just once, though."

"Do I play good that game?"

"You play good every game."

Ruth tugged on his pants again. "I'll help you," he said. "I got behind today. Boss told me I had to stay extra. I was just about to put those threads in." He walked to the sewing machine, flipped open a small drawer, reached in, and pulled out two long, thick pieces of thread. "Here," he said. He lifted them up.

From the radio in Oscar's hand came the thin voice of the announcer reporting that the Yankees had come back three runs in one inning, the Red Sox rallying only with two. The score was tied again 6–6 in the bottom of the third.

And just as Oscar reached forward and took the threads from Ruth's hands, they disappeared.

Laughter—high-pitched chirrups—sounded from the heating duct.

"What happened?" Oscar asked, his cheeks flushed with fever. "Where did they go?"

Ruth looked off in the direction of the laughter. "It doesn't make sense," he said. "Now, all of a sudden, I remember a cleaning lady who laughed like that. She came by my station. She told me to look out the window because there were fireworks. But there weren't any."

"Skinny old woman? Thick glasses?"

"Yep. It's strange, because I didn't remember it and now I do. It's like it just happened, but a while ago." Ruth shook his head, confused.

Oscar ran to the heating duct. The weasel was already ahead of him. "Thanks, Babe!" he shouted down the row of machines.

"Babe? Who's Babe?"

"You are!" Oscar shouted, using all of the air in his weak lungs. He scooped up the weasel and crawled into the duct.

Everything blurred and then snapped back into focus. Oscar and the weasel went back in time to catch Auntie Fedelma stealing the threads. By this point, it was the top of the fourth inning, and the Red Sox were losing again, 9–6.

As they started to climb back out of the heating duct into the tailor shop—Ruth down the rows, working at his noisy machine—again there was a blur and then a sharp focus. Auntie Fedelma was there, about to climb in. The sight of them startled her. Oscar grabbed her by the wrist. The weasel snapped at the threads, caught them both in her jaws, and pulled. The threads slid from Auntie Fedelma's grasp. She looked weak and exhausted, but with enough energy to pounce; and, like a cat, she swiped Oscar's arm, leaving three long scratches that beaded up with dots of blood. Oscar reared back, grabbing his arm, breathless.

But then, with a hazy blur, Auntie Fedelma and the threads were gone. She reappeared up the chute—a dirt tunnel again. She was laughing and coughing.

"How did you do that?" Oscar shouted, his voice going hoarse. He looked down at his arm. The scratches were gone, except for the one that was raw and scabby.

"Once you start meddling with time, you can

always go back and erase! That time I stole faster and got by you two before you appeared! Ha-HA!"

"What do we do now?" the weasel snapped.

"She's getting weak, since she's away from Fenway," Oscar said, "like my dad gets."

"But she can always go to the present and get her energy and come back full force."

"That's right," Oscar said, kicking at the dirt.

"We could beat her by going way back, to the moment when Keeffe took the baseball apart to set the Curse. We could get the threads from him!"

"I don't think he'd ever give up those threads. Not ever. We can just go back and warn Babe, I guess."

"Not to be distracted, to guard the threads better so that they're there when we come to trade them later."

"Exactly," Oscar said, but he didn't have much conviction in this plan. He was tired, his muscles were aching, and he had chills. Auntie Gormley was shivering in his pocket. This time travel struck him as a bad thing, a waste of time, an endless loop.

When Oscar and the weasel went back in time to tell Ruth not to leave his sewing machine, even if an old cleaning woman told him there were fireworks out the window, the Red Sox score was even worse: 11–6.

This time, though, Ruth had the pair of red threads in his hand. Oscar tried not to eye them greedily. He and Ruth had the same old conversation about the transistor radio and a similar talk about the future, but Oscar was antsy this time. If the Sox lost this game, they would be down three games to zero. One more loss and the Yankees will have swept the playoffs. Time was running out. He had to confront Auntie Fedelma once and for all.

"Can we hide nearby?" Oscar whispered. His throat was sore.

"Sure, kid," Babe Ruth said.

And so Oscar and the weasel crouched under a sewing machine in the back row while Auntie Fedelma told Ruth about the fireworks. He didn't budge. "No thanks," he said. "I been warned about you."

"By a boy and his weasel?" She was sagging under her own weight, coughing into her knotty fist.

Ruth nodded, surprised.

"Twits!"

Then suddenly Ruth said, "They came by just like you said they would. Right after that man,

Keeffe, gave me these." He held up the threads and shook them. The versions of the past were overlapping, folding in on themselves. Ruth himself looked bewildered. He said, "I think I've worked too long today. Staring at the needle, some say, can make you feel batty like this."

The score kept getting worse: 12–6. 13–6. 14–6. 15, 16, 17–6. The radio, kept at the dimmest whisper, announced a home run by Varitek, bringing in Ortiz; but it seemed way too late for a rally. Oscar was feeling desperate. It dawned on him that the Sox could lose this one; and if they did, they had all of history against a comeback.

Oscar stepped out of his hiding place and said, "Look, enough is enough."

Auntie Fedelma gasped, and that threw her into a coughing jag.

Oscar went on, "We can go on messing with time until none of it makes any sense, until there isn't a single version left. We'll wear Ruth out, make him think he's going crazy; and what good will that do to the future? Anybody's future."

"It's you," Ruth said. "You and that weasel and that tiny radio again."

The transistor radio announced a Matsui homer that brought Crosby in with it. Oscar looked down at the radio in his hand. "I can't believe we're going to lose."

"The Curse, right?" Ruth said, and he looked at Oscar as if he remembered their conversation. Oscar himself didn't know if the conversation still existed or not. So much of the past had been meddled with.

"Right," Oscar said.

Ruth looked at him with deep sympathy. He shook his head sadly, but then his face brightened. "I got an answer," Ruth said. He handed Oscar one of the threads, and the other he gave to Auntie Fedelma. "You two will have to fight for who gets the pair now."

"Oh, no," Auntie Fedelma said. "One will do just fine. He can't break the Curse with just one thread."

"I could maybe break mine in half. Get most of the job done," Oscar said, examining the thread, pulling it to see if it was strong. It was. He wound it around his hand. "I wonder what would happen then."

"There's only one way to settle this," Ruth said.

"How's that?" Oscar asked, putting the thread in his pocket.

Ruth smiled—that big, wide smile. His eyes shone. "The only real game in the whole world: baseball. How else?"

Oscar looked at Ruth, then Auntie Fedelma, then the weasel—Auntie Gormley—then Auntie Fedelma again. They both looked haggard and weak, and he knew that he did, too. "Count me in!" he said.

Auntie Fedelma's chest labored like an accordion. She sneered. "Count me in, too," she said, glaring at Oscar. "I play a little ball. Nobody knows it, but I taught Ty Cobb a thing or two."

"Ty Cobb," Oscar said. "That figures."

"Listen!" Auntie Fedelma shouted. "We don't have much time. Here's my team: me, Stickler, Weasel-man, and the Bobs—but the Bobs only count as one. Who've you got?"

"I've got, um, me, my dad, maybe Smoker."

"Oonagh and Gormley will play for you," she offered sweetly. "Put them together and they might count as one, which makes four."

"I'd rather take him," Oscar said, pointing to Ruth.

"I'll play for you, sure," Ruth said.

Auntie Fedelma smiled. "Then I'll take Cobb."

"But he has to be a kid," Oscar said. "Like Ruth here and like me."

"I'm twelve," Ruth said.

"Me, too, so Cobb has to be twelve. You can go

back in time and get him," Oscar said.

"Okay then," Auntie Fedelma said. "He'll be twelve."

"We'll fill out the rest of our teams with twelve-year-olds then—any one we can get to come with us from the past. Let's say we have two per team—two who aren't future pros—on the field at all times. Fair enough?" She took a long rattling breath.

"Fair enough. And we need a fair umpire."

"A fair ump?"

"A Hall of Famer," Oscar said, his joints aching.

"No cheats," said Ruth.

"Okay, okay. I'll get one," she said. "A Hall of Famer. Keep in mind that the Cursed Creatures can only play in Fenway Park or we'll get too weak. And if you want to break the Curse, we can't put off the game. Tomorrow night is your last chance. If the Sox lose tomorrow, then they're out and the Yankees are in. The field will be filled with outsiders between now and tomorrow night . . . so we'll all have to go into the past to play—at a time when the field was empty, all ours." Fedelma then spread her old wings and flapped them behind her head.

Ruth stumbled backward. "What are those? Is that the way we'll all be in the future?"

Auntie Fedelma bent down to the heating duct, about to slip inside. "I've got a team to get ready. Good luck," she said. "You'll need it!" With a tubercular cackle, she disappeared into the hole.

CHAPTER TWENTY

The Roster of Twelve-Year-Old Greats

AUNTIE OONAGH FILLED A BOWL with warm, soapy water and set it on the table in front of Oscar, where it gave off steam. He dipped his arm into the water, wincing. And then the pain subsided and he let his arm settle in. One of the scratch marks was stubborn—still there despite all the time travel.

Auntie Gormley was Auntie Gormley again, and the weasel was just a weasel, padding around the place mats in a nervous circle. They both seemed to feel better. Oscar's throat was no longer sore. His cough and fever had disappeared. He slipped his hand into his pocket to check on the thread. It was there, wound like a little nest.

His father put his elbows on the table and leaned in close to examine the scratch on Oscar's arm. "I don't know what's come over Auntie Fedelma," he said.

Auntie Gormley snorted and shook her head. With her eyes she signed, "Fedelma's always had this in her."

Smoker was pacing by the sink, patting down his pockets for a pack of cigarettes. He found one—crumpled and nearly empty. "We can pick anybody, you say?" Smoker asked. "Go back in the past and get any ballplayer we want when he was twelve?" He lit the cigarette and took a deep drag.

"No more smoking," Oscar said. "You've got to play, too. We all do. We need your lungs to work, Smoker!"

Auntie Oonagh snatched the cigarette from his lips on her way by and dropped it in the wet sink.

"We've got Ruth," Oscar went on. "We'll pick him up tomorrow night. We did plan that much. And we should pick up the others during the night, too, so when we take them back they'll think it was just a dream."

"The best of the best," Oscar's father said, concentrating. "Anyone we want from all of baseball history when he was twelve years old?"

Auntie Gormley sat back dreamily and smiled. "The best of the best," she blinked. "We'll get to see them play. One last time."

"I've always liked the heroes of baseball, the ones with the best hearts," Auntie Oonagh said. "Roberto Clemente, Joe DiMaggio, Hank Aaron, Lou Gehrig."

"Oh, Clemente," Auntie Gormley's eyes—wet with tears—darted out his name. She made the sign of the cross.

"And Curt Flood!" Auntie Oonagh cried joyfully.

"Yes, yes," Oscar's father nodded. "The players with good hearts! If we're going to win, it's because we've got heart!"

"They made the game a thing of grace," Smoker said. "Somehow made up for so many of baseball's ills."

There was a moment of silence then. They were all in their own worlds, thinking. Oscar was, too; and although it seemed right to go with the players with the most heart, it also wasn't quite exactly right.

Auntie Gormley seemed to come to some conclusion. She looked at Oscar and shook her head. Oscar's father took in a deep breath and held up one finger. And before he had a chance to say anything, Auntie Gormley leaned in and nodded.

Smoker said, "What? What is it?"

And Auntie Oonagh said, "What we need is a cure for our ills."

Oscar's father said, "What we need are the players with some sorrow to heal, some sorrow that burrowed down into the dirt of Fenway Park."

Oscar's father reached into a drawer, pulled out an old Red Sox roster sheet and a pen. "We'll pass around the paper. Put down the names. How many do we need? Six?" He passed the paper to Oscar. "You start."

Auntie Oonagh gave Oscar a towel. He lifted his arm from the bowl. She took the bowl to the sink. He wrapped his elbow and then wrote down the obvious: "Babe Ruth" and passed on the paper. It made its way around the table. Everyone scribbled hurriedly, and when the sheet came back it was full. "I'll read the names aloud," Oscar said. "Then we'll all have to agree on each one. Okay?"

Auntie Oonagh lifted the funnel to her ear so she wouldn't miss a word.

"Babe Ruth," Oscar said. "He's an obvious choice. Isn't he?"

"Yes, yes," everyone said. "Of course!"

Oscar put a check beside his name and read the next: "Jackie Robinson."

Oscar's father said, "The spring of forty-five. Isadore Muchnick was on the city council, and said he'd vote against allowing Sox games on Sundays if they didn't start trying out black players. So they brought in three to try out. Jackie was one of them." Oscar's father's voice broke off.

And Smoker filled in. "We were there, watching from hidden spots all around the park. Beautiful to watch. But at the end of it, someone yelled out, 'Get those niggers off the field.'"

Oscar felt the word in his stomach, in his chest. He felt suddenly hot.

Auntie Oonagh said, "He has to be on the team. There'll be no peace without Jackie Robinson."

Oscar checked the next name. "Willie Mays," he said.

"Future Hall of Famer Willie Mays," Auntie Oonagh whispered. "The Red Sox scout refused to wait out a rain delay to see black kids play, so he missed seeing Mays then. And later, when they finally had him come for a tryout, the scout said Mays wasn't *their type* of player. Ha!"

They all nodded. Oscar checked the name and went on. "Ted Williams."

"Everybody loves him now," Auntie Oonagh said. "But they hated him back then—in the stands, in the press. He refused to tip his hat because they were cruel to him."

Oscar's father said, "When he was inducted into the Hall of Fame, he said, 'I hope someday the names of Satchel Paige and Josh Gibson in some way can be added as a symbol of the great Negro players that are not here only because they were never given a chance.' He was half Mexican, on his mother's side. He knew he was lucky to be able to play at all and that others weren't."

Oscar hated the idea of those greats never getting to play in the majors. It reminded him of how it had felt to watch Little League all summer—to feel it in his muscles, his bones, but to be stuck sitting on the sidelines. All of that waste. "Ted Williams," Oscar said, making his check mark. "Next is Johnny Pesky."

"The goat. '46 series against the Cardinals," Auntie Oonagh said. "He held the ball too long on one play, hesitating on the throw home. They never ever let him forget it."

Oscar gave a check. "Pumpsie Green," he said.

Auntie Oonagh shook her head with a sad smile.

"The first to integrate the Red Sox—and the Red Sox were the last team to integrate. Dead last."

Smoker said, "When they gave him a tryout in Arizona, he had to stay seventeen miles away from the team in a boardinghouse because the Safari Motel didn't allow black guests."

"And when they finally took him on, it was ugly," his father added. "Like they wanted him to fail."

Oscar checked Pumpsie and read the last name. "Bill Buckner."

"2,715 career hits," Oscar's father said. "More than Ted Williams! About 500 more than Joe DiMaggio. But he's not in the Hall of Fame for an *error.* One ball going through his legs, one lousy mistake."

Oscar checked Buckner's name. "That's the team," Oscar said. "We all agree."

"Too bad we don't get a coach," Auntie Gormley blinked. "Good old Harper."

"The Elks Club in Winter Haven," Auntie Oonagh said. "Every year during spring training, they invited the white players for free dinners, but not the blacks. Harper brought it up to management, privately, in the seventies. When Harper came back to coach in eighty, he found out that it was still going on!"

"But!" Auntie Oonagh exclaimed. "He filed a suit against the Sox, and he won."

"We could use Harper, but we don't get to have a coach," Oscar said. "Anyway, we've got a great team."

Oscar's father looked nervous all of a sudden. "No team in all of sports history has ever come back in the playoffs from a three-to-zero deficit, except some hockey team once."

"Hockey?" Auntie Oonagh asked. "Is that the thing they play on ice?"

"Exactly," Smoker said.

"The Curse," Oscar's father said. "Each time we get close and we can taste the win, we lose."

Oscar knew the part of the Curse he was talking about. It was the ending. It was the only part that had stuck with him word for word. Maybe it stuck because it hadn't ever made sense to him before. It went: *May you be close enough to taste the win but always, truly, lose before you even begin.*

"There's only one way to lose before you begin," Oscar said.

"How?" Oscar's father said.

"You lose faith. You give up," Oscar said. "And we're not going to do that."

They looked around the table at one another, one by one locking eyes—Auntie Gormley, Auntie Oonagh, Smoker, Oscar, and his father.

"Promise not to lose faith?" Oscar asked.

"Promise," Auntie Gormley flashed with her eyes.

Auntie Oonagh, Smoker, and Oscar's father said it all together: "Promise."

CHAPTER TWENTY-ONE

Recruiting

OSCAR LEFT THE AUNTIES AND Smoker and his father behind so that they could talk strategy and maybe get some sleep before the game. Auntie Oonagh volunteered to greet the boys with hot dogs and pretzels and hot cocoa when they arrived. And so Oscar spent the night shuffling through the tunnel with his list of rhymes on a piece of paper and a flashlight to read them by.

Ruth was first:

If the ills of the Sox
are ever going to be healed,
I need to meet twelve-year-old Babe
on St. Mary's ball field.

He came up from a trench in the ground at the far edge of the field at St. Mary's Industrial School for Boys—one dug, it seemed, to put in new pipes, which sat shiny and new beside the trench. Ruth was sitting on the pitcher's mound in the dark, waiting. It was a cold night and Ruth was ready to go, wearing a glove on his left hand, which was strange since Oscar knew he threw with his left.

Oscar gave a whistle. Ruth's head snapped up, and he took off running toward Oscar. That's when Oscar saw the large, shifting shape of someone looking on from the distant tree line. It looked like a giant woman wearing a long dress.

When Ruth got to the trench, Oscar asked him who was watching.

"Brother Mathias. He runs the place. I didn't tell him, but there's no fooling him. I told him I wasn't running away this time. I told him that it was for the sake of baseball and that I'd come back by morning, and that I wasn't going to tell any of the other boys." Ruth jumped down the hole and was in the tunnel with Oscar. "I don't like skipping out like that. I don't like to let Brother Mathias down."

The name was familiar to Oscar. "You write about him in your autobiography, I think."

"I do? Figures. He's the only one I got."

Oscar said, "We'll have to find you a lefty's glove."

"It's okay," Ruth said. "I'm used to it. I just catch with it and then shake it off to make a throw."

Oscar told him to crawl toward the light at the end of the tunnel. "Auntie Oonagh will be there with something for you to eat."

I'll wake twelve-year-old Jackie from sleep.
He'll play with the others while his brothers count sheep.

The window in Jackie's room was open. The curtain billowed in the night breeze. Oscar could see the lights of Pasadena not far off. The room was filled with bodies—lean and long and strong. Oscar looked for the smallest one and gave him a shove.

Jackie woke up groggy, and Oscar's explanation of the reason why he was standing there in the middle of the night wasn't helping to clear Jackie's mind.

When Oscar told him about the Cursed Creatures, Jackie stopped him and whispered angrily, "Oh, Cursed Creatures, huh?" Jackie said. "Are they more cursed than us? Was their mother left by her husband with five kids to feed? Did they get called nasty names and almost get kicked out of their neighborhood?"

Oscar bowed his head and shook it; and then he lifted his head, smiling.

"Something funny?" Jackie said.

"No," Oscar said, but he couldn't hold back the smile.

"I'm in a gang. You'd better watch out."

"It's just that you're Jackie Robinson," Oscar said. "You're going to change the world because of all that you just said."

"Change the world? Don't make me laugh. Change *this* world? You're crazy."

"You're going to be the first black man to play in the major leagues." Oscar told him.

"Right! Sure!" Jackie said, but there was a flicker of recognition in his eyes. His jaw set differently. "So, what's this game about?"

Oscar went over it again; and when he explained about the Pooka being trapped and the aunties wanting their father back, Jackie said, "I can understand that." He looked past his brothers' sprawled bodies, off out the window. A dog barked out in the distance. "I'll do it," he said. "I'll go with you."

Before the Say Hey Kid is known,
before he plays in center field deep,
I'll find Willie Mays at twelve years old
and wake him from his dreamy sleep.

Oscar found himself in a closet next to a pair of work boots covered in red dust. He opened the door slowly. There was a boy in a bed—a small boy for twelve, scrawny and short. But his hand—stretched out on his pillow, lit by the moonlight coming in through the window—was huge, like a mitt itself.

There were the sounds of other people sleeping, not far-off. Oscar whispered, "Willie?" He shoved his shoulder. "Willie? Wake up."

Willie didn't wake up calmly like Jackie. He jolted upright, his eyes wide. "Who are you? What do you want with me?"

Oscar told him the story, as quickly as he could; and Willie interrupted him when he came to the aunties. "You have aunties?"

"Yeah, two good ones and another who's kind of sour."

"I have aunties, too, and an uncle; and they're good to me. It's just my daddy, you know, and the aunties here. My mama's gone."

“My mom’s gone too,” Oscar said.

Oscar thought of how he’d been stingy with his mother on the phone when she’d called. He’d been punishing her for leaving him. “Look, we need an outfielder who can really catch.”

“I can catch,” he said. “I sure can catch.”

As Oscar led Willie back through the tunnel to the kitchen, Willie told him all about how he was already a batboy; and how his dad, Kitty Kat, played ball in these parts and was really well known; and how he loved the game, how he loved to sprint and run and stretch to catch a ball in midair.

I’ve got to find twelve-year-old Teddy Ballgame—
The Kid, The Splendid Splinter, whatever the name.
Tonight I need his Red Sox career to begin
so that he can help us earn a true win.

There were two beds side by side—a boy in each—but it wasn’t hard for Oscar to figure out which one was Ted. He wasn’t asleep. He was lying there on his back with his hands lifted, squeezing tennis balls. His bed was covered in homemade baseballs: balled-up white rags tied with string. He wasn’t surprised by Oscar. It seemed as if he’d been waiting for someone. While they talked, the other boy, a little smaller than Ted, kicked in his sleep. In another room, not far-off, a man was snoring loudly. Ted let Oscar tell him the story while he tightened the knots on the balled-up rags.

When Oscar asked Ted if he would follow him into the future to play a ball game, Ted was quiet. Oscar looked around the room—small and unkempt, dusty, dingy. It could have used some scrubbing. There was a thin cross hung on the wall, paint chipping all around it. The dresser was missing some knobs. There was an ancient-looking chair with the cane seat blown out.

"It's a mess. Go on and say it." Ted got up and walked to the window. He looked up the street. It was dark. "She's out late," he said.

"Your mother?" Oscar asked.

"You know her?" he said. "You've probably made fun of her, ringing that bell on the street for the Salvation Army. Can't get enough of helping poor people—like we aren't poor enough ourselves. She'll want me to have said my prayers and gone to sleep a long time ago. But I can't."

"Where's your dad?" Oscar asked.

"Passed out."

He picked up some of the baseballs off the floor.

"You make those?"

"I'll hit anything. Tennis balls, rags like this. Anything at all."

"Well, how about hitting tonight."

"What? We're going to play in the dark?"

"No, under lights."

"Lights?"

"They have them rigged up. Trust me."

Ted's eyes toured the room. He paused on a photograph on his dresser: a picture of a beautiful woman with brown skin, shiny black hair. His mother, Oscar could tell. He recognized the way Ted seemed to know the picture by heart but still studied it.

Ted said, "I don't know that there's anything keeping me here."

Oscar rubbed his eyes. "Okay then. Let's go."

I need to meet Pesky at twelve years old,
when he was a boy just enjoying the game.
We have a new story to unfold,
and Fenway Park will never be the same.

With Pesky there was some confusion at first. Oscar found himself at a ballpark in the middle of the day. The scoreboard showed that the home team was the

Portland Beavers. He saw what seemed at first to be a row of ballplayers with billowing shirts; then the shirts flew up, kicked by a breeze. It was only a laundry line of uniforms. Oscar asked a kid at the end of the laundry line if he knew a boy named Pesky. He pointed to a boy sitting alone in the bleachers, watching batting practice. "He's always here. It's like he doesn't have a home or something."

Oscar walked over to him. "Are you Johnny Pesky?" he asked.

"No," the kid said, keeping his eyes on the batter.

"You aren't?" Oscar said, rummaging his pocket, pulling out the sheet of rhymes again. "Are you sure?"

"Am I sure who I am?" the kid asked.

Oscar mouthed through the rhyme again. "Yes, are you sure?"

"I'm Johnny Paveskovich. Some people call me Pesky." He said his last name with a strong accent. It was a heavy name that lingered in the front of the kid's mouth. "But it's not my real name."

"Paveskovich," Oscar repeated. "You're twelve, right?"

"Yeah. My parents are immigrants. They don't understand America," Johnny said. He looked down at the book in his arms—a baseball book—his finger hooked on a chapter about Charlie Gehringer. "Baseball's the American game. Everybody knows that. To be an American you've got to love it."

"You're the person I'm looking for," Oscar said.

"Looking for? What do you mean?"

"You feel like playing a ball game in Fenway Park?"

Johnny looked at Oscar wide-eyed. "Are you kidding me? Who wouldn't love that? I've wanted to do that all my life."

"I've got a deal for you, Pesky," Oscar said. "A real sweet deal."

Twelve-year-old Bill Buckner dreams at night
of meeting the fastball just right.
We need him playing first
if we're going to break the Curse.

When Oscar knocked his head on a pipe and tumbled out of a cabinet door onto hard floor, a boy was standing over him with a bat swung back over his head. "Who are you? What are you doing in there?" The boy was lean and muscular, with a faint mustache.

"Don't kill me," Oscar said. "I wasn't doing

anything wrong. I just came to talk to you."

It was Buckner. He'd been woken by the neighbors fighting and had been listening at the kitchen window. While Oscar explained who he was and why he was there, Buckner stayed at the open window, still listening to the fight, the bat gripped in his fists. When Oscar asked him if he'd come play, he said, "Tonight? Fenway Park?" He was tempted. "Jan's asleep. Maybe she wouldn't notice."

"Who's Jan?"

"My older sister. She keeps me straight."

The neighbors started up again. The man was cursing now at the top of his lungs.

"Don't you hate that. Who can sleep through it?"

"You could shut the window," Oscar said.

"No," Bill said. "Then I couldn't hear them, you know, if the woman needed help or something. . . ."

"Oh," Oscar said.

"I can't leave," Buckner said, gripping his bat, his eyes fixed on the neighbor's house. "Not until it dies down at least or the old man out there runs out of steam. He's drunk. He usually just gives up, but you never know. What if I'm the only one paying attention? The only one who can help her?" he said. "Can you wait?"

Oscar nodded. "Sure," he said. "I'll wait."

And so they did. They drank milk and talked baseball while Buckner kept watch at the window. He was right. Finally the old man gave up. They both stood at the window and watched the woman walk through the house, straightening furniture, turning out lights.

Then Buckner put the bat under his arm, pulled on a ball cap. "Okay," he said. "Now we can go."

I need to find Pumpsie Green
before he's even turned thirteen.
I'll find him all alone at night, wide-awake,
and tell him there's a curse to break.

Pumpsie was the only one Oscar couldn't convince to come along. Oscar spotted him through a crack in the closet door—a boy with dark skin and dark eyes, sprawled out on a tired sofa but, like Williams and Buckner, not asleep. When Oscar stepped out of the closet, Pumpsie wasn't afraid.

"Is this part of some prank my brothers put you up to? Look, I'm tired. I've been working all afternoon, working for my mother—on the farm, in the neighborhood. I'm so tired I can't sleep. My legs are twitching. I almost have enough to buy a baseball glove. A three-finger one. A Caledonia." He smiled and leaned back and closed his eyes. "A Caledonia."

"No, this isn't a prank," Oscar said, and he told him the whole story—the Curse, the ball game—and why he needed him. "I need you," Oscar said. "The Red Sox need you."

"The Red Sox need me?"

"In the future."

"You know the future? Is that what you're saying?"

"Yes, see, you're going to be the first black player on their team one day."

"Not me," Pumpsie said. "I'd like to play for the Oakland Oaks, but the majors? No. I'm just a kid." Pumpsie paused. "You think they're going to let black players play in the majors?"

"Yes," Oscar said. "Jackie Robinson is going to be the first. He's going to meet with Branch Rickey, and Rickey's going to talk Robinson through being turned away from hotels, dining rooms, and railway cars, and prejudiced sportswriters and fans. And then he's going to get right up in Robinson's face and ask him what he's going to do when some angry player hauls off and punches Robinson right in the cheek. And Rickey's going to pretend to punch him, and he'll shout at him, 'What do you do?' "

It was quiet for a moment. "And what is Robinson

going to say?" Pumpsie asked.

"He's only going to whisper, 'Mr. Rickey, I've got two cheeks. That it?' "

Pumpsie stared down at his shoes. "And is that going to be it?"

"No," Oscar said. "That's just going to be the beginning."

Pumpsie sat up then, swung his feet to the floor, rested his elbows on his knees. He looked really tired now, suddenly, like an old man. He shook his head. "I don't know. I just feel like I'm about to get punched. I feel all tight inside. Have you ever had that feeling?"

Oscar nodded. "Yeah, I know what you mean."

"I can't play for you tonight," Pumpsie said. He shook his head and stared at the floor.

"I understand," Oscar said. "I know. It's okay."

CHAPTER TWENTY-TWO

The Lineup

WHEN OSCAR CRAWLED OUT THROUGH the doorway of the Door to the Past, everyone was there, waiting for him in the warm kitchen.

Buckner was standing with his bat still clutched under his arm. Willie's eyes were darting around nervously. Pesky was jumpy, too, fiddling with the strap on his glove. Auntie Oonagh had warmed some hot dogs, and Jackie was putting his plate in the sink. Ruth picked up two more hot dogs and finished them off in big gulps. Auntie Gormley and Smoker watched the kid eat, a little awestruck.

Pesky pulled Oscar aside and whispered urgently, "That's Babe Ruth right there." He pointed to Ruth, who was chugging a glass of milk.

"I know," Oscar whispered back, and then he raised his voice. "Okay, here we all are. Except for Pumpsie."

"Pumpsie Green?" Buckner asked.

"Right," Oscar said. "He couldn't make it." He glanced up at his father, who seemed to understand that it hadn't been easy with Pumpsie.

"We don't have time to replace him," Auntie Oonagh said.

"Nope, we'll just have to go forward," his father said.

Oscar cleared his throat and went on. "So, here we are: Babe Ruth." Ruth bounced his eyebrows. "Jackie Robinson." Jackie nodded solemnly. "Willie Mays." Willie flashed a smile while sizing up the team. "Johnny Pesky." Johnny gave a salute. "Ted Williams." Ted tipped his cap nervously. "And this is Bill Buckner."

Buckner looked stunned. He leaned over to Oscar. "You didn't tell me who I'd be playing with!"

"I know. I know. Sorry," Oscar said.

"Don't say you're sorry," Buckner said, slapping Oscar on the back. "I don't know how it's possible. I have no idea! But I like it."

Oscar went on with the introductions. "And me, Oscar Egg. My dad, Malachi Egg. Auntie Oonagh.

Auntie Gormley, and Smoker."

"Ruth is going to pitch. Buckner's on first. Jackie's on second. Willie Mays plays center. Pesky is shortstop. I'll be catcher. Smoker will play third—the hot corner. My dad will play left field. Ted will play right. Auntie Oonagh and Auntie Gormley will be our subs. Got it?"

They all nodded.

Auntie Oonagh started pacing. She said, "Oh, I don't know! I just don't know!"

"Know what?" Oscar asked.

"I look at these boys and think of all the wrongs that are going to be committed. The Red Sox, oh, so much of this they've brought on themselves! I don't know if the Curse can be reversed." Her cheeks flushed with sudden anger. "I don't know if it should!"

"If they're so bad," Jackie said, "I don't know if I want to help them break the Curse."

The other boys nodded.

Willie said, "Why should we, anyway?"

Oscar looked up at his father. His father stared back at him. *Why should they?* he seemed to be asking with his eyes. Oscar thought about how much his father had disappointed him all of these years. He thought of the sickly man hunched over the wrong order at Pizzeria Uno who hadn't ever fought to be with his mother, with him, and who'd just let the Curse be the Curse all of those years. But ever since he brought Oscar here into this world, he'd been a great father. He was truly a good man, only cursed. And how could Oscar not forgive him for that? Oscar didn't know the whole story of what had happened between his father and mother, and he knew he never really would; but, right now, he could feel his forgiveness rising up. He felt it tighten his chest.

He turned to the group of boys. He said, "It's better to forgive people. It's better to forgive them for their future wrongs. It's better to go out there and let that forgiveness make things right. Ugliness and racism and meanness have ganged up to make things wrong. It's only forgiveness—your forgiveness—that's stronger than this curse."

The boys looked around at one another. Some were nodding already. Others still weren't so sure.

"Plus," Oscar said, "this is a taste of what's going to come your way. You'll get to see a little of your future, and maybe knowing what's to come will give you the confidence you'll need later to get you through."

Willie just got on with it. "Okay," he said, "who are we playing against? I like to know the competition."

Oscar's father smiled at him. The boys were in, for good. Oscar smiled back. Oscar's father told Willie, "It's time to go find out."

And so, one by one, they herded through the doorway of the Door to the Past—all of the ballplayers Oscar had collected first, then Smoker, Auntie Oonagh, and Auntie Gormley holding tight to the weasel.

Oscar and his father were about to head through next, but Oscar stopped. It was just the two of them in the kitchen now. Oscar said, "There's something I want to know before we go on. I want to know if you were surprised."

"Surprised? By what?"

"Were you surprised that you'd adopted a mixed-race child. I mean, maybe you got tricked; maybe you didn't know."

"I knew, Oscar, from the beginning," his father said. "And I was surprised too, because the moment I held you, you were mine. I didn't know it would feel like that." He leaned down and kissed Oscar on the forehead in a way he hadn't done since Oscar was little. When Oscar looked up at his father, he saw that his father's eyes were wet with tears. His father smiled broadly. "Go on now," his father said. "We've got a game to win."

Oscar crawled in through the doorway. His dad followed. They huddled in the tunnel with all of the others. Oscar pulled out his piece of paper and read the final rhyme he'd written:

We need to meet Auntie Fedelma's team in the past
so that we can break the Curse at last.

CHAPTER TWENTY-THREE

Auntie Fedelma's Team

OSCAR AND HIS TEAM EMERGED from the Red Sox dugout and stood in a loose row near home plate. The field stretched out before them, broad and green, the lines white, the bases gleaming. All around, the stands seemed to be leaning in. The moon was up in the sky, straight up, gazing down at them unblinkingly. The lights too seemed to be watching them. One of the slits in the Green Monster was lit up by the Pooka's glowing eyes. Surely he was inside, winding the cursed ball.

This was Fenway Park on an off night in the past, but there was no mistaking that in the present reality it was also Game 4 of the Red Sox–Yankees playoffs. Auntie Oonagh had brought the transistor radio with her, and it squawked from a corner of the dugout. The park felt electrified. The seats were empty, but there was still an intensity of energy all around the players.

Clem, the umpire, was pacing behind home plate. He wore a bow tie and a black cap with a button on top. The other team was warming up. The pitcher—a lanky twelve-year-old—was lobbing slow pitches at the catcher: Auntie Fedelma, bulked up by a chest protector. She'd loosened her wings and was using them to flutter up to catch a ball that bounced off the front edge of home plate. How? Oscar wondered. She was nearly blind!

The Bobs were at third, scooping up grounders and throwing across the diamond to first. Weaselman pointed to Oscar's team from the visitor's dugout and Stickler laughed, but Oscar couldn't place the other players. They were fierce and quick and tough—anyone could see that at a glance, could feel it. They were a menacing group of boys, almost frenetic, lit from within.

"Who are those kids?" Willie asked.

"I don't know," Oscar said.

Auntie Fedelma bounded toward them, chasing a ball bobbling toward their shoes. As she straightened up, Oscar saw that she was wearing her red thread as a necklace tied around her throat. Oscar reached into his pocket and made sure his was still there—it was becoming a nervous habit. “So, you showed up,” she said. “That’s a surprise.”

“How did you see that ball?” Oscar asked.

“I have power. I play by my senses, including my sixth sense,” she said smugly.

Oscar’s father looked at Auntie Fedelma tenderly. “We don’t have to do this. We could just talk it out. This isn’t going to prove anything.”

Auntie Gormley nodded fiercely, jostling the weasel curled in her arms.

“Old Boy is right,” Auntie Oonagh said, reaching out and touching her sister’s shoulder.

But Auntie Fedelma shrugged her off. “Who do you have here?” she asked, pointing at the boys.

“You tell us who you’ve got out there first,” Oscar said.

“Some of the best competitors of all time. Pete Rose for one.” She pointed to a shaggy kid in left field. “And he’s putting his money on us,” she said. “He’s no dummy.” Rose sprinted after a ball thrown into the outfield and chased it down. “We’ve got Chick Gandil and Eddie Cicotte.” She pointed to two boys on the right side of the infield.

"White Sox? 1919? They threw the World Series!" Jackie said.

"My boys!" Auntie Fedelma said with a smile. "We thought of Nettles, Cash, Sosa, and Hatcher, but a guy who just corks his bat, well, he isn't thinking big enough."

"That's cheating," said Ruth.

"We want players who aren't afraid to win. At any cost," Auntie Fedelma said. "It was hard to pick the best cheating pitcher of all time, but we did what we could. We've got Gaylord Perry on the mound."

"Tsk, tsk," Auntie Oonagh said, wagging a finger.

"So many spitballs and goops to choose from," Auntie Fedelma said, "so little time!"

"Who's that?" Oscar asked, pointing to a dark-haired boy in right field.

"Canseco," Auntie Fedelma said. "He's a bit of a tattler—a little lily-livered to stick with a good cheat; but the others, well, you can't be sure."

"Steroids?" Oscar asked.

"What are steroids?" asked Jackie.

"Are they robots from the future?" asked Ruth.

"Drugs to make you play better," Oscar explained, and all of the boys nodded. "It's cheating. Some of the new players will say they broke your records, but it was only because they were on drugs," Oscar explained.

"My records?" Willie Mays said, trying it out. He seemed to like the sound of it.

"But he's not on steroids now," Oscar's father said, pointing to Canseco. "He's just a skinny kid."

"I want the players who are willing to go all-out, who have strong convictions," Auntie Fedelma said. "Like Pinky Higgins."

"Auntie Fedelma!" Auntie Oonagh said. "Pinky Higgins? He's the worst racist of them all. How could you?"

"He understands that change isn't always good. He understands." She looked fragile for a moment. She teetered in her cleats.

"Are you going to cheat?" Oscar asked.

She glared at Oscar with her milky eyes. "I'm going to win," she said.

"Who's that?" Johnny asked, pointing to a kid in center field. He was the meanest looking of them all. His face was already streaked with dirt. He was scuffing his cleats in the grass like a bull, flexing his knees and elbows as if preparing for a fight.

"That—oh, well, that's my old buddy Ty Cobb," Auntie Fedelma said, pressing her mitt to her heart. "Look at him! Just look at him! What a boy!"

There was someone new on the field—an antsy twelve-year-old boy in a shiny uniform with a brand-new mitt. He was talking to Canseco. Pinky walked over and was talking now, too.

"Who's the rich kid?" Williams asked.

"I don't know," Auntie Fedelma said. But now they could see that Canseco was taking a wad of cash, stuffing it into his jeans, and walking off the field. He gave a hearty wave and walked back to the dugout tunnel.

"Don't worry!" the rich boy shouted. "It's me! Tommy Yawkey! That other kid is going on home! He doesn't feel well all of a sudden! I'm going to play instead!" He smiled at Pinky and slapped him on the back as if they were old friends. "I belong here as much as anybody!" he shouted happily.

"Yawkey?" Oscar said in disbelief. "He's going to play?" Yawkey had been the owner of the Red Sox during the bleakest period of racism. He and Pinky's racism ate up the Red Sox for ages.

Auntie Fedelma sighed. "I guess he is. You can't say no to him."

"Is Frazee going to show up, too?" Oscar's father asked.

"Frazee doesn't care about baseball," Auntie Fedelma said. "He wouldn't show his face here."

Jackie Robinson looked down at the ground and muttered something under his breath.

"What was that, boy?" Auntie Fedelma asked. "You got something to say?"

Jackie shook his head. "Let's play," he said. "Let's just start the game."

Auntie Fedelma smiled. "Don't you know you've already lost? This Curse can't be broken. You are all a lost cause. Haven't you read the Curse? Don't you know it in your hearts?"

"I know exactly what's in my heart," Oscar said. He had faith. It was more than a feeling. It was something real, stored up inside of himself.

"You don't know what's in somebody else's heart," Willie said. "That's only ours to know."

"Like Jackie said. Let's play ball," Ruth said angrily. "Let's just play."

CHAPTER TWENTY-FOUR

The Game Between the Greats

Opening Innings

OSCAR'S FATHER FLIPPED A FAT silver coin, which slapped the light in glints and then landed in the dirt just as Auntie Fedelma called, "Tails." The coin landed head up. The bad guys were up to bat first. Auntie Fedelma called them in.

Oscar suited up in the rest of his catcher's gear. The shin pads were long for his legs and banged above his knees. The chest protector made him feel as if he'd fallen into a well. The padding on the catcher's mask didn't fit his face, and he looked out at his team on the field through its thick black padding and metal cage. He tugged on his catcher's mask, picked up his mitt off the bench, and was just about to jog out to home plate to catch Babe Ruth's pitches when Teddy Williams called out to him, "Hey, aren't we going to sing?"

Oscar was confused for a moment. Teddy pointed at the flag flipping in left center field. "Oh," Oscar said, "I forgot." He meant that he'd forgotten to sing, but also that Williams was going to grow up to be a war hero, serving in both World War II and the Korean War. He looked over at Auntie Fedelma. "We're supposed to sing the national anthem!"

Auntie Fedelma rolled her eyes.

Oscar's father said, "Let's sing."

And Auntie Fedelma's team stepped out of the dugout. They all turned and faced the flag. Oscar sang softly at first: "Oh, say, can you see." The voices around him—all of these boys plucked from different towns across the country, from different times, standing tall with their hands on their hearts—well, it made him proud. His voice swelled. "And the rockets' red glare." And the voices all around him rose up, too. "Oh say, does that star-spangled banner yet wave" . . . Auntie Gormley mouthed the words. Auntie Oonagh trilled. "And the home of the brave."

Now it was time to play.

Oscar's team took the field just like the Red Sox were, at this very moment, on the same field at a different moment in time. Ruth looked tall on the mound for a twelve-year-old. His pitches came in fast and hard, stinging Oscar's palm. Ruth had two pitches: a fastball and a smooth curve. Ty Cobb was the first batter up. Ruth struck out Cobb while he was looking at one of those slow curves.

Oscar watched as his teammates shifted nervously, an edgy readiness in their feet. Willie Mays called from the outfield, "Say who, say what, say where, say hey!" He was smiling and laughing all the while. Jackie Robinson was a picture of concentration. Buckner worked his mitt with his fist and, at different times, put his hands on his knees and then, deciding against it, stood tall again.

Ruth got through the first inning without allowing a base runner. Oscar met him at the steps of the dugout.

"This is fun," Ruth said. "We should do this every day!"

"You will, you will," Oscar said.

Gaylord Perry took the mound, his back pocket bulging with tubes of goop. Everyone knew the ball was going to get some doctoring. But it's difficult to control a greaseball. Perry walked two runners in the first, but Oscar's team couldn't get a hit.

In the second inning Pete Rose ripped a ball down the left field line. It took one bounce and ended up in the bleachers. That wiped the happy grin off Ruth's face. Yawkey hit a nubber off the end of his bat that dribbled to Jackie. Yawkey was out at first, but Rose moved over to third. On the next play Fedelma hit a grounder to short, and Rose broke for home.

Pesky never hesitated. He fired a strike to Oscar.

Oscar wanted to stop everything. He wanted to shout to Auntie Fedelma, "Did you see that? Did you see how he did that perfectly? He wasn't the goat!" But, no, Oscar thought. No one would stop to admire the perfect execution of that play. They expected it; and Pesky would go on, like Buckner, to be branded by one mistake instead of being praised for thousands of perfect plays.

There was no time to stop. Rose was charging at him like a steam train and plowed into him, knocking Oscar backward. When the dust cleared, Oscar sat up—Rose standing over him in disbelief. Oscar's mask had been knocked off, his shin guards had spun to the sides of his legs, and his jaw felt as if it was swelling; but he held the ball in his puffy mitt. Rose was out.

Oscar could hear Mays whooping and yelling from center. Oscar looked out to left field where his father stood, grinning, giving Oscar a thumbs-up. In the dugout, Auntie Gormley and Auntie Oonagh clapped wildly.

In the top of the third the Bobs put all four hands on one bat; and to everyone's surprise, they got a hit and wobbled miraculously to first base—safe. Ruth challenged Cobb with a fastball, but Cobb was ready. He crushed Ruth's pitch over the Green Monster. It was a beautiful sight, the sure crack of bat on ball, the soaring arc, the white speck noiselessly disappearing from view. The Bobs came in panting. Oscar looked out for Cobb. He had a deep respect for Cobb's ability, and he smiled at him as he crossed the plate.

"Sucker," Cobb said, and he spat on the ground at Oscar's feet. A thrill of rage ripped up from Oscar's stomach to the back of his throat. He marched toward the pitcher's mound with a new ball.

"That guy will not get another hit in this game, you got that?" Oscar said to Ruth.

Ruth was mad about the pitch, but he winced at Oscar. "I got it, boss."

"Good," Oscar said, and he slapped the ball into Ruth's mitt.

Chick Gandil sidled up to the plate. Oscar had read about his part in the Black Sox scandal of 1919. He didn't like him. Gandil struck out on three pitches. Oscar wondered if he was trying to throw this game just like he had a long time ago. How could you trust him? He eyed Oscar after the strikeout with a look of disgust—for Oscar? For himself? Oscar couldn't tell.

Oscar's team was still struggling to hit Perry's junk balls. Willie Mays returned to the dugout shaking his head. "It's like trying to hit a butterfly with a baseball bat," he muttered.

Oscar watched as Perry pulled an oily tube from his back pocket. He slathered the ball. Oscar's father never got the bat off his shoulder. The third strike stuttered from Perry's hand across the plate. Oscar's father swung and missed.

The Middle Innings

RUTH GOT THROUGH THE FOURTH allowing only a single to Fedelma, and Oscar took off his gear quickly for his second turn at bat against Perry. On the radio, the announcers talking through the Red Sox–Yankees game were reporting the same score: the Yankees up by two.

"Come on, we can beat these guys," Oscar said. Mumbles of encouragement came from the other players.

Oscar stepped into the batter's box and saw Perry wipe a syrupy goo from the underside of his cap's visor onto the ball. Perry rubbed it in and then reared back and threw. As Oscar watched the pitch veer away from the plate, he relaxed. At the last moment, though, the ball sneaked back over the outside corner.

"Strike one!" called the umpire. Oscar couldn't believe it.

The second pitch looked the same.

"Strike two!"

Perry snickered and went to his visor. This time, protecting the plate, Oscar lunged at the outside pitch; but instead of sliding back toward the plate, the ball swerved even farther outside. Oscar stumbled to keep his balance, and that's when he heard the laughter coming from the empty stands. At first it was just Perry and Auntie Fedelma, but then the whole place seemed to swell with the taunt.

"You're going to lose," Auntie Fedelma said. "Everyone knows it."

Oscar retreated to the dugout, passing Williams on his way to the batter's box. Oscar fastened on his catcher's equipment. His eyes burned. He remembered Drew Sizemore in the line for gym the last day Oscar had been at school. "Who's your daddy?" Oscar looked down the bench at his teammates. They struggled to meet his eyes.

"You think I dragged you guys here to lose to this bunch of cheaters? You think we're going to let Perry throw that junk and fool us?" Oscar kicked the ground. "We're going to play within the rules, and we will win this game. You understand?"

No one said anything.

"Do you?"

They looked at each other up and down the bench and nodded.

Another round of ugly hooting and laughter erupted from the stands as Williams flew out to center. They all watched Williams march back into the dugout. "It's like they're wolves out there," he said. "Wolves in the stands."

"Let's do the best we can," Oscar's father said, almost apologetically, his hand on Oscar's shoulder, his wings giving a quiver under his shirt.

"No. Let's go get 'em," Oscar said, staring at his father, wanting him to straighten up, to be a hero.

"He's right." The voice came from behind him.

Oscar turned. Pumpsie Green stepped out from behind Buckner.

"Pumpsie!" Oscar said. "You came!"

"I just couldn't help it," Pumpsie said. "I could hear you all—the echo of the game, far-off—coming from the closet. And it seemed like I should follow it."

"We need you," Oscar said.

"I don't know how or why," Pumpsie said, "but I feel like I can do something good here, somehow."

Williams nodded. "Glad you're here."

The other players smacked him on the back.

"Pumpsie, you go in for Smoker at third," Oscar's father said with an ease in his voice that calmed Oscar.

Perry lost control of his goopy baseball in the bottom of the fifth. He walked Buckner and Jackie. Then when Willie grounded out, Buckner raced to third. There were two outs in the inning when Pesky shot one through the right side bringing Buckner home, and then Perry walked Oscar's father. With the bases loaded, it was Babe's turn to bat.

"You know what to do," Oscar told him.

"Yes, I do," said Babe, a smile on his face.

Babe scuffed at the dirt and cocked his bat. Perry wound up and threw a menacing curveball.

But Babe watched it all the way in and smoked a line drive up the middle that sent Perry sprawling and his hat flying off his head. The gooped-up cap clotted with dirt. Jackie and Pesky pounded around; Oscar's team took the lead, 3–2.

"Yeah! Yeah!" Oscar cried, as his teammates clapped one another on the back in the dugout.

Oscar overheard the radio at that moment. It reported a turn in the fourth game of the Red Sox vs. Yankees playoffs. David Ortiz had just singled with the bases loaded to push the Sox ahead of the Yankees.

"Yes," Oscar said, clenching his fist. But he was up now. He felt sick. He grabbed his bat and stepped into the batter's box.

Perry fumed. Oscar struck out swinging at three straight pitches. He looked at the other team. Weasel-man and the Bobs couldn't hold his gaze. Neither could Gandil nor Cicotte.

Oscar returned to the dugout as an eerie sound rose from the stands and the field itself—not one voice as with the laughter, but a thousand nasty voices, full of gripe, full of bile and bitterness. Ghostly forms appeared in the bleachers, shaking their fists, swearing, booing. Words were hissing from their mouths: "Darkies," "Coloreds,"

"Losers." The voices were ringing and rising. One group started to chant, "Goat! Goat! Goat!" and then another, "Who's your daddy? Who's your daddy?" Among them, Oscar could clearly hear a voice with a slow, Texan drawl, louder than all of the other jeering voices: Woodall, the scout who had passed up watching Willie Mays. He was refusing to watch black ballplayers in the rain. And then it was Pinky's voice, grown-up but saying a famous line: "There will never be any niggers on this team as long as I have anything to say about it." The sentence echoed on and on. Then another voice said, "It's our policy. The Safari Motel doesn't allow colored guests." It quickly blurred into another voice saying something similar about the Elks Club of Winter Haven. And that voice blurred into the Floridian Hotel, and then another and then another. Pumpsie tightened up and narrowed his eyes in concentration. The voices burned in Oscar's ears and in his chest.

Oscar's father said, "Maybe this is what Fenway has to do. It has to let it go somehow."

"Why are they yelling all of this stuff at us?" Pesky said.

Oscar's father was pale. He said, "I don't know why. I just don't know."

“They want us to crack,” Pumpsie said.

“We can only beat them if we don’t give in to it,” Jackie said.

“We’ve got to rise above it,” Willie said.

“It’s the only way we can really win,” Oscar added.

With one out in the sixth, Rose tripled to center field. Yawkey came to the plate, waving his arms to stir up the crowd.

“Knock it off,” Oscar told him. “Just play the game.”

“Hey, this is the fun part,” Yawkey said. “You hear that crowd? They love us. We’re their team. We’re not the bunch of misfits you’ve got. We belong.”

“You’ll spend your whole lousy life trying to fit in, Yawkey!” Auntie Oonagh shouted from the dugout. “You’re as much of a misfit as any of us!”

“Shut up! Just shut up.” Yawkey charged Auntie Oonagh, but Oscar stepped in front of him. Yawkey shoved Oscar backward. Oscar’s father quickly got in between the two boys and pulled them apart.

“We belong; they love us,” Yawkey said, bawling.

“Look,” Oscar said, “we all belong.” He thought of his old home with his mother above the dry cleaners and his new home under the pitcher's mound with his father. It was true. He *did* belong.

Pinky hollered from the dugout. "What's this? What's going on?"

"Just play the game, son," Oscar's father said to Yawkey.

"Don't call him 'son.' He ain't your son," Pinky said.

Yawkey didn't say anything. He just stepped back and gave a sneer.

"Play ball," the umpire said.

Yawkey wiped his face on his sleeve. And when the pitch flew in, he hit it past Pumpsie at third. Pesky dived—his body shot out long and lean—and he knocked the ball down, but that was all he could do. Rose scored, and Yawkey hopped up and down on first, safe.

The game was tied at 3, but only for a moment. Ruth was rattled and threw a wild pitch, allowing Yawkey to advance to second base. After he stole third, Fedelma hit a single, and Yawkey came sprinting home. Yawkey yelled at Oscar's team, "See, you're going to lose! It's already over!"

There was another infield hit, and then Pinky strutted up to home plate and shouted, "You can't pitch!"

Ruth seemed jangled by it all and walked Pinky to load the bases, but the Bobs weren't as lucky this time. They swung out of sync and grounded out to end the inning.

The Final Innings

AFTER THAT, NEITHER TEAM COULD score. The seventh and eighth innings flew by with nothing to show for them on either side.

With Auntie Fedelma's team up and no one on base in the ninth, Pinky ripped a grounder toward Buckner, who was playing deep at first base. The ball was hit so sharply that Buckner didn't have time to charge.

Oscar saw in his mind the video clip everyone in Boston knew by heart. The hobbling, adult Bill Buckner staggering to the line, bending to the ball, and then lifting his hands in disgust as the ball rolled between his legs and dribbled to a stop in short right field. This time Buckner fielded the ball cleanly and raced to the bag. Pinky beat him by a step.

"Buckner blew it again!" Auntie Fedelma barked. "He's to blame for keeping the Curse alive. He deserved to be driven out of Boston. Billy Buck couldn't field a simple grounder."

"That's not true! The runner would have been safe, anyway. The Mets would have won the '86 World Series even if Buckner had made the play," Oscar shouted, but it was no use. Fedelma just laughed at him. He gave up arguing. "I've got a game to play."

Oscar knew his team needed a runner. They were trailing, 4–3, in the bottom of the ninth. Jackie Robinson was up. "When you get on, you'll have to steal second," Oscar told him.

Jackie remained all business. "That's right; then I'll score if anyone gets a hit."

"Yup, easy as that."

But it wasn't going to be that easy. As Jackie walked up the dugout steps, a black cat was thrown at him from the stands. A voice, disconnected, rang out across the field. "Look, it's your cousin!" the voice said, laughing. The heckles rose up the grandstands.

Oscar reached over and took the cat from Jackie, whose arms were shaking. He petted the cat's soft head. "Never mind all that. Just concentrate," Oscar said.

"Do we have to do it all alone?" Jackie asked. "Where are the good guys?"

Oscar shrugged. "I don't know." He set down the cat, and it darted quickly off the field.

Jackie strode up to home plate, took some practice swings. And that's when Oscar first heard a different kind of voice: someone cheering. Jackie heard it, too. He looked out into the stands and gave a smile, a nod.

Oscar jumped up the dugout steps and followed Jackie's eyes. He saw the hazy figure of a man sitting by himself, off to the edge of the bleachers. "Who is it?" Oscar asked.

Oscar's father appeared at his side. "It's Izzy Muchnick," he said.

"Who?"

"He was the city councilor who pushed the Sox to integrate. He and Jackie became good friends. Muchnick wouldn't miss this for the world."

Then some other ghosts, black and white, walked up the bleacher steps and sat around him.

"Do you know those guys, too?"

"I think that's Branch Rickey and Bill Veeck. Reporters, too: Wendell Smith and Sam Lacy," he said, and he smiled. "The good guys are here."

Jackie found his steely focus, and Perry seemed rankled by it and walked him. He kicked the rubber as Jackie jogged to first base. Perry pulled another tool from his back pocket. He hunched over the ball, the muscles in his arms flexing with effort. Oscar watched, amazed, and then felt a nudge at his elbow. It was Ted Williams. "It's taken me a little while to figure this guy out, but I think I've got him now. I can see the stitching on the ball when it comes out of his hand." And with that Williams strode out and took his spot in the batter's box.

Williams made his smooth warm-up strokes across the plate. Jackie danced off first. Perry threw to first to try to keep him close.

Everyone in the park knew Jackie had to steal second, including Perry, including Gandil. Perry threw over to first again, and Gandil tried to kick Jackie's hand away from the base; but Jackie seemed to know it was coming and hugged the bag with both arms. Gandil pretended to throw the ball back to Perry; but, actually, the ball was still lodged in his glove.

"Hidden-ball trick," Oscar yelled. "He's got the ball!"

Jackie nodded at Oscar and didn't take his hands off the base until his foot was on it, firmly.

"Not Jackie," Oscar's father said to Oscar. "He's too smart for that."

Jackie's savvy irked the ghosts in the stands. Slurs reverberated off the walls of Fenway Park.

Something old seemed about to crack.

By the time Gandil gave up trying to outsmart Jackie Robinson and Perry had the ball back in his glove, the ghostly crowd was rabid. Oscar looked over at his father and smiled. Then Oscar's father said, "Jackie's going to steal second, and Ted's going to drive him in."

"Sounds good to me," Oscar said.

Perry led into his windup, stepping toward home plate. Jackie took off. Oscar watched the ball dart toward home plate. It was Perry's first fastball of the game, and it was wide.

"Pitch out!" the whole team yelled in unison from the top step of the dugout. Auntie Fedelma had been waiting for the ball to be pitched wide. She caught it and fired a bullet to second.

Oscar saw Jackie's cleats turning up the dirt, his sleeves flapping, his eyes glued to second base. Auntie Fedelma's throw was right on the money, slapping Pinky's mitt with conviction. Pinky dropped the tag down toward Jackie's outstretched hand, but Jackie got there first.

"Safe!" the umpire yelled.

"Safe!" came the cry from the bench.

Oscar looked at Williams now, who smirked and nodded and turned his attention back to Perry.

Williams looked at the next few pitches as if he were conducting a science experiment and the results interested him. On the fourth pitch, Williams leisurely cocked his bat and cracked the ball on a line drive to center.

Jackie was already sprinting for third when the ball cleared the infield. Ty Cobb fielded the ball in center, but all he could do was lob it back to his pal Pinky in the infield. Jackie came home.

Game tied, 4–4.

Oscar ran over to the radio and cranked it up just as the announcer was reporting that the Red Sox and the Yankees were now tied, too. Oscar could feel it—all of the years clicking into place; the two games were locked together now.

Jackie smiled for the first time in the game when he met Oscar on the dugout step. "I told you" was all he said.

"I told *you*!" Oscar said, and then let Jackie pass into the swarm of his teammates.

The voices in the crowd were battling now—the bad against the good. The roars got so loud, Oscar could feel them in his ribs. The air was pulsing. His team loaded the bases but couldn't score another run.

* * *

THAT'S WHEN OSCAR NOTICED THAT the stands were filling up. Children—other twelve-year-old boys and girls—had started to appear. They hung over the railings and shouted and cheered. They were wearing their pajamas, as if they'd been woken up, too, and had rushed here in a hurry.

"Where did they come from?" Buckner asked.

Oscar called to one. "What's your name?" he asked.

"Ellis!" the boy shouted back proudly.

"Ellis who?" Oscar asked.

"Burks!" the boy said.

"I'm Jim Ed Rice," said the boy next to him.

Another boy jumped in. "I'm Mo Vaughn. I play baseball, too."

"I know you do!" Oscar said. "I know you do!"

And then Oscar saw some girls cheering in the stands, too. One of them caught Oscar staring.

"We're here, too, you know! This game isn't only for boys!" she said.

"You think you own this sport?" another yelled out. "I can play with anybody!"

The girls introduced themselves—Doris Sams and Marcenia Lyle.

Oscar smiled and nodded. "Okay," he said. "I'm

glad you're here!" The park seemed buoyed by the kids. The jeering and booing was being drowned out by their giddy whooping.

Ruth mowed down Fedelma's team in the tenth, and Oscar's team couldn't get anything going in their half. Oscar did finally hit the ball; and even though it was a line drive out to Pinky at short, Oscar was proud to have made good contact.

In the eleventh, Ruth went through a bad stretch, allowing the bases to get loaded. Yawkey was up, and Oscar walked out to the mound.

"We've got two outs. No way this kid beats us," Oscar said.

"I don't know. I kind of feel sorry for him," Ruth said. "It's going to hurt."

Oscar turned to look at Yawkey. He looked small and mean. "What's going to hurt?" Oscar said.

Babe's face broke into a mischievous grin. "How bad he's going to lose this game."

Oscar walked past Yawkey and settled into his squat.

Yawkey reared back and swung at Ruth's fastball with all his might.

He connected, and the ball rose into the night, graying with distance as it soared toward center field. *No,* Oscar thought, *it can't end this way. It just can't.*

But Oscar had forgotten about Willie Mays.

As the ball began to careen back to Earth, Oscar caught a glimpse of the hatless Mays dashing toward an intersection with the ball. *He can't possibly catch it,* Oscar thought; *he has too far to go, and the ball is sinking fast.*

But Mays covered the ground, grass clods flying at his back, and then he leaped and seemed to float on air, arms outstretched, toes pointed, miraculously converging with the ball. Above the sludge of nasty shrieks from the stands there came a subtle pop, and only one sound known to man makes it.

Willie Mays ran across the outfield grass, the ball raised in his gloved hand, the smile impossibly wider than his young narrow face.

Auntie Fedelma was so angry that the cords of her neck were stiff, straining against the red thread.

Even though Mays walked in the bottom of the eleventh and stole second, Oscar's team could not get him home.

So they went to the twelfth inning. Ruth gave up another single to Fedelma but then got three outs in a row.

Oscar stumbled toward the radio, picked it up, thumbed the volume knob. When he lifted the radio to his ear, he wasn't surprised to hear that the Red Sox and the Yankees were also playing in extra innings in the present, still tied 4–4.

Oscar's father was up. The count was three balls, no strikes. He only needed one more ball to get the walk. And, according to the radio announcer, that was the same exact position that Manny Ramirez was in.

Perry's pitch came in wobbly, looking as if it would be a good bit outside, but Oscar's father cocked his bat to swing. Oscar put the radio down on the bench. He wanted to yell, "No, you don't have to!" But his father was already swinging.

It was a hit to shortstop. His father started running. Pinky bobbled the ball. Oscar's father wouldn't make it, though, even with the bobble. Oscar could tell. Then something strained against the fabric of his father's shirt. The shirt tensed and then ripped, and two wide wings unfolded from his father's back. They whipped open—soft, dun-colored feathers. They spread and began to beat, lifting his father slightly off the ground, speeding him to first.

Oscar had never seen anything so strong and graceful in his life. How could his father have ever been embarrassed by those wings? The ball sailed across the infield, but Oscar's father was safe.

The bench went wild. Oscar shouted and hooted. His father looked the most surprised of all. He smiled and waved, his wings open, lush and full. He stood tall, ready to take off to second.

Ruth strode to the plate. He shuffled the dirt in the batter's box, slid his hand up and down the bat to make sure it was clean, and rested the bat against his thigh.

Then Ruth did something Oscar had only seen one other player do: Ruth rubbed his palms together, separated them, and then made a tremendous clap. A vibration rippled the dusty air.

It was a sign, even though Ruth didn't know it. It was a sign to Oscar, and he knew exactly how to read it.

The clap was David Ortiz's clap.

Oscar had seen him do it all summer long watching games on NESN on the little black-and-white screen. Oscar held the radio to his ear again. The announcer was talking about Ortiz, who was up at bat; but Oscar was watching the batter's box. Ruth raised his bat and pointed out a spot in right field.

Jeers and taunts exploded from the stands, but so did the good voices; and the twelve-year-olds were screaming. Everything stirred. The grass seethed. The air buzzed as if filled with hornets.

The Red Sox announcer made the call: "Ortiz, so many times the hero for the Red Sox, trying to have the ball club jump on his back one more time. Here's the 2–1 pitch."

A jolt went through Oscar and echoed through his body. He watched Ruth swing the bat with all of his might. The crack of bat on ball came simultaneously from the field and, at the same moment, through the static haze of the radio's tinny speaker. Oscar rushed up to the top step of the dugout and watched Ruth's ball fly out of sight. From the radio gripped in his hand, he heard the announcer shout over the noise, ". . . deep to right, way back, and this ball is gone! Jump on his back, fellas. The Red Sox win!"

CHAPTER TWENTY-FIVE

Broken

EVERYONE RUSHED BABE RUTH AS he crossed home plate: Oscar's teammates, his father, Auntie Oonagh, Auntie Gormley, and Smoker, Oscar jostling among them. They leaped around on Ruth, hugging him and one another, shouting and whooping. Everyone was going wild in the stands too: Muchnick, the reporters, and all of the boys and girls in pajamas.

But, amid all of the wild celebration, something strange caught Oscar's eye.

The red thread.

It had uncoiled and was rising in the air, weaving through the rowdy joy of his teammates, across the infield. Oscar took off running after it.

Auntie Fedelma was running away from her team, too, across the field. Her thread had come off of her neck and was spiraling now as if caught by the wind.

"No," she shouted. "Stop!"

The threads were quick, slithering through the air. They were headed for the slit in the Green Monster—still lit by the Pooka's eyes. Just as Oscar and Auntie Fedelma reached the wall, the threads slipped through the slit.

Oscar collapsed on the grass, staring back across the field to his team. "What now?" he said.

Auntie Fedelma, breathless, leaned against the wall. "No," she sputtered. "No, no."

And then the door opened. The Pooka stepped out, hunched over his cupped hands. He opened them, and there was the ball—wholly intact—wound up tight, its skins perfectly stitched. He tottered on his hooves. "Look," he said. "Look!"

Auntie Fedelma backed away from him. "Stay there," she said. "Don't come near me!"

The Pooka said her name, softly. "Fedelma, my girl."

His voice took her breath away. And she and Oscar stared as his large horse head grew smaller. His nostrils shrank and faded. His mane disappeared. His legs became manly. His hooves turned into feet, and then became covered with old leather shoes. A hat appeared on his head. Suddenly he was wearing woolen pants. A shirt flipped over his back and buttoned up the front. He was an old man, weathered but still tough. He grabbed the cuffs of his sleeves. They were held together by red thread. "How is it possible?" he asked Oscar.

"Those are fakes," Oscar said. "The real threads are in the ball."

Fedelma started to cry. She shook her head and stared at the man before her again. "Father?" she said. "Is it you?"

He nodded. "'Tis," he said. "Indeed. All of these years."

Fedelma charged him then, like a tough little girl, arms wide. She buried her face in his shirt. "You've got to come and see the others," she said. "Come on!"

"First things first, my dear," he said. And he turned to Oscar and held out his hand. "Thank you, sonny. You come, too."

Oscar took his hand, and they walked toward home plate.

"I have a date," Keeffe said. "A dancing date to keep at dawn."

"With the Banshee?" Oscar asked. It was all clear to him now.

Keeffe gave a nod, his eyes teary.

"Come now," Auntie Fedelma said. "We've missed you."

Auntie Oonagh and Auntie Gormley saw him from a distance. And then Oscar's father noticed. The three of them walked away from the mad celebration, slowly at first, not sure that they were seeing it correctly: Auntie Fedelma on one side and Oscar on the other and the aunties' old father beaming at them in the middle. But when they trusted the vision to be true, they began to run.

Oscar's father got there first—because of his large wings—and the two men wrapped their arms around each other. Auntie Oonagh got there next and then Auntie Gormley.

None of them said a word. They hugged the old man and touched his face and seemed struck by the miracle of it all.

And then Oscar's father picked up Oscar and set him on his shoulder. "The Curse is broken," he said.

"But the Red Sox still have to win the rest of the playoff games and the World Series," Oscar said.

“Now they can. Now it’s up to them! You made it possible!”

“Not alone,” Oscar said. “Not by myself.”

As if his teammates had heard him, they turned and saw Oscar. Pesky and Pumpsie. Teddy and Buckner. Willie and Jackie and Ruth. They cheered and whooped and broke out into a run—each of them sprinting toward Oscar—and it seemed as if they weren’t charging toward him as much as each one of them was charging toward his own undeniable future.

EPILOGUE

OSCAR AND HIS FATHER WATCHED the final game of the World Series, which was being played in a Missouri ballpark, on a small television that Weasel-man had picked up in the Lost and Found. They all gathered around it.

The Bobs were now two separate individuals, each wearing his own tweed jacket, sitting quite happily on two opposite ends of the row of bleacher seats.

Weasel-man had set his weasels free, to lead their own lives. (One weasel had decided to stay behind and spent most of her days curled up on Auntie Gormley's lap, purring with her soft, whistling purr.) Weasel-man sat next to Auntie Fedelma on one of the bleacher seats, nice and close; and she didn't seem to mind.

Smoker had quit smoking for good. He was still a nervous man, however, and paced in the kitchen for most of the game.

All of their heads were hornless. The horns had melted away as soon as the cursed baseball had stitched itself back together. No one would have been able to tell that the horns were gone, however. They all still wore their Red Sox caps.

Auntie Gormley and Auntie Oonagh sat on either side of their father, Keeffe Egg, each locked onto one of his arms, as if he might disappear again. But he never went anywhere except for one appointment every day at dawn. He met with his long lost wife and danced with her in the outfield. The Curse was broken, but it couldn't bring her back to life. She was no longer a wailing banshee, but she was still a banshee nonetheless: a beautiful, ghostly banshee.

And Oscar and his father sat on the floor right in front of the television so they wouldn't miss a single play.

When the game ended, they could hear joyful hooting and car horns from the streets of Boston overhead. Oscar knew that none of the other Red Sox fans would ever know about the real curse and how it was broken. They would never know about the underbelly of Fenway Park—the mice had quickly dispersed, the nettles had shriveled away—or the once-cursed creatures who lived here. It didn't matter.

Oddly enough, there wasn't an uproarious celebration in this small parlor beneath the pitcher's mound. No. It was a calm moment. A sweet moment. Relief. They all knew that from now on everything would be different, and they weren't sure what to do with their new freedom. They all stood up and looked at one another, and then they hugged and cried a bit. Auntie Oonagh kept saying, "Well, now! Well, now!"

And then the phone rang. Oscar's father walked to the kitchen and answered it. He appeared in the doorway with his hand cupped over the mouthpiece. "It's your mother," he said to Oscar. He was smiling. He'd cut holes in most of his shirts so that his muscular wings could breathe. They were curled over his shoulders, making him look taller and stronger than before. He handed Oscar the phone. "Tell her that I miss her," he said.

Oscar took the phone, and his mother was on the line. "They did it!" she said. "They did it! You were right! You had faith in them, Oscar!"

"Eighty-six years," Oscar said. "It's been a long time."

"I'm coming home," his mother said, her voice cracking. "I need to come home."

"We miss you," Oscar said.

"Who do you mean? We?" she asked.

"Dad and I. We miss you."

She didn't say anything at first. "You both miss me?" she asked.

"Yep."

There was another pause. "Eighty-six years is a long time," she said. "It's important to always have some faith." And then she laughed a little, nervously, and Oscar could hear the rattle of her beaded necklace. It was a sign, and he knew how to read it. He knew that his birthday wish would come true, that when he turned thirteen, they would all be together.

Oscar closed his eyes. In the distance he could hear the Banshee singing, but each note was full of hope—as clear and sweet as a struck bell.

HISTORICAL NOTE

IN 2004, THE BOSTON RED SOX made it to the American League Championship Series against the New York Yankees. They hadn't won a World Series title in eighty-six years. They were within three outs of being swept in four straight games. In that fourth game, they won, 6–4, in twelve innings. It stands as one of the great games in baseball history. They went on to do what no other professional baseball team had ever done. They came back from a 3–0 series deficit to win, and then went on to become World Series champions.

AUTHOR'S NOTE

I REALIZED EARLY ON WHILE writing *The Prince of Fenway Park* that to write about the history of baseball with accuracy, I would have to make a commitment to writing about racism.

Although *The Prince of Fenway Park* is a work of fiction, it relies on and intersects with history. The word *nigger* appears in this novel three times—on pages 177, 257, and 299. In each of these cases, I was relying on facts and real quotes.

I believe that the word *nigger* is the most hateful word in the English language. Although it is morally wrong to use this word, censoring it would be an attempt to sanitize the past. I refuse to do so—for the sake of children or any readers, for that matter. When we try to alter history, we cannot truly understand and learn from our mistakes, and we are guilty of diminishing the truly great acts of heroism in the battle against racism. So it was with careful thought and consideration that I used *nigger* in my book.

For the children who read this novel, if I could whisper one thing that would ride beneath *all* of the words in this book, it would be this: *Go forth. Create a greater nation, a better world. Show us how it's done.*

EXTRAS

A Q&A with Julianna Baggott

Batter Up! Three Writing Exercises

Red Sox Trivia!

A Q&A with Julianna Baggott

Julianna Baggott is the author of sixteen books, including the Anybodies trilogy under the pen name N. E. Bode, novels for adults, and collections of poetry. She also has written for the *New York Times*, the *Boston Globe*, the *Washington Post*, and read her work on NPR's *Talk of the Nation*. She's a professor of creative writing at Florida State University and lives in Florida with her fabulous husband, four rowdy kids, two sweet dogs, and one mean cat.

What made you want to write about the Red Sox?

I believe that the world is a very strange and mysterious place. If you're paying close enough attention, you'll see all of those oddities with your own eyes. I love writing about those mysteries that surround us—sometimes hidden just out of view, sometimes hidden in the underbelly of a legendary baseball park.

When my husband was a kid he loved the Red Sox, and so he was the one who suggested that I write a Red Sox book. I said that I didn't really want to write a sports book. I reminded him that I like to write wild and wooly magical fantasy, but, at the same moment, it hit both of us that the Red Sox are magical. They were cursed (for eighty-six years). That Curse was reversed. What if I found the boy who broke the Curse?

And that is how this adventure started. . . .

This book deals closely with racism. What would you like your readers to consider when reading *The Prince of Fenway Park*? What do you want them to learn?

In some ways, this was a hard novel to write. The history of racism in baseball is a difficult thing to tackle. There's so much pain and suffering and injustice there. But what made it so satisfying to write about was the fact that there are great, real-life heroes who changed history—Jackie Robinson, Hank Aaron, Izzy Muchnick, and many more. It was an honor to write about these heroes.

Why do you think some kids, like Drew Sizemore, are bullies?

Bullies are cowards. They have to prove that they're worth something by asserting power over others. They're sad examples of how to live a life. A lot of kids who are bullies are bullied at home. It's how they've been taught to exist in the world. So bullies aren't just kids. They come in adult form, too. The world has plenty of them. We have to stand up against them, be brave, and if we stand up together, shoulder-to-shoulder, all the better.

Why is it important to *know the past*?

How else can we learn from our mistakes but to know the past and try not to make the same mistakes again?

What roles do magic and mythology have in this book? How do these relate to baseball?

Well, it's no coincidence that the Red Sox are Boston's team and that Boston was home to many Irish immigrants, and that the Irish are quite fond of blessings and curses. It made a whole lot of sense to me that Irish mythology and their creatures were probably in some way tied up in the curse. I was right, and, as a result, the book is filled with characters that show up in Irish mythology—Pooka with his horse head, glowing eyes, and human hands; the banshee who cries and keens before each loss; the horned creatures who exist in Fenway Park's underbelly. It's all tied up in the Curse!

Many kids grow up with parents in separate homes. What are the challenges of this for Oscar?

In many ways, Oscar is a kid who wants his family to be whole again. Yes, he's a diehard Red Sox fan. Yes, he loves baseball. Yes, he's caught up in a crazy curse that he alone must reverse. But, deep down, he is just a kid who wants his family to be put back together. Even if your family is still together you can relate to that desire—a mother, a father, a place called home.

If you could have a special ability like being able to read signs or break codes, what would you want your gift to be?

I have the gift that's most important to me. You have it, too. The imagination.

Get the Red Sox Writing Rampage Up and Running

A Note from Julianna Baggott:
Writing exercises are just like baseball exercises, except you don't have to run to first base or field grounders. But if you want to sprint down the line or barehand a bunt or two—if this gets blood to your brain—then by all means, do it. And now, let's get ready to write!

EXERCISE ONE—Blessings and Curses

Way back, when I didn't yet know much about the Curse on the Red Sox, I knew I wanted to write about something magical—as I always do—but I also wanted a story that was grounded in the real world. The Curse on the Boston Red Sox seemed like the perfect territory to start digging for a story. But the part that was the most fun was recreating the Curse itself. I've written in the Curse on Fenway Park, below, the one that appears in the novel so you can get a feel for what an old Irish curse sounds like . . . because . . . YOU are going to write a story that has a Curse inside of it.

But first, I want you to think of your hero, the person who is going to break the Curse. Is it someone like you? Is it someone who's brave? Is it someone who's afraid? Or both? And then I want you to think of your bad guy. If this is a baseball story—and it doesn't have to be—is it one team who's trying to curse the other? Is the person who writes the Curse a manager, a player, an angry fan? If this is not a baseball story, then who or what is being cursed: a neighborhood, a school, a bus, a cafeteria?

And now, I want you to write the Curse itself. To give you

a feel for it, listen to the Curse below. Pay attention to the sound of the rhyme. Your Curse can rhyme, but it doesn't have to. Do you want to create strange creatures into your Curse? Go for it. Would you prefer to write a blessing—one that creates a different kind of story altogether? Have at it! Once you have your Curse (or blessing) written, do you want to go on and tell your story about the kid who saves the day? Please do!

And here is the Curse that you will find in *The Prince of Fenway Park*:

May you be cursed, Fenway Park.
May horned creatures reign the dark.
May a Pooka roost in your hill.
May the banshee cry and keen at will.
May weasels nest
and nettles infest.
May herds of mice swarm
and evil managers do harm.
May you be close enough to taste the win
but always, truly, lose before you even begin.

And now, before I send you off to write, here's a little writerly blessing:

May the muse be in your brain today.
May you think of brilliant and strange things to say.
May your glittery mind sizzle and glow.
May your story dazzle and snazzle and flow.

EXERCISE TWO: Writing Baseball Action!

Choose your favorite baseball player of all time. What if you could play a game of baseball with that player? What if he was your age at the time you played with him? Write an adventure scene in which you and the famous player play side by side or maybe on opposing teams. Make the scene jam-packed with excitement.

How, exactly, do you make a scene jam-packed with excitement? Well, you have to remember that your main character—who might be you!—perceives the world through the senses. In this scene, make sure you:

1. Let your eyes see! Are things shiny or dull? Dirty or sparkling? What colors are there all around you?

2. What does the scene smell like? There's grass and dirt and breezes . . . is a storm coming? Use your nose!

3. Listen up! If you're playing in a ballpark or an old worn field, the game of baseball is filled with all of these rich sounds. Describe them.

4. Feel the game. There's a feeling in your hands after a ball smacks your glove or as you connect a ball with a bat or as you charge and slide.

5. Taste. Is there anything in your scene that has a taste? Probably! Write that, too.

You also have to remember that your character has a body. What does the heart feel like in your chest when you're playing a game? What do your lungs do? How do your legs feel as they carry you around the bases?

EXERCISE THREE: Create Creatures!

The Prince of Fenway Park mentions many magical creatures that are part of Irish mythology and folklore. Find out what a Pooka and banshee are, and what roles they play in the Irish imagination. What other creatures do you find in Irish mythology and folklore?

And now . . . invent your OWN creatures! Use wings, beaks, hooves, fire, tails—anything you want! Create three—use bits from other creatures if you want to invent something wholly new and all your own! Use your writing skills to describe the creature and then, if you want, draw pictures.

Red Sox Trivia!

1. What Boston Red Sox player was recently named to the National Baseball Hall of Fame?
2. Who was the manager of the Red Sox when they won the World Series in 2004?
3. How many home runs did David Ortiz hit in the 2004 playoffs? (Hint: Not just in the World Series.)
4. How many times have the Red Sox played in the World Series from 1967 to the present?
5. What is David Ortiz's nickname?
6. Which Red Sox Nation fan favorite was traded in the middle of the 2004 season?
7. Who was the last player to hit over .400 in Major League Baseball in a single season?
8. In which city is the National Baseball Hall of Fame located?
9. Which player has his bloody sock enshrined in the National Baseball Hall of Fame?
10. Which eight players in Red Sox history have had their numbers retired?

Answer Key:

1. Jim Rice; 2. Terry Francona; 3. 5; 4. 5; 5. Big Papi; 6. Nomar Garciaparra; 7. Ted Williams; 8. Cooperstown, NY; 9. Curt Schilling; 10. Bobby Doer—#1, Joe Cronin—#4, Johnny Pesky—#6, Carl Yastrzemski—#8, Ted Williams—#9, Carlton Fisk—#27, Jackie Robinson—#42